"Are you okay?" David asked.

Gracie pressed her lips together, took a breath. "I'm good. I should get back." She slid off the horse and made her way back to the fence where they'd come in.

"Gracie. Wait."

She turned just as they reached the fence. He was close. Reaching out for her. She took a step back. Not that she didn't want him to touch her, but that she wanted it too much.

"Don't," she said.

"I thought you were having fun. I thought the horses were a good thing. Decker won't really be mad."

"It's not that. I just need you to stop."

"Stop what? I don't understand."

"Stop...this." She knew that made no sense. "Stop... apologizing and stop defending me and stop getting me a horse to get me through a bad day. And stop delivering kittens in the barn and kissing my grandma on the cheek and...and...stop coming to dinner and being so nice. Okay?"

Dear Reader,

There are few perfect matches in this world. Peanut butter and jelly. Salt and pepper. Mac and cheese. Tom and Jerry.

Wait, Tom and Jerry? Yep, even though they fight like cat and, uh...well, mouse...they simply can't be one without the other. Some might say they're quite fond of each other, even if on the outside their fondness looks much more like animosity.

Similarly, David and Gracie might look like enemies but may, in reality, be something else entirely.

Sometimes, your greatest adversary can be your past. It can be the promises that you made to yourself. It can be the hurt that you just can't let go. Often, love's greatest enemy is fear or mistrust or vulnerability.

And sometimes, you just have to let go of the defenses that keep you most comfortable when you realize that they could also be keeping you from your happily-ever-after. If David and Gracie can do just that...they might find a perfect match in each other.

One more perfect match? Harlequin readers and Harlequin Heartwarming romance, of course!

Thank you for reading. Enjoy!

Jennifer

THE VETERINARIAN'S PERFECT MATCH

JENNIFER BROWN

Harlequin
HEARTWARMING

Harlequin® HEARTWARMING™

Recycling programs for this product may not exist in your area.

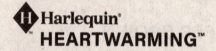

ISBN-13: 978-1-335-46008-0

The Veterinarian's Perfect Match

Harlequin Enterprises ULC
22 Adelaide St. West, 41st Floor
Toronto, Ontario M5H 4E3, Canada
www.Harlequin.com

Printed in U.S.A.

Jennifer Brown is the award-winning author of several middle-grade and young adult novels, including her acclaimed debut, *Hate List*. Additionally, Jennifer is the author of four Love Inspired novels, including the *Publishers Weekly* bestseller *Kidnapped in Kansas*. Jennifer is also the nationally bestselling author of women's fiction novels under the pseudonym Jennifer Scott. She lives in Kansas City, Missouri. Visit her at jenniferbrownauthor.com.

Books by Jennifer Brown

Harlequin Heartwarming

A Haw Springs Romance

The Cowboy's Dream Family

Love Inspired Inspirational Mountain Rescue

Rescue on the Ridge
Peril at the Peak
Hunted at the Hideaway

Love Inspired Inspirational The Protectors

Kidnapped in Kansas

Visit the Author Profile page
at Harlequin.com for more titles.

For Scott, my perfect match.

Acknowledgments

I am lucky to have so many “perfect matches” in my corner when it comes to writing books.

Thank you to my perfect-match agent, Cori Deyoe, at 3 Seas Literary Agency, for endless wisdom and enthusiasm, for all the smiley faces on my manuscripts and for teaching me more about horses than I ever thought I would know.

Huge thanks to the entire Harlequin team for helping me bring Haw Springs to life, and especially to Johanna Raisanen for helping me find and refine what exactly makes David and Gracie the perfect match that they are.

Thank you to my family and friends—you are boundless in your support, and I love you all.

Finally, thank you to my readers, who come to the page eager to find a perfect match of a story. I, quite literally, could not do this without you.

CHAPTER ONE

DAVID'S MUCK BOOTS squelched across the soggy pasture with every step. The late summer rain had made the ground a goopy mess, and in some spots his heels sank into hungry patches of mud. Ordinarily, he would watch where he stepped, try to keep himself decent for when he returned to the office, but the distressed crying from the barn sounded urgent, and urgent times called for urgent measures. And, sometimes, urgent measures meant an afternoon in muddy scrubs, whether he was wearing muck boots or not.

The alpacas were excited to see him. They met him halfway across the pasture and flanked him as he walked.

"Hang on, guys. I promise I'll give you attention. I've got to check on Norma. Sounds like she's having a time of it." He felt a nudge on his shoulder blade and turned to find himself nose-to-nose with the alpaca behind him. "In a minute, Sam. Be patient. Betty, can't you keep him under better control?" As if she understood completely, Sam's alpaca partner, Betty, fell back a few steps, causing Sam to lay off. "Thank you, ma'am. Extra pumpkin for you today." *If I have time to get your pumpkin at all,* he thought, doubting that he would. Call it the hunch of an experienced veterinarian. He also knew that he would feel a little guilty about not delivering on his promise—the experience of a lifelong animal lover.

Generally, David didn't mind being the star of the farm when he arrived. The animals came to him, and he rarely had to go hunting for someone to make sure they weren't lost or injured somewhere on the property. Since most of the time he was caring for Vera Langhorst's animals on his lunch break, time was of the essence. His office was getting fuller and fuller, his patient list longer and longer. Sometimes he had a hard time pushing his way through the waiting room when he got back. He gave up his lunch breaks because he had a soft spot for Vera, whose property butted up to the ranch he'd grown up on, and who was his first and most loyal client. He just tried to be quick about it.

But today, as soon as he heard Norma's cries, he called the office to let his receptionist, Renee, know that he would likely be late, and she may need to do some rescheduling. Then he went back to his truck to grab his emergency kit and carrier. He had a feeling Norma was going to need more than a little extra help.

The barn was dim and dusty. Henry and Henrietta, Vera's resident surly geese, honked warnings at him from their pen as soon as he entered, lazily swaying their way to the fence. David loved animals, but he did not love geese. He could still remember his early days right out of vet school when a goose took a good gnaw at him, leaving him with an angry bruise that lasted for days. He especially didn't love Henry, who was as mean as the day was long and would love nothing more than to get his beak around some skin to prove it. *Henrietta*, David had said more than once. *You'll pardon me for saying this, but I don't get what you see in that guy. You could do better.*

He pulled a length of reflective Mylar scare tape out of his pocket and held it up, wiggling it to keep them at bay as he walked. "Henry. Henrietta. Good afternoon. That's enough out of you two."

Norma's cries seemed to get weaker and more erratic as David got near. This was not a good sign. He let his eyes adjust to the dim barn light and peered around the stacks of hay bales, trying to discern where she was hiding. Could be anywhere.

"Norma," he said softly. "Where are you, mama kitty?"

Norma yowled in response. Unlike Henry, Norma thought David was pretty great, and always greeted him with purrs and rubs when he ventured into the barn.

"I hear you. Where are you?"

He began stepping up on bales and peering into cracks and corners. The barn was Norma's domain, and she was no stranger to finding hiding places in the stacked bales on a normal day; who knew where she would have gone when she went into labor?

"I'm coming for you. Where are you? Keep talking to me."

Fannie, the Langhorst spirited, mixed-breed farm dog, entered the barn, all snuffles and playful energy. She bumped into the backs of David's knees, stamping his scrubs with muddy paw prints, and let out an airy *woof* for attention. David turned and gave her ears a quick scratch. She licked the air trying to get at his hands.

"Hey, Fannie, do you know where Norma is?"

The dog stilled, mid-lick, her ears perked, as if she were really considering his question. And if you asked David, she probably was. Dogs were smart, and Fannie was a smart dog. She didn't tend to give Norma any grief, and often David arrived to see them playing a little game of hide-

and-pounce on the hay bales or resting together in the sun on Vera's back porch. He guessed that Fannie's arrival in the barn was only partially to greet him. She'd probably been hanging around for as long as Norma had been in labor. Norma's cries were probably distressing to her, too.

Norma cried again, and Fannie's ears twitched in a different direction. She whirled and put her nose to the ground, then started sniffing in the completely opposite direction from where David was headed. Good. They could cover the barn more quickly this way.

He found Norma in a soft triangular bed of hay created by two bales and the barn wall. As soon as she saw his face poke over the hay, she let out a wail, then laid her head down, panting.

"Oh, goodness, mama kitty, you're having serious trouble, aren't you?" He reached down and stroked her neck to let her know that it was going to be all right and then commenced giving her the once-over. It didn't take long before he knew what was wrong. And he also knew that he didn't have a lot of time to act.

His cell phone rang. Leo, his veterinary assistant, was calling.

"Renee said there's a problem. How can I help?" Leo asked as soon as David picked up.

"I'm going to be a minute," David said. "Can you handle the next couple appointments?"

"Absolutely. Everything okay? Renee said it's Norma. Is it dystocia?" Leo was just about to graduate vet school and was smart as a whip. Easily the best assistant David had ever had. He hoped to someday make Leo a partner in the practice, if he could find someplace and expand before Leo got a better offer or decided to open up shop for himself. David didn't love the idea of having Leo for competition.

At the moment, though, expanding was out of the question. He had plans to stick to, and he wasn't quite ready to branch out.

"It would appear to be dystocia, yes. She's stopped having contractions."

"Do you have Pitocin?"

David flung open his emergency kit and rifled through. "I do. But her ears and feet are cool, her breathing rapid."

"She's in shock."

"Yes. Exactly. I have no idea how long she's been in labor, but my gut tells me she won't make it through an induction."

"Emergency C-section?"

David began laying out a sterile blanket while they talked. "I think there's no other choice."

"I can prep for it."

"I don't think we have time for the drive back into town. I'm going to have to do it here."

"I'll prep recovery," Leo said, and disconnected. David knew that Leo was disappointed that he wouldn't get to assist, or at least watch, the surgery, so he quickly flipped to his camera and hit record, then propped the phone against a bale of hay. He would talk his way through the procedure, and Leo would be able to watch everything when David got back.

Fannie nosed her way in, and he gently nudged her away as he unzipped his field surgery kit. "Not now, girl. This is serious."

Fannie, smart as always, took two steps back and sat, watching.

Norma didn't even protest when David reached down into her space and didn't fight him when he picked her up. "It's okay, little mama. We're going to get those babies out right now." He doused his hands with sanitizer, hoping that it would be enough to keep infection at bay later.

David worked quickly, letting his training take over, trying not to miss anything, but also trying not to overthink things. Both could be equally disastrous when facing an emergency in the field. The few times that he'd lost a patient, he'd been devastated. He knew what the animals meant to their owners, and losing one was income lost or companionship lost, or in some cases, both. His job was both blessing and curse. In moments like these, he hoped and prayed for blessing, but mentally prepared for curse.

He didn't need to give Norma the sedative he would usually give to calm a cat. Instead, he went straight to anesthesia, gave her belly a quick shave, and delivered her four kittens, setting each of them on a clean towel that he'd extracted from his kit.

"Congratulations, Norma," he said to the sleeping cat. "Everyone looks healthy and hungry. Let's get you all to the office, pronto."

His hands flew on autopilot as he flushed and sutured the incision, then carefully moved Norma into the pet carrier. He found a nearby box and, one by one, laid the new kittens inside, on top of their towel. It was a twenty-minute drive from the Langhorst property to the office, and a good five minutes' walk to the car from the barn. He needed to let Leo get these kittens onto a warming pad and get Norma into recovery.

He tossed his tools back in his bag. He could clean and sterilize everything later.

"Fannie, tell the others that lunch will be a little delayed today," he said. "Tell Betty I'm sorry about the pumpkin. And don't you worry. Your pal Norma will be just fine. You'll have four new buddies to play with soon."

Fannie's ears lifted as she paid close attention to everything he said, and then she lunged at him playfully, her muddy paws now stamping the front of his scrubs, too. *So much for staying clean and professional*, he thought.

He gave Renee a quick call. "We're on our way. Have Leo fire up the warming pad for these babies."

"How many we got?" Renee asked.

"Four."

"I'll work on some temporary names for our new visitors. I'm thinking North, South, East and West. What do you think?"

"I think you need to run it by Norma. She's incoming."

He stuffed his phone back into his scrubs pocket, tucked the box of kittens under one arm, then picked up the cat carrier in one hand and the emergency kit in the other. He would have to come clean up the messy blanket and anything he might have dropped later.

He didn't even see the silhouette step into the barn entryway.

But he heard the cock of the shotgun.

That sound was unmistakable.

"Don't move a muscle, thief," the silhouette said.

David froze.

GRACIE LANGHORST MIGHT be a city girl now, but she was born and raised in the country, and there were two things she wasn't afraid of: animal thieves and pulling a trigger. She knew her way around a shotgun—her Grandma Vera made sure of that—and this barn thief was about to find out the hard way that she once beat out every boy on the Buck County High School trap team to win a $1,000 cash prize at the fall skeet shooting competition. When she was ten.

Everyone underestimates a small girl, until she's blowing clay out of the sky like it's no big deal.

A breeze picked up a lock of her thick, wavy, auburn hair, and pushed it in front of her face. She shrugged it back over her shoulder without taking her eyes off the thief. He was only a shadow in the back of the barn, but she had a good aim on him, and she could hit a shadow just as well as she could hit anything else.

"Put down whatever it is you're stealing, and I might let you get out of here with all your body parts intact," she said. "Take one step toward me, and I shoot the foot that stepped. Don't think I can't do it."

"Okay," the thief's shadow said. "Easy."

The shadow slowly lowered what he was holding onto a nearby hay bale, then straightened with his hands up at his shoulders.

Gracie's eyes had begun to adjust to the dark. The thief was unusually well kempt, with dark brown hair carefully combed back, and trimmed stubble that marched obediently from his sideburns downward, barely concealing the cleft in his chin. He wore light blue scrubs that were covered with muddy paw prints. Gracie suppressed a smile. *Good job, Fannie. Way to slow him down.*

"What are you stealing, anyway?" She gestured to the box that he'd set down. It looked like a pet carrier. "Chickens?" But she didn't hear chicken chatter coming from the box. And, besides, her Grandma Vera didn't keep chickens in the barn, if she kept chickens at all anymore. Gracie hadn't gotten the chance to make the rounds on the farm since she got back the night before; she wasn't sure exactly what sort of livestock her grandma kept.

"I'm not stealing anything," the shadow said, taking a tentative step towards her.

The closer he got, the more handsome he got. But also…

"What is that all over you?" She knew very well what it was. Alarm coursed through her, making her trigger finger tighten. "Stop right there."

He wasn't just covered in mud. He was covered in blood, too.

She pointed the gun right at his chest. "I said don't move."

Obediently, he stopped walking, his hands still

at his shoulders. "Okay. I'm not moving. You don't have to…you can put the gun down. I'm not dangerous."

She let out a laugh. Her shoulders had begun to ache from holding the gun locked in place for so long, but she ignored them. It felt good, actually, to feel her body working. She didn't get a lot of that behind her desk up in Kansas City. "Fat chance, thief. Or should I say killer? What animal did you kill? If it's Sam, you'll have worse problems than me. You'll have my grandma to answer to. She loves that alpaca."

"I'm a doctor, not a killer. Or a thief," he corrected, speaking slowly, calmly. His voice had an undertone of warm, decadent butter to it. "Doctor David McBride. I'm a veterinarian. And I love that alpaca, too, for what it's worth. I came to feed and check in on the animals like always, and Norma was in distress. I delivered her kittens."

Gracie's ears perked at the word *kittens*. Her gun began to slowly, almost imperceptibly, lower. "Right here in the barn?"

"If I hadn't delivered them here, it was likely that Norma and her kittens would have all died. But they're not entirely out of the woods yet. I need to take them into town. Care for Norma's incision. Warm up the kittens. I need to do it right away, miss. So if you could put the gun down and let me pass, that would be great."

Gracie caught the barrel of her gun lowering on its own, and lifted it again. "Where are they? The kittens?"

He nodded toward the cardboard box he'd lain next to the pet carrier. "Can you hear them?"

She stayed silent for a moment, and sure as the world, she did hear tiny mews, as if the kittens were looking for their mother. The sound made her sad. *I know what that's like, little guys,* she thought. *I know all too well.*

This time, she purposely lowered the shotgun, as she tiptoed closer to the box, craning her neck so she could see the tiny, squirming, wet balls of fur inside. She let out a little noise, a cross between awe and anguish.

"Miss, I really need to go. Timing is important here. These kittens are going to get cold, and the office is half an hour down the hill there. You can tell Vera that David McBride took Norma and her kittens. She'll know exactly who you're talking about."

"David McBride? Didn't you live on the ranch next door? You and a brother. Donald?"

"Decker. And, yes. Can we catch up later, though?" He picked up the boxes while he was talking, as if he was confident that she wasn't going to shoot him after all. Or maybe he was willing to put his life on the line for Norma. Either way, Gracie suddenly lost the energy to be menacing. She tried her best, though. After all, she and the McBride brothers had hardly been friends, and she probably wouldn't have recognized David McBride after all these years even if they had been. And she'd spent a lifetime training herself not to believe anything at first blush. Especially not someone covered in blood appearing on private property with no warning.

She lifted the gun again and half-heartedly aimed it at him.

"Fine. But you better bring them back."

He bustled past her. "I don't have the space to keep a cat and four kittens around, trust me."

"And in the future, I'd appreciate it if you don't show up unless you're invited," she called to his retreating back.

"I'm always invited," he yelled back without turning around. "Ask your grandma. I'll be back later today."

Thanks to her good-for-nothing parents, Gracie wasn't quick to trust anyone. Sure, the man claiming to be David McBride may have been handsome. And, sure, he may have saved the cat and her kittens. But just because he said he was welcome on the farm didn't make it so. Besides, Vera was not herself right now, so even if she gave him her blessing to be there, her judgment could have been off. For all Gracie knew, this man could be conning her grandma out of her animals, her land, and who-knew-what-else. No, Gracie was going to need more than his word for it.

She let the gun fall to her side, and watched all the way until he loaded the boxes in his car, then got in, brought the car to life, and drove away.

Gracie didn't particularly love her skeptical side, and sometimes worried that it was a tool that she used to keep herself from getting too close to people. But she was who she was. And she'd learned to accept that.

If Gracie was going to protect her grandma in her dying days, she was going to have to watch over everything carefully. Which meant she was going to have to watch David McBride carefully, and that was all there was to it. She rested the gun against her shoulder, barrel pointing to the sky, as she made her way back to the house.

CHAPTER TWO

BROTH, BROTH, BROTH. Her grandma must be sick of broth, Gracie thought as she placed yet another steaming bowl on a serving tray and started toward the living room. She'd only been here twenty-four hours, and all she'd seen the woman eat was broth. And precious little of it, at that.

Gracie knew that this was what the end stages of stomach cancer looked like, and she knew her grandma's prognosis could be counted in months rather than years, and it nearly broke her heart. Grandma Vera was a widow before Gracie was even born. She was tough and fierce and, once upon a time, she was a force to be reckoned with. Now, she was literally withering away, light and angular as a stack of kindling, reminiscing about meals past as if they were lost loved ones, sipping broth and fighting to keep it down. Even though Gracie had returned to Haw Springs to be with her grandma during this final stretch of illness, she was still in denial that it was really true that her grandma would be dying soon. But all this broth made it hard to ignore.

Still, she was here to help. She was here to bring some brightness to her grandma, and to pay her back for all those years of caring for her after her parents split. So she pasted on a smile as if broth was something to be excited about, and chirped as she walked into the living room, "Dinnertime!"

Vera sat in a recliner, covered with blankets, only the toes of her thick socks sticking out at the end. The television was playing old black-and-white sitcom reruns. Vera had a remote control loosely clutched in one hand, but she hadn't changed the channel in hours. Maybe not at all since Gracie arrived. Vera's hair was thin and wispy and flew out from the crown of her head as if it was already trying to get to heaven without her. She turned her head and gave a smile when Gracie entered.

"Oh. Hm. You can set it right there," she said, pointing at the end table next to her chair.

Gracie knew what this meant. She was no more planning to eat the broth than Gracie was. "You have to eat something, Grandma," Gracie said softly, even as she deposited the soup on the table per instructions. "You have to keep up your strength."

Vera snorted. "I think we're past that, honey.

That's why you're here, remember? Just the two of us against the world. I want your face to be the last thing I see before I go."

"Okay, well, this face is going to be here a good, long while, because you're sticking around. Does something else sound better? Macaroni and cheese? Toast? I'll make whatever sounds good to you."

"Goodness, no." Vera laid her head back against the chair and closed her eyes. "I'm fine, sweetheart, I'll eat the broth. Did you know, I had the most vivid dream this afternoon. It was about your great-grandma, Irene. You probably don't remember her at all, do you?"

Gracie shook her head.

"She was very old by the time you were born," Vera said. "Boy, was she a pip. No bigger than you are, but she was downright terrifying when she wanted to be. Nobody took Granny Irene for granted, that was for sure, and everyone took her seriously. If they didn't, they might end up with an earful. Or a belly full of buckshot."

Relatable, Gracie thought, remembering the heft of the shotgun in her hands just a few hours earlier.

"Anyway, Great-Grandma Irene was sitting right here in this living room, right where you are. And she was telling me that I was late, and that I needed to get my suitcase packed right away. And I asked her where we were going, because I couldn't remember, and she never would answer me. But I knew she was right. We had a trip to go on, and I was excited to go, but I couldn't find my suitcase for the life of me."

"Grandma," Gracie said softly, and then trailed off. Hospice had warned her of this. As a person gets closer to dying, they sometimes begin to see loved ones from their past. They sometimes start talking about taking a big trip. "What do you say I get you some oyster crackers to put in that broth?" she asked around a very dry throat. She didn't know what else to say. She certainly didn't feel tough and terrifying at the moment. She only felt terrified.

When you could count on one and only one adult in your life to not let you down, what was supposed to happen to you when that adult died? Even though Gracie lived hours away, the fact that Vera was still in this world meant she wasn't alone, and she supposed she counted on that, even as she held people at a distance. Gracie felt silly to feel this way, but with Vera gone, she worried that she would be completely and utterly alone. She could already feel it pressing in on her. She'd walled herself off and had no true personal connections in this world, and she knew it.

Vera reached over and patted the back of Gracie's hand. "Oh, honey, it's all going to be okay. Death is part of life."

"How...how about yogurt? I think we have some." She felt like a fool, continuing down this path of trying to get food into her grandmother, but she was stuck on repeat. She'd spent too long away. There were still stories to hear. There were still stories to tell.

She needed more time.

What was she doing, playing big-city lawyer while precious years zipped away at home? Creating a life of safe, easy loneliness for herself, pouring every ounce of herself into a big-city job that she hated, that's what.

"Do you know that you even look just like your great-grandma Irene?" Vera asked. "You have her thick red hair, and you're built exactly alike. Small, but mighty. She could chop wood and bale hay and ride bulls. And I once saw her stare down a bouncer at the bar in town so that she could go in and drag your daddy out. She literally pulled him through the door by his ear." Vera gave a chuckle, and Gracie couldn't help herself—she laughed, too. The idea of someone making Farley Langhorst, Father of the Century, leave a bar was the stuff tall tales were made of. "She wasn't afraid of anything. Just like you."

Not true, Gracie thought. *I'm scared of plenty of things. Not the least of which is losing you.*

"But, you know, deep down she was soft and gentle and kind and full of love to share. She was just afraid to let that side of her show. Just like you," Vera said.

There was a thumping noise, and Fannie barreled through the dog door, all oversized muddy paws and strings of slobber hanging off a lolling tongue. The shotgun that was propped against the wall next to the door fell over with a clatter. Gracie jumped, hands flying over her head, half expecting the darn thing to go off. She'd propped it there for easy access, not even thinking about Fannie.

"Fannie," she scolded as she got up to move the gun. "Slow down, for goodness' sake. And you're getting mud everywhere!" She grabbed a wad of paper towels and commenced chasing down the hyper dog. "Grandma, how on earth do you handle this wild child all by yourself?"

Vera snickered as she watched the chase ensue. Gracie found herself giggling along with her grandma as the mud situation got worse and worse with every lap. Fannie was having a grand old time of it.

Finally, Gracie captured the dog and wiped down her paws and hindquarters. Fannie stood and let herself be fussed over, but she panted impatiently. Gracie hadn't been joking—she truly had no idea how her grandma could have possibly been taking care of these animals by herself. It dawned on her that maybe the so-called vet she'd run across in the barn was on the up-and-up, and this was why he was hanging around. *Maybe*, she thought. *But that doesn't mean he's not also helping himself under the guise of helping her. People are like that.*

"Why is that thing out, anyway?" Vera asked, pointing toward the gun, which Gracie had absently laid across the coffee table in her quest to capture Fannie.

"Huh? Oh. There was someone in your barn earlier. I took care of it."

Vera's brow creased. "What do you mean, someone in my barn? What were they after?"

Gracie finished and released Fannie, who took off like a shot, made two quick laps around the house, and then darted back out the dog door. Gracie sighed as she tossed the muddy paper towels in the trash. All that work for nothing. That silly mutt would only come back in just as filthy as before.

"It was David McBride," she said, returning to her grandma's side. "He was delivering kittens. Not like, bringing you kittens. *Delivering* them."

Vera's eyes grew wide. "Norma had her babies?"

Gracie shrugged. "I guess so. He said she was having problems, and he acted all in a hurry to get her and the babies to his office. He said he's a veterinarian, which I guess he must be, since he was performing surgery on a cat. But it seemed sketchy. You didn't call him. I didn't call him. And it's not like Norma called 9-1-1. Why would he be in your barn to see that Norma was having trouble in the first place?"

"You held him at gunpoint?"

"Just while I was questioning him. I let him go."

Vera chuckled, laid her head back, and closed her eyes again. She was getting tired, Gracie could tell. And yet the bowl of broth remained right where she'd set it. No longer steaming.

"He's been taking care of my animals for years. When I told him about the cancer, he started coming every day to help me out. And over time, I stopped being able to get around as well as I once could, and he just started doing it all, without even being asked. Free of charge. He's a wonderful man."

A little too wonderful, Gracie thought. In her experience, nobody did much of anything out of the kindness of their heart. Life was all about quid pro quo. People always had their hand out for something in return for their "good deeds." Her good-for-nothing daddy taught her that there was no such thing as a pure heart, and where he left off, her job in the legal system picked right up. Three-quarters of Gracie's career was dealing with quid pro quo gone wrong.

Driving all the way out from Haw Springs to the county farms every day just to feed some old lady's alpacas was beyond kind. It was unbelievably kind, emphasis on the *unbelievable* part. It didn't take a mathematician to solve this equation. Old, dying lady, seemingly all alone in the world plus random man suddenly willing to go far, far out of his way to do things for said old, dying lady equaled thief dressed up as a Samaritan.

Well, Gracie had news for this *wonderful* man. This old, dying lady was not all alone in the world. He may have gotten away with his act thus far, but he was messing with the wrong granddaughter, and if he thought he would fool her, he had another thing coming. Irene may be gone, and Vera may be joining her, but this redheaded force to be reckoned with was going nowhere.

Vera opened her eyes and sat a little straighter. "You know, you should meet him properly." She arched an eyebrow. "Without the shotgun."

"What? Why?"

"Well, for one, I'm sure you scared the daylights out of him. But also because he's kind and handsome and funny. I really think you might like him if you got to know him."

"Might *like* him. Very doubtful. Grandma. I'm not looking to *like* anyone. I'm just fine on my own, thank you."

"I'm not saying you should marry him."

"Good. Because I don't want to marry anyone. The last thing I need is some deadbeat man hanging around for me to take care of just so that he can split later and leave me high and dry."

"Now, Gracie. That's unfair. Not all men are like your father."

"Enough of them are."

"And I'm sure enough women are like your mother," Vera said. Gracie didn't love having her grandma admonish her, but she didn't mind the spirit that it was bringing out. This was much better than the dozing, starving grandma watching the same episode of *I Love Lucy* for the hundredth time. "But David McBride is nothing like either of them, and I think it would be nice of you to apologize for holding him at gunpoint in my barn. He's very understanding. He will be forgiving, I'm sure. He'll probably see the humor in it."

"I wasn't trying to be funny."

Vera cocked her head. "Well, then, you *really* need to apologize."

Gracie set her jaw. "Fine. I'll say I'm sorry." She supposed she probably had jumped to conclusions a little too quickly with him, and if nothing else, it wasn't the best manners to greet someone with the barrel of a gun. "If I see him."

"You'll see him, because tomorrow morning, you'll drive into town to check on Norma and her babies."

"I thought he comes here every day."

The arched eyebrow made a reappearance. "Would you come back here if you were him, given the greeting he received today?"

"Not if he's got half a brain." Gracie sighed. "Okay. I'll check on the cat. I'll say hello and reassure him that I'm probably not going to shoot him if he comes back to the farm."

But he won't come back to the farm, she thought. *Because I don't trust his intentions in the least, and nobody is saying I can't make that clear as well.*

"Good," Vera said, leaning back and closing her eyes again. "We need him here."

Gracie got up and took her grandma's cold soup back into the kitchen. *Speak for yourself,* she thought. *I don't need any man anywhere.*

NORMA WAS RECOVERING like a champ.

David, on the other hand, was a zombie.

He was a notorious early riser, known for puttering around the office hours before anyone else arrived, but today he was last in, and trudged through the front door, yawning, his large Dreamy Bean latte already mostly empty and still not doing a thing for him.

Renee glanced up from the front desk, then did a double take and smiled wide.

"How's our patient? And how are the babies?" she cooed, coming around the corner to take the cat carrier from him. He yawned again. "Well, good morning to you, too, David. I suppose I don't need to ask how you are. I thought maybe you'd run off to Vegas. I was about to call the police for a well check." She peered into the carrier.

"Tired," he said. "I was up all night checking on them."

Renee placed the carrier on the counter and opened it. "Oh, no," she said in a baby voice to the kittens. "Was something wrong?"

"Me," he said on another yawn. He made his way around to the other side of the counter and glanced at the calendar. "I'm what's wrong. I was so busy worrying about them I couldn't sleep. And I was worrying about the others on the farm, as well."

Renee poked her finger through the carrier door and stroked Norma's tail. "What's wrong with the farm?"

"There was a welcoming committee that I didn't care for yesterday."

"Uh-oh, coyotes?"

"Something like that. Only more vicious." He

sank into the empty office chair. He hadn't gone back to the farm after his run-in with the redhead, and Vera didn't answer his texts, which was not unusual. Like many elderly farm folks, Vera treated her phone as an emergency lifeline only, and kept it turned off and ignored most of the time.

He fretted all night about the animals, hoping that Little Miss Shotgun at least fed them, since she'd run him off from doing so. He spent most of the night sitting on the bathroom floor, listening to the kittens mew as they fought for a spot to milk on exhausted Norma, and feeling bad that he'd gone back on his pumpkin promise to Betty.

"You look bright-eyed and bushy-tailed this morning," Leo said, coming in from the back. He opened the first file for the day's appointments and gave it a quick read. "You sure you're not the one studying for the license exam right now?" He dropped the file on the desk and let his head loll back in defeat. "Pug toenails."

Renee gave a knowing smile. "Not just any pug. Ralphie the Screamer."

"Oh, come on. At eight o'clock in the morning? Why do you hate me, Renee?"

"I'm just trying to give you all the experiences. I don't think David has Ralphie energy today."

“He doesn’t,” David said.

“Don’t worry, I’ll help you.” Renee patted Leo’s arm. “I’ll take Norma to the back. Is she going home today?”

“That will depend on if Vera ever answers my texts. I’d like to keep her a few days more, just to keep an eye on her and let her incision heal before she’s rummaging about in the barn. In the meantime, I don’t think there’s anyone boarding. Let her have the cat room to herself. Nice and calm in there. What else do we have this morning?”

Leo picked up another file and opened it. “Well check on a hound dog.”

David nodded, watching out the window as a familiar young woman, Annie Allbrook, struggled to keep an eager hound from pulling her across the parking lot. David knew Annie and the hound well. Annie was one of the volunteers on his brother’s riding therapy ranch, and June was his brother’s dog. June wasn’t used to leashes and was very excited to take in all the new smells. “I believe said hound dog has arrived,” he said.

June bounded through the doorway before Annie even had it all the way open.

“Ope! That’s a lot of dog. Let’s go, Norma,” Renee said, and disappeared into the back.

David gathered all his energy and called out

to Annie. "My brother sure stuck you with a job," he said. "You can let her go. There's no one else in here."

"I didn't get stuck," Annie said, breathlessly. She let go of the leash, and June sniffed and wagged her way around the perimeter of the waiting room. "I volunteered. Mr. Decker did say to give you a message, though."

"Okay?"

"He said you have two and a half months to come up with a date to the wedding, and that the color is officially going to be yellow. I have a sunflower bridesmaid dress. It's really pretty. He didn't tell me to tell you that last part. That was me telling you."

David laughed. "Well, two and a half months isn't very long. I guess I'll have to go as an eligible bachelor. But luckily, yellow is my color."

"Miss Marlee says yellow isn't anybody's color, unless you're a banana. But I think that's because Miss Marlee doesn't like her dress. It isn't as pretty as mine because it's plain and doesn't have any sunflowers. You're not supposed to look flashy and pretty when you're a maid of honor, at least that's what I read in a wedding magazine. You'll overpower the bride if you do, and nobody's supposed to overpower the bride."

"I think you mean overshadow."

"Yeah. That. But, also, Mr. Decker said to tell you that coming as an eligible bachelor is a cop-out. He must have guessed that you'd say that."

David tilted his head back and laughed to the ceiling. "I'm sure he did. After fighting it for years, he finds the woman of his dreams and suddenly everyone needs to be engaged."

Annie let out an uncomfortable breath that David supposed was meant to be a laugh. Annie didn't always understand sarcasm. But she had gotten good at pretending she did.

The waiting room door opened, and Leo made a smooching noise at June, who eagerly disappeared into the back with him.

"So you're reading wedding magazines, huh?" David asked, flipping through June's file for a refresher. She was a farm hound; she was sturdy and hardy and could live off a diet of beetles and bark if she had to. This was going to be a quick, easy check-up. Which was good, because he wasn't sure he had much more than quick and easy in his reservoir tank this morning. And Ralphie the Screamer was coming in to get his nails clipped. Ugh. "Does that mean that you and Ben are finally talking about tying the knot?"

Annie blushed deep red and refused to make eye contact. Ben Werth was Decker's farm hand, and his right-hand man when it came to running his program for kids on the autism spectrum.

Both Ben and Annie were on the spectrum, and the two were also obviously in love. "No, sir. We would never overshadow Mr. Decker and Miss Morgan's wedding with our own wedding news," she said.

"That doesn't mean there isn't any wedding news..." he teased, but he trailed off when he saw another familiar shape storming across the parking lot. He hadn't gotten a good look at her yesterday, what with all the fear and adrenaline pumping through him, but that wild red hair was unmistakable.

Well, at least she's not carrying a gun, he thought.

Annie followed his gaze, a curious crease in her brow. "Who's that?"

"Just a visitor on the Langhorst farm. Why don't you go on in and wait with June," David said, putting on a reassuring smile. "She'll be in room one. I'll join you shortly."

"Okay." Annie gave one last uncertain glance to the parking lot, and then disappeared through the door June had just gone through.

Suddenly, David was wide awake, his heart thumping. This woman was a loose cannon if he ever met one.

The door opened and she stepped inside. For the first time, he got a good look at her. Her auburn hair framed a sweet, heart-shaped face, with pouty lips against creamy skin, and a smattering of freckles sprinkled across her cheeks. She gazed around the lobby with light gray eyes the color and intensity of a wolf's eyes. David shuddered, feeling her stare to his core. That sweetheart face with the natural plump pout was very deceiving. This was the kind of girl who could worm her way inside of you and never let go.

She saw him at the desk, gave a quick nod and strode to him in a few easy steps. Her white, fringed boots were impractical, her flannel was pressed and tied in a knot at her stomach, her denim shorts were crisp. This was no cowgirl; this was a magazine version of a cowgirl. Someone playing dress-up.

Yet she handled that gun like she knew exactly what she was doing.

There was more to this woman than she let on. The only thing David knew for certain was that there was probably no such thing as ever knowing anything about this woman for certain.

"Hi," she said.

He nodded, too tired, too confused and too stunned to speak.

She tossed her hands up, looking around. "Turns out, you're legit."

"Yep. Contrary to popular belief—or maybe it's just *your* belief—not just anyone off the street can perform an emergency C-section on a ten-pound cat in a dimly lit barn. Successfully, I might add. Norma's doing great, if you're curious. So are the kittens. Four of them."

"Good to hear," she said. "I'll tell my grandma."

"If you don't mind, that would be great. Tell her I'll keep them here for a day or two. Let Norma get some rest. Let the kittens get established. Make sure everyone's doing okay. Free of charge, of course." He wouldn't need to tell Vera that, but for some reason felt the need to clarify with this woman.

"I'll pass it on."

"Appreciate it."

There was an awkward pause, during which she seemed to be working on a speech. David was more than just tired; he was weary. And he didn't have the patience for this.

"I've got a hound dog waiting for me," he said. "Renee can take you back to visit Norma, if you like. Thanks for stopping by."

"Listen, I don't want to take up a bunch of your time. I'm just here to apologize," she blurted. "For what happened yesterday."

"Okay."

"I mean, I'm not sorry. And I would do it again."

"Interesting apology. Needs some work."

She tossed her hair over her shoulder and planted her hands on her hips. He had a feeling that she often did this to make herself appear larger and more intimidating. It…worked, actually.

"I'm sorry that I pointed a gun at you. Well, not that I pointed the gun in the first place. I would do that again, too."

"You do know what the word *apology* means, right?"

"I'm getting there, okay? Just hear me out. I'm not sorry for pointing the gun, because my grandmother lives out on that land all alone, and thieves are a real thing, and so are murderers, and sometimes bad guys can even look like friends, and you can never be too careful."

He frowned, failing to follow where this was coming from. Or going. He gave one nod. "Okay. Forgiven. Gotta go."

"What I'm sorry for is holding you at gunpoint once you told me what you were doing there. That was maybe not as necessary. Although, in my defense, I had no idea who you were, and you had blood on your clothes and were literally taking something out of the barn. So, you know, technically, you *were* a thief."

"A thief who will bring back more cats than I took. If we're being technical about it."

"Point taken. Anyway. I'm not sorry about what I did, and I would do it again, because I had good reason for it. But I apologize for… I guess for making you uncomfortable."

He let out a laugh. "Uncomfortable?"

"Were you not?"

"Yes! I was! Have you ever had a shotgun pointed at your chest?"

"Not exactly, no."

He picked up the stack of folders and tapped them on the counter to make them even, then set them down again. "She made you apologize, didn't she? Vera?"

"I'm a grown woman, Mr. McBride."

"*Doctor* McBride." David was the last person to insist that people call him *doctor*. Pretentiousness irritated him, and he often skipped professional events for that very reason. But if she was going to unapologetically threaten to shoot him, he might as well get something out of the deal.

She cocked her head to the side and set her jaw. But he could see the tiniest amused uptick at the corners of her mouth. "So sorry. *Doctor*."

"Seems a little less than genuine, but I'll take it. Apology-ish accepted. Like I said, I'll be bringing Norma back in a few days or so, depending on how she's doing. I'll check on all the other animals later today, during my lunch break. Now, if you're done apologizing, I've got work to do." He turned from the counter and started toward the back.

"That won't be necessary."

"I'll decide what's necessary for my patients."

"No, I mean it won't be necessary for you to check on the other animals. I'll take care of that. You can leave the cats on the porch and I'll make sure everyone gets what they need. I'm relieving you of your duties."

He stopped and turned back to her. Her nerve had stopped being intriguing and had spilled over into annoying. "I owe Betty some pumpkin."

"Okay."

"So I need to bring her some pumpkin today."

"I know what a pumpkin is, Doctor McBride. I'll take care of Betty."

"Vera and I have an agreement. I've been looking after her animals for years."

"And I grew up with her, so I would guess my years trump your years. And you may have an agreement with her, but what I'm not sure about is whether that *agreement* benefits you more than it benefits her, if you know what I mean."

"No. I actually have no idea what you mean."

"What with her about to die and all."

David bristled. *About to die.* This was a thought that he'd been actively avoiding. He had a very soft spot for Vera Langhorst, and he couldn't face the reality that she'd been getting weaker. Dwindling.

"She's worse, then? The cancer?" The words felt like barbed wire being dragged out of his throat.

"Yes. The cancer is getting worse. Much worse, and I'm afraid she doesn't have long."

"Oh, no. I'm so sorry to hear that. What can I do?"

"You can stay away. I'm here to help my grandmother, and I'm more than capable of doing that myself. I'm also more than capable of protecting her. And, make no mistake, I will continue to protect her after she's gone. So if you saw her illness as a good opportunity, you're mistaken, and you can drop the act."

"It's not an act. Vera and I have been friends since before she had cancer. I didn't think that she had family but, to me, that just meant she needed extra help."

Gracie's eyes narrowed, self-righteous and stung. "What do you mean you didn't think she had family? I grew up next door to you."

A memory tried to tickle the back of his brain, but it was elusive, and slipped away before he could grab hold of it. "I think I remember that now. But we didn't hang out together. You weren't in my class. I haven't seen you around in a long time. Maybe not since high school. So you'll forgive me if I thought she was all alone and needed extra help." He thought he saw a slight wince flash across Gracie's face, as if he'd treaded on a sore subject.

Renee popped around the corner. "Norma is resting comfortably in the cat room, and Leo is ready for you in exam one."

"Thank you, Renee."

"Well," Gracie said in a small voice. "She has family. Me. I'm her family."

"And I'm glad of it." He picked up June's folder and held it against his chest. "I'll be by later today. We have an agreement. It benefits the animals. And unless Vera herself tells me to stop coming by, I'll be there."

The redhead opened her mouth to argue, but he didn't give her a chance. He turned and walked into the back, realizing only as he put his hand on the doorknob that he was sweating.

She was demanding and rude and as cynical as the day was long. She was maddening.

And, he had been right; she was already under his skin.

CHAPTER THREE

"OH, MY GOODNESS! Oh, my goodness!"

Ellory DeCloud, owner of The Dreamy Bean coffee shop, zipped out from behind the counter as soon as David walked through the door. She came at him with her arms outstretched, the tiny bells on her ankle bracelets jingling as she walked.

As soon as she reached him, she bent to peer into the cat carrier.

"You brought them! Oh, my goodness!"

"I told you I would. Norma's all healed and they're going home today."

"Can I see them?"

He set the carrier down on a bench. "Sure." He opened the latch. Norma gazed out at him warily. "Don't worry, Mama, we're just browsing." Immediately, one of the squirming babies—the one he was already thinking of as the dominant one, full of curiosity, orneriness and attitude—began mewing and clumsily crawling toward the open door. They'd been tumbling around the cat room for over a week now, and their personalities were starting to show.

Ellory clasped her hands under her chin in anticipation. She gasped and cooed at the kitten. "You're so cute. I would definitely call you Latte. Does he need a home?"

David smirked. "Unfortunately, he already has one. He's a barn cat. He has a job to do."

"But they have three others. They won't even know he's gone."

"Oh, I'm certain the guard dog will know he's gone. And I don't mean Fannie. I mean the two-legged guard dog."

Ellory raised her eyebrows. "That sounds like a story."

He waved her away. "It's just Vera's granddaughter. I didn't even know she had one." *Not true*, he thought. *You just forgot, and you can't pinpoint the memory.* "Anyway, she's very protective. Not in a good way. For me."

"I know exactly who you're talking about. She's been in here a couple times. She's intense, all right. I always feel like I need to try and talk her into decaf." She giggled. "She's just a little closed off. I figured that she hasn't settled in yet, and she'll open up when she's more comfortable. All I've gotten out of her is that her name is Gracie and she likes cranberry scones."

Gracie. A quiet, serene name for a raging spitfire.

"Well, she's settled in enough to know where the guns are. She's followed me around with a shotgun at her side for a week now."

"What? Why? Have you talked to Vera about it?"

He shook his head. He couldn't get anywhere near Vera. Gracie stayed ten paces behind him everywhere he went, silently watching as he tended to the animals. If he turned to see if she was still there, she glared back at him defiantly, snapping to attention, but never said a word.

The one time he'd made toward the house to see Vera, he heard the gun cock behind him. When he turned toward the noise, she had it pointed at him.

"I thought you weren't going to do that again," he said.

"Actually, I apologized, but said I *would* do it again," she responded. "Sorry, not sorry."

"You can calm down," he said. "I just want to check in with Vera."

"Remind her that you exist so she doesn't forget to leave you in the will, you mean? And don't ever tell me to calm down."

"You've got some serious trust issues, do you know that?"

Gracie faltered a little, the gun wobbling in

her hands. He'd struck a chord. She recovered quickly and steadied herself. "You're a psychologist now, *Doctor* McBride?"

"Doesn't take a psychologist to know that this..." He gestured toward her and her firearm. "Isn't exactly healthy. Or normal."

"It's normal around here, now that I'm back. Don't you forget it. I may be letting you feed the animals, but you're not getting to her."

Today, though, he intended to get to Vera regardless of Gracie's determination to keep him away. She wouldn't actually shoot him if he just kept walking—he was ninety percent sure of that.

Okay, maybe seventy-five percent sure.

Sixty percent?

Still a majority.

"Anyway," David said, closing the cage door. "I've got to get moving. Can I get my usual?"

"Bye, Latte," Ellory said in a tiny, sad voice. She straightened. "Of course. Coming right up."

"How's the wedding cake going?" David asked, following her.

"I have a sample," Ellory said, hurrying behind the counter. She washed her hands. "I've settled on vanilla almond, I think. And I'm getting much better at roses." She nodded her head toward a plate full of brownies, each adorned with a jaunty yellow icing rose.

"Wow, much better," David said. "I should take one to Vera."

Ellory shut off the water, took a knife and plate to a nearby cake pan, and cut out a square of white cake. She handed the plate to David. He took a bite and let out a little groan.

"That's perfection."

Ellory beamed. "I think so, too. Morgan still has to taste it, but I'm pretty sure it's the one. You think Decker would like it?"

"I think Decker just wants to get married, and if I know my brother, he is going to leave all of the decisions about vanilla almond cake and yellow icing roses to Morgan. But, yes. He'll love it. I know I would, if it was my wedding."

"I'll keep that in mind for when you get married," Ellory said, pushing buttons on the coffeemaker.

He let out a laugh. "A hundred years or so from now."

"Or soon," she said. "I could see a wedding in your future. You never know." She handed the coffee over, then expertly tucked three brownies into a bag. "One for Vera, one for you, and one for Gracie."

"You're too kind. And, trust me, I know that there's no wedding in my future. I've got work to do. The last thing I have room for in my life is love and marriage." He checked his watch, jumped, crammed the rest of the cake in his mouth, and set the plate back on the counter, along with a twenty. "Speaking of work, I've gotta go." He kissed his fingers, chef's kiss style, picked up his coffee and brownies in one hand, the cat carrier in the other, and headed out.

He chuckled as he started his truck. "A wedding in my future…that's a good one."

As he drove to Vera's house, sipping his coffee, he pondered the impossibility of the very idea of him getting married. In order to get married, he would first need to get serious with someone. And he couldn't even take the first step toward that.

Not that he didn't get lonely on occasion. Of course he did, just like anyone would. But he had worked so hard to get his practice up and running—he was too busy, too singularly focused to even go on a date. He wanted to get established before turning his mind toward dating. But then he got established quickly—too quickly!—and now he was overrun with patients. With this came a new, singular focus: Growth.

Finding a place so he could expand.

Except he couldn't find a place.

And, okay, maybe he was a little afraid of expanding. Maybe his brother's impending wedding scared the daylights out of him just a little, because if Decker could get past the damage their parents had inflicted on them, what was going to be his excuse?

After all, their parents were hardly the model of a perfect marriage. When their mom walked out, their dad never got back on his feet. Not totally. David had it in his head that he couldn't possibly even consider love and marriage unless and until he was totally stable—better than stable!—in every possible way. That way if someone pulled the rug out from under him, he could still keep his balance.

So maybe he didn't feel ready, and was a little bit afraid that he never would be.

Maybe, just maybe, he had decided to write off love and marriage completely.

Vera was sitting on her porch, a crocheted blanket spread across her lap when he pulled into the long, gravel driveway. She lifted a bony hand to wave. He gave a hearty wave back. It was good to see his friend. It had been a while.

Gracie appeared to be nowhere around; David silently congratulated himself on making the right move. He'd remembered Vera once telling him that she loved to have a cup of tea on the front porch in the afternoons and guessed that switching up his routine might throw Small But Deadly off his trail.

He grabbed the cat carrier and brownies and

crunched up the gravel driveway to the front porch.

"Hello," Vera called. Her voice was as weak as the rest of her looked. It had been a while, but not that long. She'd declined a lot in a short amount of time. "What do you have there?"

He came up onto the porch, set the carrier down, and opened it. Norma cautiously stepped out and went directly for Vera, brushing up against her leg. The kittens mewed loudly at the absence of their mother.

"Well, look at you, Mama," Vera said, reaching down to pet Norma. "Congratulations. You sure gave David a scare, I would reckon."

"Yes, ma'am, she did." He sat on the porch rail so he could intercept a wandering kitten if they should manage to find their way out of the carrier. "But she's a trouper."

"That's my girl," Vera said. "Tough little mama. And the kittens?"

The one Ellory called Latte was first out of the carrier. David scooped him up and handed him over.

"Oh, my, I can see orneriness in you, little one. The mice aren't gonna know what hit them."

"All four are healthy," David said. "He's just the explorer. The girl at the coffee shop is head over heels."

"Well, who wouldn't be? Look at that handsome face." Vera held Latte to eye level and made silly faces at him, kissed his nose and then handed him back. David shut him in the carrier, much to Latte's chagrin.

"Speaking of handsome faces, how come I haven't seen yours around?"

Ah. So Gracie hadn't told her grandmother that he'd been there. He scratched the back of his neck uncomfortably. "Well, you have a very effective guard dog."

Vera frowned. "Fannie's been giving you trouble? That's odd. She loves you. She's never gotten after you before."

"Fannie does love me. Gracie, however… seems to love to get after me."

Vera giggled. "Oh. My granddaughter is protective."

"Maybe a little on the *over*protective side?"

"She means well."

He nodded. He couldn't argue that. At the base of Gracie's attitude was love and care for her grandmother, he supposed. When she wasn't actively enjoying bullying him, that was.

"She has it in her head that I'm only here to get something out of you. I hope you don't think that's true."

"Of course not." Vera held her hand out. David took a few steps forward and took it. Her fingers were bony and cold, her skin soft and delicate.

"You've been such a help to me here. And you never ask for a thing in return. So kind, like a son."

"Well, I don't know about all that. I'm just doing what a friend would do."

A voice came from the other side of the screen door. "I should have known."

GRACIE LANGHORST WASN'T afraid of big, bold moves. Sometimes, she felt as though her life was nothing but one big, bold move. Not that she'd always wanted it that way. You just had to play the hand you were dealt, and her hand was make a big, bold move, or be moved. As if her parents had birthed her only to turn her out into the world to figure it out on her own—be brave or be dead.

Well, she would choose brave every single time.

Of course, that wasn't fair to her grandma. Gracie may have had to jump in the deep end long before she'd learned to swim, but at least her grandma was there with a life preserver. Even when Gracie felt like she was drowning, she knew she wouldn't, because her grandma wouldn't let her.

She supposed she spent her entire life mentally preparing herself for this moment—for the time when she would truly be on her own. She'd fooled herself into thinking she was ready for it. But now that she was faced with the reality of her life preserver being gone, she was reeling. She was lashing out, being unfair, and she knew it. She just couldn't stop it. She was hurting. She was making big, bold moves, in hopes that she would become unmovable.

But it wasn't working. For the first time since she was a kid, she felt like she was drowning. And soon there would be no one there to keep it from happening.

When she'd told Jem, the managing partner at her firm, that she needed to take a leave of absence to care for her grandma, the reaction was swift and fierce.

You have clients.

Andrew can handle them without me. He lives to take over. Now he won't even have to bully me down. It'll be like a vacation for him.

Jem had rolled her eyes, showing off her perfectly glittered eyelids. Jem was immaculate in every way, as if she slept absolutely still with her hands placed at her sides, like a corpse in a coffin. Gracie always imagined her waking every morning with little to do but knock a single stray hair back into place. Sort of like a vampire. *You, with the victimhood again.*

It's not victimhood. And what do you mean again? *You know what, I don't want to know. The fact of the matter is that I have a right to take a leave of absence in the event of a family member needing palliative care, and my dying grandmother needs palliative care. Andrew wants to be lead, and if I'm in Haw Springs for a few months, there's nothing holding him back.*

And what if being in Haw Springs, Jem said the words *Haw Springs* as if they pained her, *holds* you *back?*

So be it, Gracie said through gritted teeth.

And if I say no?

I'm not asking for permission, Jem. I'm telling you that I'm going.

Gracie was the most successful young attorney the law firm had seen since Jem herself first stepped through the front doors. But one thing about being a successful young attorney in a successful, mammoth law firm—you had to fight your way every single day. Not just to win cases, but to stay in a position of being given cases to win.

Gracie was good at fighting. Gracie had been fighting since she was a toddler.

Gracie was tired of fighting.

She needed a break from all the fighting.

Part of Gracie didn't want to fight anymore at all.

Which is what made this veterinarian's presence all the more maddening. She stepped out onto the porch, where he was currently holding her grandmother's hand, turning on the charm. Goodness knew what kind of promises he was making. All she knew was she'd heard her grandmother say he was *like a son*, and him say something about being her *friend*.

Gracie let the door slam shut behind her. *Need to fix that door*, she thought. But, for now, it got the point across, so she was glad she hadn't. David dropped Vera's hand and stepped back.

"I was wondering where you were today," Gracie said. "Had my gun all oiled and everything, but you never showed up."

David gave a sardonic smile. "Sorry to disappoint you. Maybe tomorrow I'll get out of line, and you can scratch that itchy trigger finger of yours."

Gracie mimicked his smile. "One can dream."

"David brought Norma home," Vera said. "And there are four kittens."

"How nice of him," Gracie said, and she tried to mean it, for her grandma's sake. Whatever hold this guy had over her was working—her grandma was definitely buying into it. And, Gracie begrudgingly admitted to herself, there was a certain charm to him. A tenderness. He talked to the animals as if they were friends, his hands working the fur of their cheeks and chins, drawing out looks of contentment from them. He was confident enough to cut open a cat on a hay bale, but gentle enough to stroke a newborn kitten to life.

He was fearless enough to stand in front of the barrel of a gun, and still come back the next day. And the next.

And, well, she would be a fool not to notice that set to his jaw that whispered, *Bring it on*, whenever she threatened him. The devilish grin that he wore when they were verbally sparring. Almost as if he was enjoying it.

But, still, it was the devilish grin and that charm that whispered to her: *Keep your guard up. Don't trust this one.*

"I say you should let the girl in the coffee shop have the kitten," Vera said.

Gracie's ears perked up. "Absolutely not." The words popped out of her mouth before she realized she'd opened it. She actually found The Dreamy Bean to be quite charming, and Ellory to be the exact right balance between starry-eyed and savvy. She'd encouraged Ellory to consider franchising, bringing some Dreamy Beans up to the city. Ellory had demurred, said she liked the speed of Haw Springs better than money. A coffeehouse cat made perfect sense for The Dreamy Bean.

Gracie liked Ellory.

Everyone liked Ellory.

A part of her was afraid that it was the simple

fact that David apparently also liked Ellory that made her have such a reaction.

Which was utterly ridiculous.

What did she care about who David McBride liked?

"That's *your* cat, Grandma. You don't need to give your animals away. Besides, what if I wanted that cat?"

"Well, you can visit the cat anytime you go get a coffee," Vera said. "Plus, we'll have three more in the barn in case you get so bereft you can't make it into town."

She could see David suppress a smile. He must have been loving this, watching her grandma tease her. She felt small, like a child. She hated feeling like a child. And she hated overreacting to everything like a child.

"Besides, she gave it the cutest name—Lola."

"Latte," David corrected.

"Latte," Vera said.

"Grandma," Gracie said, kneeling down next to her grandma's chair. "You don't need to do something just because he says so."

"I didn't say so," David said. "I didn't even ask."

Gracie shot darts at him with her eyes. "You're taking advantage of an old, dying lady. Squeezing things out of her while she's incapacitated.

Manipulating her into giving things to your girlfriend."

"Ellory? She's not my girlfriend. I don't have a girlfriend."

"Fine. Friends. Whatever. That's not the point. Can't you see that my grandma is not strong right now? You should leave."

Vera patted her arm. "Honey, I have stomach cancer, not terminal idiocy. I know what I'm doing. Give me a little credit."

Gracie's face burned, as the smile that David was fighting to suppress won. He rubbed his chin to hide it, but Gracie saw it all the same. He was loving every minute of this little victory. That tiny voice in the back of her head that was always telling her not to trust, not to give in, was practically shouting that her instinct had been correct.

Well, he can love it.

He won't win in the long run.

She needed to be strategic about it. Let the kitten go. Approach the subject of her concerns about David later, when she and Vera were alone. Right now, just get along. Watch him closely, but smile when he smiles, nod when he nods, pretend when he pretends. Do it for her grandma who, for whatever reason, seemed quite attached to this guy.

He cleared his throat. "Well, the kittens still

need time with their mama. That way, you have plenty of time to change your mind. And I won't say anything to Ellory until they're ready to wean."

"We're keeping them in the house in the meantime," Gracie said, unsure if that was what her grandma wanted. There wasn't even a litter pan inside. "That way, Grandma has a chance to get attached, if that's what she wants. And you can't just waltz in here and take one away."

"It was wonderful to see you, David. Thank you again for taking care of everyone while I'm incapacitated." Vera gave Gracie a little side-eye.

He leaned over and kissed Vera on the cheek—another manipulative power move that enraged Gracie. At the same time, she felt that gentle kiss on her own cheek—a tingle that warmed her and threatened to leach the rage right out of her. She tipped her face to the floor, afraid that it was flushed. *Okay, so that was weird.*

"The animals are all doing great. Don't you worry about a thing." He picked up the cat carrier and handed it to Gracie. "If it's okay with you, I'm going to go about my chores now. I'll be in the pasture, the barn and the coop. I don't need supervision, but of course, that's not going to stop you. So come on out. Wear work boots and gloves. I'm sure I'll have some chores to put you to." He gave a wink, spun, and hurried to his car, his muck boots crunching along the gravel.

"Wait a minute," Gracie said to his back. "Put me to chores? Who are you to put me to anything? Huh?" *That wink, though.* "And don't go winking at me. It's…it's…" *electric.* "Presumptuous!"

Vera put her hand on Gracie's arm. "Honey, it's okay. He was teasing you."

"Well, I'm not in a teasing mood." Gracie set down the cat carrier and stormed to the edge of the porch. "This is not your farm!" she yelled.

But he was already in the car with the engine started. He gave her a quick wave and a thumbs-up, and was gone.

"And, you know what? He's not even as good-looking as he thinks he is," Gracie muttered.

Vera chuckled. "Not sure where that came from. Nobody was talking about his looks."

Gracie could feel herself blush. Sometimes her mouth was her worst enemy. "Well… I can just tell that he thinks it. He…thinks loudly."

"Somebody was thinking it, I suppose. Just not sure it was him," Vera said. "Sweetie, why don't you have a seat? Enjoy the beautiful day with me. You only get so many of those in life. Take my word for it. I have precious few of them left."

Gracie's shoulders slumped. "You know I hate it when you talk like that." But she obeyed, making her way to the chair on the other side of her grandma and plopping down gratefully. She'd spent the morning on the phone, arguing with Jem about whether or not Andrew was royally messing up every case she'd left in his care, and she was already exhausted. So tired of arguing and fighting. So why was it that she couldn't stop? "It's depressing and bleak."

Vera smirked. "You should try dying sometime, if you want depressing and bleak."

"Grandma!"

"What? I'm just dropping what you young people call *truth bombs*. Give me one of those kitties, would you?"

"Truth bombs? Where did you get that?" Gracie couldn't help letting out the tiniest giggle. She leaned forward and opened the cat carrier. She pulled out a squirming, warm kitten and handed it to her grandmother. Vera cupped it in her lap and began stroking its fur with shaky fingers.

"It's pretty amazing when you think about it," Vera said.

"What's amazing?"

Vera paused for so long, Gracie thought maybe she hadn't heard the question. But after the long pause, she shrugged and held the kitten up to her face. "The way life ebbs and flows," she said. "I remember being your age like it was yesterday.

Falling in love with your grandfather. Ready to get life up and started. Dreaming of a farm just like this one. I never thought I would be running it alone just a few years later, of course. And with a baby on my hip. You don't think in those terms when you're falling in love. Which is what makes falling in love so wonderful. You only see the hopeful and exciting part of the future."

Gracie had a feeling she knew exactly where this was going. She was not nearly as naïve as her grandmother thought she was. She knew about love. She knew about loss. And having her heart broken. She knew about hopefulness, and she knew how hopes got dashed. She was thirty-two, not thirteen. She'd lived life. She knew that the one constant of love was loss.

You simply couldn't have one without the other.

After all, she'd lost her mom when she was a little girl. And then, only months later, lost her deadbeat dad to prison. And then lost him again when he got out of prison and "reunited" with her, only to steal her blind while she was at work. She'd been forced to kick him to the curb—a whole scene that involved the Kansas City police and a return to jail—and had vowed to never speak to him again, for as long as she lived.

"I'm sure back then you didn't expect that you'd have to raise a granddaughter on this farm," she said.

Vera gave a slow nod. "No, I didn't. That was one of life's delights."

Gracie made a skeptical noise. "Farley Langhorst is not a life delight. No offense."

"None taken. I don't blame you for seeing him that way. My son certainly had his struggles."

"*Has* his struggles," Gracie corrected. "I mean, I would assume. I haven't seen him in years. But you know what they say about tigers and their stripes—they don't change. I very much doubt he's changed his."

There was a long pause between them. Gracie felt guilty for her attitude. She didn't want to fill her grandmother's final days with negativity. But, for some reason, she couldn't help herself. She felt…off. Like something in her life was just not right lately, and it had nothing to do with her grandma.

"Grandma," she said. "Did Great-Grandma Irene have…a soft side? Or was she just…tough all the time?"

Vera reached over and stroked Gracie's hair, just as she'd been stroking the kitten. Gracie leaned into it. "She had the softest side," Vera said. "She just hid it well. It was hard for her to let her guard down. But if you needed someone to hug away a hurt, she was there with an open heart and open arms."

"Had she been hurt?"

Vera's look turned sorrowful as she ran her fingers down the length of Gracie's hair. She nodded slowly. "Something else you two have in common."

"How did she get past it?" Gracie was practically whispering.

"I don't suppose she ever did." Vera went back to stroking the kitten's head. It had begun to fall asleep in her lap—something Gracie had done more times than she could count. "Some hurt is very hard to get past. But somehow she found a way to open herself up despite her fear of being hurt again."

Gracie let out a sniff.

"I'm a little worried about you, Gracie."

"You shouldn't be. I'm fine."

"I want you to be better than fine. I worry that you're lonely. You work awfully hard at keeping people out."

"I'm not lonely."

"Not lonely and busy are two different things, Gracie. You're very busy."

Gracie's mouth felt cemented shut. She'd been aware of this for some time, but hearing her grandmother say it somehow made it even more true—she kept busy to avoid being lonely. Sure, she'd dated a few men, but her real relationship was her job. But what Vera didn't know was that she was sick of being married to a desk and a computer. The problem was, at least she could trust her desk and computer.

"I'm not keeping people out. I'm just not interested. It's okay to be alone."

"I suppose that's true."

"Some people are all alone and totally fulfilled."

"I suppose that's true, too. Funny that you're talking about *some people* and not yourself, though."

"I'm fine, Grandma. Really. And so are you. You've been doing much better." The words felt cold and icy making their way up her throat. "Maybe you've got more time left than you think you do."

"Well, now you're just telling stories." Vera held the kitten up so that its nose was touching her nose. "Can you believe these stories she's telling? Me, either."

Gracie checked her watch. "What can I get you for lunch, Grandma? Broth?" She could barely get the word out of her mouth without making a face.

Vera set the kitten down on her lap and waved Gracie away. "No time for that."

"What? Why not?"

"You need to get out there." She nodded toward the pasture, where David appeared to be conversing with the alpacas.

“Why?”

“I don’t know. You tell me. You’re the one who makes a beeline for that man every time he comes by. The one who’s not as handsome as he thinks he is.”

“I do not,” Gracie said, but she’d stood up without even realizing it.

“My bad,” Vera said. “That’s the way you say it, right? *My bad?*”

Gracie suppressed a smile. “Grandma, where are you getting these phrases?”

“Hey, I’m hip and cool,” Vera said. “I may be dying, but I’m not dead yet. Plus I watch a lot of television. Oh, that’s what we should name you.” She held the kitten up to look into its face again. “Remote. It has a ring to it, doesn’t it?”

“Sure,” Gracie said, distracted. David had moved into the barn. She hated when she couldn’t clearly see what he was doing.

“You know what, honey? I forgot to tell him that Henry’s honk sounded odd yesterday. I need him to check that out. Do you mind running out there real quick before he moves on from the barn?”

“His honk sounded odd,” Gracie repeated skeptically. “Really? That’s the best excuse you can come up with?”

Vera nodded somberly. “I would go tell him myself, but I’m much too slow. By the time I got up there, he would be gone for the day. And I would need someone to carry me back. I'm feeble now, remember? Very, very—what was the word you used? *Fragile.* I'm very fragile." She gave a weak cough.

"I know what you're trying to do. And it isn't going to work."

"I have no idea what you're talking about," Vera said. "Do you, Remote? No? Neither one of us knows. I just know that my goose possibly needs assistance, and there's a veterinarian right out there who could help him if only he knew."

"Fine. Okay. You can stop laying it on so thick," Gracie said. "I'll go tell him about Henry's weird honk. Any other messages you need me to pass along? Is Fannie's woof sounding strange? Sam's…whatever you call that noise an alpaca makes?"

Vera appeared to think it over and then shook her head. "Just Henry. You're a peach, sweetheart."

"Uh-huh," Gracie said, heading off the porch. "You're a terrible actress, Vera."

But she couldn't help noticing that, as she bounded down the stairs and headed across the driveway to the pasture fence, she felt the most energized she'd felt all day.

CHAPTER FOUR

THE TINY LOBBY was barking, squawking, grooming, panting chaos. Gracie paused before pulling open the door, afraid that she might accidentally let an animal escape. David McBride appeared to be the only veterinarian in Haw Springs, and he was certainly enjoying his fair share of business.

Renee, the receptionist, looked up when Gracie entered, a wary glint in her eye. Gracie felt bad that she often saw that same wariness on people when she walked into a room, as if she had arrived only to give someone trouble.

So often, she gave people trouble. The wariness wasn't unwarranted. Once upon a time, she was proud of her ability to hold her own. She considered it a gift that had been bestowed upon her, a necessary trait for her career. But, over time, the novelty had worn off. She'd begun to hate her gift and wish that she could allow herself to be softer and more vulnerable with people other than the woman who raised her.

You need to smile more, Gracie, her grandma

had often said, so she pasted on a smile that felt unnatural, and from the alarm on Renee's face, didn't look any more natural than it felt. Did her smile look like a grimace? Was she grimacing? Ugh, she didn't mean to grimace.

So much for Grandma's wisdom.

She let the smile drop and replaced it with a confident stride instead. Gracie was good at confidence.

Or at least at the appearance of confidence.

But even that was temporary.

She tripped over a Weimaraner who happened to pull out of his leash, and practically fell into the desk, knocking a jar of dog treats onto the computer keyboard below. The Weimaraner's owner jumped up, shouting the dog's name and issuing apologies, and the whole fiasco triggered a relentless bark from a trembling Chihuahua. Out of nowhere, a cockatoo swooped in and landed on Gracie's shoulder, giving a squawk that wrenched a return squawk out of her.

What in the world was happening?

"Can I help you?" Renee asked as more dogs joined in the barking. She was calm, as if this was an everyday occurrence in her world, but Gracie was sure she saw a slight twitch in the corner of Renee's eye as she scooped the spilled treats back into the jar.

Gracie shrugged her shoulder, trying to oust the bird, but he stayed put.

"Is it always like this?" she asked.

"Like what?"

Gracie looked around, astonished that Renee even had to ask.

"Oh, this chaos?" Renee asked. "Absolutely."

Gracie shrugged at the bird again. No avail. A gray-and-white cat jumped up on the counter and sauntered toward her. The bird squawked, and Gracie braced herself for a bird-cat tussle with her right in the middle, but the cat simply blinked sleepily and lay down. Right on Gracie's car keys, which she'd absently placed on the counter.

"You can't be serious," she mumbled. She tried to edge her hand under the cat, but every time she came close, the cat glared at her and she snatched her hand back.

"Do you have an appointment? Or…you know…an animal?" Renee asked.

"No, and no," Gracie answered. "I'm here for food."

She heard a door open and shut behind the reception desk and out popped David. He took one look at her and tucked his chin down to suppress a smile. That didn't work, so he ended up covering the lower half of his face with the file folder he was holding instead. Gracie gave an impatient shrug and the bird finally fluttered from her shoulder.

And landed, instead, on top of her head.

This elicited an audible chuckle. "I've got this one, Renee," he said. "Do you mind taking Sugar on back? Get her on the scale for me? Leo's busy with some ear mites."

"Sure thing," Renee said, giving a half-hearted wave at the bird, which only hopped in place and squawked at her. She shrugged at Gracie apologetically and scurried away.

Gracie wasn't great at playing it cool to begin with. She had no idea how to play it cool with a bird on her head and her car keys currently warming under the belly of a cat. Still, she gathered herself up and pasted on as serious a face as she could muster.

David's face…not so serious. *He is loving this*, she thought bitterly. *Just another reason to dislike him. What kind of man delights in someone else's discomfort?* Extreme *discomfort.*

"Miss Langhorst, what can I do for you?"

"Really? You're really asking that?"

He raised his eyebrows innocently. "You're here for a reason, I presume. How can I help you?"

She pointed up at the top of her head. "You can get this thing off of me for starters. Its toenails are sharp."

"Talons."

"Whatever they are, they're sharp. Please get the thing off my head."

He winced, then leaned in and whispered, "Ethel doesn't like to be called a thing."

"Oh, she doesn't?" Gracie whispered back. "I'm so sorry."

"It's okay. You can apologize to her later. She's a pretty forgiving old gal."

Gracie leaned over the counter, and gestured for him to lean closer to her. She could smell the spice of his aftershave, and couldn't help noticing that his smile was quite nice.

Didn't matter.

"Get it off my head," she said, her voice loud and commanding.

"Her," he countered, laughing.

"Get it off!" She didn't want to yell. She didn't intend to yell. When she arrived today, she had no inkling that she might yell. Yet here she was, yelling, setting off a whole new series of barks. She took a breath and let it out, slow and steady. She closed her eyes. "Please remove Ethel from my head."

"Okay," he said. "Why didn't you say so? Come on, Ethel, you prankster. Not everybody is into fun and games." He made a noise with his mouth, and the bird flapped from her head to his shoulder. He pulled a handful of birdseed out of his pocket, and sprinkled it across the length of the counter. The bird hopped down to the counter and pecked at the food he'd sprinkled.

Like it was no big deal. Easy. Something that happened every day.

To be fair, around here, it probably did. In a law office, not so much.

"Thank you," Gracie said through gritted teeth. "Also…" She pointed at the sleeping cat.

David's eyes followed where she was pointing. "Sarah? What about her? She can't possibly be offending you. She's napping."

"My car keys are in there," Gracie said.

"In there? Sarah *ate* your car keys?" Now he looked alarmed.

"No, it's sleeping on them. Every time I try to get them, it gives me a look."

"There's that word again," he said. "It."

"Can you just get my keys out from under the cat, please?" Gracie's patience was running thin.

He slipped a hand under the cat and had the keys out before the cat's eyes were even fully open. He gave them to Gracie, his hand lightly brushing against hers. She ignored the jolting sensation she got when their hands touched. That…was not supposed to happen.

It was adrenaline. Had to be. She was just on high alert because of the animals. Who wouldn't get a little agitated with a strange bird's tiny talons digging into their scalp? Except for David, of course. Nothing seemed to rattle him. He could have an ostrich balanced on his head and would just go about his business like it was no big deal.

"Food," she croaked, bypassing any more niceties. She just needed to get out of here before she completely lost it.

Again, his eyebrows raised. "Are you asking me to lunch? I haven't had any yet. But I have to say, this is unexpected, given the whole gun situation previously. And, you know, the fact that you don't like me at all and think I'm always up to something shady. Are you thinking of poisoning me?"

The very thought of having to have lunch with David rattled her even further. It didn't sound like the worst idea in the world. There had to be something wrong with her that she was cozying up to him. *It's probably his relentless...niceness*, she thought bitterly.

She couldn't play along. Not anymore. She just needed to get out of there.

The look on her face must have telegraphed her struggle, because the levity fell from his, and he hurried to the cabinet behind him.

"For Fannie, I assume?" he asked, pulling cans down. "I just asked Vera yesterday if she needed more and she said no."

"She must have forgotten," Gracie said, grateful that he'd turned away and taken some of the spell with him. She still felt off-kilter, but at least she could speak again.

"Not like her." He grabbed a plastic bag and tossed the cans inside.

"Well, she's not exactly herself right now. Not that I would expect you to know." Good. Her snark was back.

So why did that also make her unhappy?

He shooed the cat away and set the bulging bag on the counter. "I am a little out of touch with Vera." He leaned on the counter, and again Gracie began to feel that wooziness press in on her. Why was he so intoxicating? "But that's because someone is standing in the way. Literally. Are you keeping all of her friends away, or am I special?"

"Oh, you're special, all right," Gracie spat. "A special pain in my neck. I overheard you with her on the front porch. All your whining about needing more space for your office, as if that's her problem. You're very transparent."

"I never said it was her problem. I was chatting. Catching up. She's my friend, Gracie. We chat and catch up. That's what friends do."

"She's your dying friend who just happens to be sitting on a fat plot of land. You walk around there acting like you care."

"I do care."

"And you talk to her like you care."

"I do care."

"Are you sure you're not just hoping that she'll go ahead and die so you can get your hands on that land for free? Hoping that she'll leave you a little something in her will?"

"I am most definitely not. And, honestly, I feel a little sorry for you."

Gracie balked. "Sorry for me?"

He nodded. "It must be really sad and lonely to walk through life feeling so jaded and distrustful. Are you always this way?"

Gracie blinked, surprised at the sting she felt. "Am I always in touch with reality? Yes."

"Not my reality. My reality is that Vera and I are friends, and that I don't want anything from her. I'm happy to help her. Maybe you just can't relate because you're sad and lonely."

"I'm actually quite happy. Fulfilled."

Gracie wasn't even sure what she was saying anymore. She only knew that, as long as she kept talking, she would remain immune to what he was saying. Because the truth was, it was all hitting a little close to home. Her chest had begun to feel heavy.

"I know how people work, David, and you're no different. People are greedy and always looking out for themselves. The truth is, I'm a little unexpected wrench in your plans. Now you've got to charm her extra hard, and I'll tell you what, if you want to charm my grandma, you're going to have to first get through me. And I am not charmable." She paused, realizing that maybe she'd made it sound as if she wanted him to charm her, which was actually the last thing she wanted. She also realized she was breathing hard, and that tears had threatened to sprout in her eyes.

No. She was not going to cry today. Not in front of him. Never in front of him.

She'd stared down some of the hardest opponents in court, had been flustered beyond belief, fighting for her client, knowing she was about to lose, and never—not one time!—had she ever cried. She couldn't even imagine the amount of torment she would receive from Jem if so much as a single tear slid down her cheek in the middle of the fight.

Andrew called her The Great Wall of Stitchknot, Goodwell and Reese—a nickname that both pleased and insulted her. She wanted to be soft. Kind. The type of friend that people came to for a shoulder to cry on. The person she believed she could be on the inside. But she wasn't those things on the outside. Good, bad or otherwise, it was just reality.

She blinked hard to will the tears back inside, and somehow, it worked.

David, however, looked as hurt as she felt.

Well, that was what you wanted, Gracie, wasn't it?

I'm not sure what I want anymore, she thought. *I just want to get out of here*.

She grabbed the bag of dog food in one hand and opened her purse with the other. "What do I owe you?"

David shook his head. "Nothing. It's on me."

"No. This stuff is expensive. How much?"

"I don't know how else to say this. Vera is my friend. I want nothing from her. I haven't charged her since she got sick. And I'm not going to charge her through you, either. Take from that what you will." He turned and walked into the back, just as Renee reappeared behind the desk.

Renee watched David leave, concern on her face, and then turned to Gracie. "Is there anything else I can get you, sweetie?" Maybe Gracie was reading into things, but that *sweetie* felt loaded with something else. Why was everyone so protective of this man?

Gracie cleared her throat and pulled herself up taller. "I just need to pay for this," she said, her voice cold, clinical.

"Is that for Fannie?" Renee waved her away. "Doctor McBride never charges Vera anything. All on him. He's a big old softie, especially when it comes to that silly dog and those two alpacas."

"The Langhorsts don't do charity," Gracie said. She reached into her purse, grabbed a twenty and tossed it down on the counter, then turned on her heel and left before Renee could say anything more. She tried not to notice the eyes that followed her out of the clinic, everyone having just heard all of her dirty laundry spilled right there in public.

She pushed through the door and paused, eyes closed. She took a few breaths. She'd finally told David exactly what she thought. Actually, what she *knew*. And she'd let him know that, under no circumstances, was she going to let his scam fly.

So why couldn't she get the dejected look on his face out of her mind?

And why did she feel so rotten? Like maybe *she* was the one in the wrong?

TWO RINGWORMS, an eye infection, a urinary tract infection, three new puppy visits and a nervous licker. And still all David could think about was what Gracie had said about his relationship with Vera.

After her for her land and money. How could she possibly think that about him?

He was offended. But, more than that, he was hurt. The idea that Vera might also think these things gutted him.

A class had just ended when he pulled into the

McBride Pathways parking lot, and there were kids everywhere. Ever since Decker brought Morgan West on board, his equine therapy business had boomed, with families coming from Oak Hollow, Spearville, and even as far away as Riverside. Morgan was good at her job. And, more than that, she was good at loving Decker. David had never seen his brother so happy.

Decker was in the barn, helping Ben and Annie untack the horses. He glanced up when David walked in.

"Make yourself useful," he said, nodding in the direction of one of the horses, which was cross-tied and waiting.

David walked over and began unbuckling the girth. "How are the wedding plans going?" he asked.

"About there," Decker said. "Morgan's getting really nervous. Wanting everything to go perfectly. You know."

David chuckled. His little brother was not a nervous perfectionist kind of guy. He must be driving his fiancée nuts with his laid-back demeanor.

"I don't know what you're laughing about," Decker said. "If she sees you, she's gonna make a beeline. She's got a whole checklist of best man duties that she plans to throw at you. You have a date yet?"

David pulled the girth off the horse and tossed it over his shoulder. "Man, you get right to it, don't you?"

"If I don't, she will."

"I promise you, not having a date will not hinder my performance as your best man."

"Just ask Renee. She'll go with you."

"I can't do that. She works for me. I don't want her to get the wrong idea. And it would be weird, anyway."

"Ask Ellory."

David considered this. When Ellory first moved to Haw Springs and opened her coffee shop, she made it no secret that she was interested. And he would have been a fool to not have his eye caught by her—beautiful, sweet and talented. But two minutes into a coffee date, they both agreed that they were destined for friendship over romance. Ellory was his buddy.

"Little sister material," was all David said. This time Decker laughed, because he knew the whole story.

"Well, little sisters can go to weddings." Decker finished up his horse, disconnected him from the cross-ties, and led him to a barn stall. All locked in, he came back to David and clapped him on the shoulder. "Listen, man, you know I don't care if you come alone. Just show up on time, in your suit, and hold the rings. Job done." He scuffed away to begin untacking the last horse. "So what brings you over tonight?" he called. "I haven't seen you in a while."

"Been busy." David lifted the saddle and pads off his horse and slung them over his arm. "I have a question for you. You know the Langhorst farm next door, right?"

"Yeah?"

"Do you remember when we were kids, there was a kid over there? A girl?"

Decker stood, removed his cowboy hat, gave his head a scratch, thinking, and returned the hat. He scrunched up his face. "Yeah. Maybe. She didn't go to school with us, though, did she?"

David set the saddle on the ground and stretched his back. It had been an extraordinarily long day and he was ready to call it a night. "She did, but a few years behind us, so we didn't really pay her any attention." She wasn't the kind of person you could ignore, though, so how that was possible, he didn't really know.

Ben appeared at Decker's side, and took over untacking Decker's horse. Simultaneously, Annie arrived at the horse David had just untacked. The two brothers turned over the work and walked out of the barn and into the crisp evening air together. Seemed like fall had just begun to arrive, and already it was passing them by.

"Why are you asking?" Decker asked.

"This girl…this woman. She's back. It's kind of impossible to get to know her on any level. She's Vera Langhorst's granddaughter, and she's truly terrible to deal with. Bad attitude, in your face all the time, held me at gunpoint."

Decker stopped short, his eyebrows lifted. "She held you at gunpoint?"

"More than once. Heck, more than a couple of times. And I can't get a single word with Vera without this woman accusing me of trying to wrestle Vera's land out from under her. I can't seem to get her to understand…well, anything. But especially not that I've been Vera's vet for a long time, and that I'm there helping out as a friend. She does nothing but toss her red hair around and clench her tiny fists and come at me like a mad hen, and I seem to remember running into her over there when we were kids. She wasn't pleasant then, either. I remember being up on the ridge and she was on the other side of the fence, picking something. Blackberries, maybe? And I remember her telling me that just because one of the blackberry bushes had grown through the fence onto our side, it didn't make it ours, and so I got off my horse and started picking them just because she—what? Why are you looking at me like that?"

Decker was grinning at him knowingly. "You seem awfully worked up about her is all," he said.

"She's been in my space everywhere I go and—did you not hear me say she held me at gunpoint?"

"Morgan used to give me fits, too."

"Give you fits with a shotgun in your face?"

They stood in the circle of light that shone out from the barn, the soft whinnies of the horses in the background. David thought he could hear Henry honking in the distance.

"I'm just saying, you remember a lot of details about her…and her tiny fists full of blackberries."

"That's a childhood memory."

"One you've obviously been thinking about a bit."

That, David couldn't argue with. He had been thinking about Gracie a lot. He told himself he was just trying to place where he'd seen her before, but he was starting to suspect that she'd somehow wormed her way inside his thoughts, not only a storm cloud stomping into his office and trailing him across Vera's pasture every day, but a clap of thunder following him home, too, in his mind.

"I didn't ask for her to appear in my life," David said. "I'm just doing my job, and she's always right there. Right." He waved his hand in front of his face. "There."

"To be fair, I didn't ask for Morgan, either. But

then, all of a sudden, she was." Decker waved his hand in front of his face. "Right. There. And now I can't imagine my life without her." *Wave, wave*. "Right. There."

"Well, I can definitely imagine life without Gracie, that's for sure. It's a calm life. It's a quiet life."

"Too calm? Too quiet?"

David raised his eyebrows. "You been in my office lately? Calm and quiet are relative. And the last thing I need is another...squawker."

Decker laughed and clapped David on the shoulder again. "I promise I will never tell her that you called her a squawker. Listen, brother, if she's that much of a pain, why don't you stop going over there? Vera's not paying you. She just wants someone to feed and check in on the animals. Sounds like Little Miss Blackberry is more than capable of doing that. Just let her have it. Vera will be on her way, and Gracie will go on her way, and the animals will...well...they'll find a place for them, I'm sure."

"That's why I can't do it," David said. "I've bonded with them. I can't bear the thought of Sam and Betty going off to some strange farm where nobody will tell Betty that her new hairdo looks beautiful or ask Sam about the weather."

Decker screwed up his face at his brother.

"What?" David shrugged. "You can't tell me

you've never had conversations with Tango. Or June."

"Oh, he has them all the time." A voice cut through the darkness. Morgan was walking down the hill from the main office toward them. She was holding her son, Archer, who had his head resting on her shoulder. "He thinks I don't overhear it, but I do. *Tango, do you think my bride is going to make you wear flowers? She's going crazy with the flowers,*" she mimicked as she stepped into the light. *"Just because her sister's a florist, I don't know why we have to have so many flowers."*

"You heard that, huh?" Decker pushed his hands into his pockets and ducked his head.

"I hear everything." She turned on David. "And what's this I hear about you not having a date to the wedding?"

David shrugged. "I'm going as the eligible bachelor best man."

"I can find someone for you. Just say the word."

"And here we are again," David said. "Gotta go."

"I'm sorry," Morgan said. "I don't mean to press."

"Yes, you do." David leaned over and gave her a kiss on the cheek, then gave Archer's hair a quick ruffle. "But I know you do it out of the goodness of your heart. And you know that I'm not interested in finding someone right now. My life is just too busy for that." His phone buzzed in his pocket. He pulled it out and shook it in the air. "Speaking of. I've gotta run."

"Bye," Decker said, knowing better than to try and pick up his fiancée's case.

"Wait. Are you going to the Haw Games Day?" Morgan asked.

David had forgotten all about Haw Games Day, the Saturday in September when the whole town turned out to celebrate the return of autumn by competing with one another through feats of strength and skill and silliness.

"Oh, I might stop by," David said. "Haven't been in a year or two."

"He hasn't been since he realized that he can't beat me at any single competition," Decker said. "He's been sore about it for years."

"Ah," David said. "Yep, that's what it is. I'm sore that I can't beat you at slingshot target practice and riding a child's tractor."

"See? Sore."

"You do sound a little sore," Morgan said, chuckling. "I'm excited about it. Haven't been since I was a kid. I forgot Haw Games Day even existed. I think Archer will love it. It's fun people-watching. You should come out. Even if you don't compete."

Decker snickered. “Yeah. Even if you can’t compete.”

“Now, that’s not what I said.” Morgan slapped at Decker’s arm. She rolled her eyes. “Brothers.”

“I’ll think about it,” David said, just as his phone buzzed again in his pocket. “Gotta go.”

“Convenient,” Decker said on a fake cough.

“I said I’ll think about it,” David said, though he had no intention of doing anything of the sort. For starters, if he wanted to compete in Haw Games, he would need a partner. And he most definitely didn’t have one of those.

CHAPTER FIVE

WHILE SHE HADN'T done it in a while, it wasn't unusual for Vera to call David when she needed something. She heard coyotes in the field and wondered if he could check on the animals, or she hadn't heard the rooster in a few days, or she thought maybe Betty had a little bit of a limp. Any number of things could cause her to summon David to the ranch.

And sometimes, when he was sitting at her kitchen table, finishing up a bowl of homemade chili, checking his watch, texting Leo to go ahead and start the next visit without him, he wondered if he wasn't being summoned simply because she was lonely.

Still, he was happy to oblige. Vera was the closest thing to a mom he'd ever had.

But it was unusual for her to call these days.

Which was why he hurried to answer when his phone buzzed a second time as he was pulling out of Decker's driveway, concern tugging at his gut.

"Hello? Everything okay?"

"It's about time you picked up." Gracie, not Vera. Since her visit to the office a few weeks ago, Gracie had given him a bit of space—still there, still following him, still glaring, but from across the field or the front porch or the pasture gate. Seeing her always filled him with indignation, underlined by the strangest sense of calm, as if everything was right with the world as long as she was in his orbit. "Do you always ignore your phone calls, Doctor McBride? Seems very undoctorly of you."

"I don't think that's a word."

"What if I was calling because my dog was stuck in a well?"

"Then he's not going anywhere, and can wait for me to answer my phone," David said.

"You're not funny."

"I wasn't aware that this was a comedy show." He pinched the bridge of his nose between his thumb and forefinger. "Can I help you in some way? Is Vera okay? Why are you calling from her phone?"

"Ironically," Gracie said, "I called from her phone because I didn't think you would answer if I called from mine. I figured since you and Grandma were *such close friends*, you'd pick up right away if she called. But you didn't. Maybe your friendship has been a little exaggerated, after all."

"I don't know if you realize this," David said. "But in order for us to be talking, I had to answer my phone. Just because you didn't get to talk to me at the exact moment that you wanted to…you know what? I'm wasting my breath. Is Vera okay?" He was starting to get annoyed. At this point, he could drive over and see for himself what was going on with Vera. "Do the animals need something?"

"She's fine. They're all fine. Impatient. Sheesh."

"Thank you for finally answering my question."

"I live to serve." She was being snarky, of course, but David could hear an undertone of something else there—enjoyment? An attempt at playfulness, maybe? He decided to play back.

"So why are you calling? Just wanted to hear my voice?"

"You caught me. I just didn't think I was going to be able to sleep tonight without the soothing sound of you berating me."

David's eyebrows flew up and he gripped the phone, pressed it closer to his ear. "*Me* berating *you*?"

"Yes, it's what you appear to do best, even though you're supposedly good with animals or something."

"*Me?* Berating *you*?"

"Is there an echo in here—oh, hang on." There was mumbling in the background, during which David once again mouthed, *Me, berating you. Unbelievable*. Then Gracie came back on the line, sounding forced and slightly under duress, although again, David could hear something softer beneath. Or maybe he was just imagining the softer part. Maybe Decker was right, and there was something about this girl that he liked. Maybe she was right, and he enjoyed their little banter. But if that was the case, why did he always feel such irritation when they talked?

Ah, but you also feel exhilaration, don't you?

"I think you can add the word *berating* right under the word *apology* on the list of words you clearly don't know the definition of," he said.

"*Anyway*, the reason I'm calling you is to invite you to dinner."

David paused. This was such a shift, he felt like he was spinning. One moment, Gracie was accusing him of berating her, and the next, she was inviting him to a casual hangout. "You want me to come to dinner."

She sighed, the gust muffling the phone. "Why are you always repeating what I say? Is this a bad connection? Yes. Dinner. The thing where you pick up silverware, get food on it, put it into your mouth and chew. Actually, I'm assuming you use silverware. Maybe you just gnaw food off of your plate like the alpacas. In fact, if you'd prefer, we can just sling your food out into the field and let you do just that."

David stifled a laugh. She was creative; he had to give her that. "Betty will be so excited to have a guest," he said.

"Is that a yes?"

"It's a why. I don't understand. You haven't exactly rolled out a welcome mat for me, and now you're inviting me over?"

"Maybe I've changed my mind about you."

"Is that so?"

"No. The invitation is coming from my grandma."

"Ah, I see. In that case, when?"

"Tomorrow. Six o'clock."

He rubbed his forehead. If Vera was asking, of course he would be there. However, he didn't exactly want to have dinner with Gracie Langhorst. But then again, he kind of did. And he couldn't explain why, even to himself. But if Decker got wind of this, he would never hear the end of it. And if Morgan found out, he would have a date to the wedding in a matter of seconds. "Can we make it six thirty? Six forty-five if you want me to change clothes. And you probably do."

He heard murmuring, and then she came back on the line. "We'll go with seven, so you can shower, too, if you'd like. Actually, I require you to shower."

"I thought I was eating with Betty. Shouldn't we ask her?"

"Don't push it or you will be eating with her." David became aware that he was smiling, and tried to tamp it down. "Does that mean you're coming?"

"Sure. Why not? I'm honored that you're willing to stoop so low as to eat dinner with a thief."

"What can I say, I'm a real humanitarian. To keep my life from being sad and lonely and all that."

"Ah, and are you planning to hold your gun on me the whole time?"

"Of course I am."

The line went dead.

David stared at his phone for a long moment, unsure of why he was smiling while he did so. When he was sure that the disconnection hadn't been a mistake or fluke, he thumbed his phone off and tucked it into the breast pocket of his scrubs. "Looking forward to it," he said aloud, and, surprisingly, found that he was.

GRACIE HAD NO idea why she was bustling around so much all day. Dusting this, polishing that, and why on earth was she fussing over dinner, anyway? It wasn't like her grandmother was going to eat it, and she was the only one at this little dinner party who mattered.

Are you sure about that? a tiny voice in the back of her mind piped up.

"Yes, I'm sure," she said aloud, spraying window cleaner onto the dining room window. She gave it such a good scrub, her arm felt tired. And, if she was being truthful, the window looked exactly the same as it did before she began scrubbing it.

Maybe you're working too hard to impress him.

"And maybe you need to mind your own business." She commenced polishing the window frame, aware that she had just admonished herself aloud.

She knew what Vera was up to. And she knew it wouldn't work. Not in a million years. He may be handsome. And smart. Funny. Accomplished. Somewhat charming. But she was not interested.

Right. Because who wants all that in a man?

She stopped. "You know, you're really starting to get on my nerves."

"Who are you talking to?" Vera asked from her spot on the recliner. Gracie startled. She had thought her grandma was asleep.

"Nobody." Gracie swiped at a missed smudge. "Myself. Sorry."

"No need to be sorry. I wander around this

place talking to myself all the time." Vera chuckled. "My mother used to say that was the only way she could get an intelligent conversation. I guess you come from a long line of solo conversationalists." She went back to her show.

Gracie pushed her hair out of her face with the back of her hand. She never thought of herself as a solo conversationalist, but now that she pondered it, she did do quite a bit of talking to herself.

Because who else are you going to talk to, rattling around your apartment by yourself all the time? You're afraid to admit that you're lonely, and you make up for it by talking to an invisible audience.

Gracie clenched her jaw, refusing to acknowledge the little voice. Hoping it would go away, even though she knew it wouldn't.

You're also afraid to admit that you think David McBride is very interesting, and would be a great person to talk to. A much better person than yourself.

"Okay, that's enough. You don't know what you're talking about," Gracie spat, unable to keep her thoughts inside. Vera chuckled again, but didn't say anything.

If it wasn't for her grandmother, this dinner date would never be happening. Gracie just didn't want to let her grandma down by fighting her on anything. She could see that Vera was weakening. Her final days loomed over them like an unwanted houseguest. So when Vera said she needed dog food, when there was clearly enough food to feed Fannie for a lifetime, Gracie went and fetched food. When she insisted that Gracie continue to allow David to visit the farm, Gracie allowed David to visit the farm. And when she proposed a dinner...*well, here we are.*

She'd decided on chicken and dumplings, because that seemed the closest thing to broth that she could make for everyone to enjoy. Dumplings were light and easy on a stomach, right? In the back of her mind, though, she knew it didn't really matter. She knew that her grandmother would be unable to eat the meal, no matter what it was, and that she would use that as an excuse to abandon Gracie at the table with David.

Gracie was already logging a list of non-confrontational small-talk subjects for when this happened. *Were you born and raised in Haw Springs? What do you think of this weather? Why did you decide to become a veterinarian? What's your favorite breed of dog?*

As boring and bland as broth, but it would get her through the meal. She would survive, her grandmother would be happy and everything would be fine.

She finished polishing the windowsill and went back to the kitchen to check on the chicken. It was just coming to boil, the fragrance of onion and garlic that she'd dropped into the pot beginning to rise into the air. She inhaled deeply and smiled. She wasn't much of a cook—she didn't need to be. She mostly existed on convenient takeout and gallons of coffee at home.

But her grandmother had taught her to cook in this very kitchen, and the chicken smelled exactly as it was supposed to smell. She was happy—and somewhat surprised—to discover that she hadn't lost her skill.

The doorbell rang.

She checked her watch and frowned. "That better not be him," she mumbled, her hand flying to her unruly hair that she'd only partially trapped into a loose ponytail. "Who shows up for a dinner party so early?"

She hurried to put the cleaning supplies back in the cabinet, seeing all the places she neglected to clean along the way, and yanked the ponytail holder out of her hair. She sniffed at her flannel shirt, decided to ditch it by tossing it down the laundry chute in the mudroom, and hurriedly tucked her T-shirt into her jeans as she walked.

She gave her hair one more smooth-over and swiped the dewy sweat from under her eyes with her fingers before opening the door. She couldn't tell if the flurry of heartbeats racing around in her chest was excitement, nerves or irritation.

Probably a mix of all of the above.

"That's fair," she said, then lifted her chin defiantly, reached out, grabbed the doorknob and pulled open the door. "How rude of you to show up so early. I would expect nothing less." She stopped short.

"Hi, Gracie."

The man standing on the porch in a dirty pair of chinos, a dingy white T-shirt, and a grimy trucker cap was familiar to Gracie only from photos, a few grainy memories, and one incident from a few years ago that she had made every effort to forget. But she would recognize him anywhere. The stench of stale booze and old cigarette smoke surrounding him. The steel-gray eyes that she inherited—only his peered out at the world flat and dead, always assessing the weak link, the injured prey, the next target. The sharp jawline with the scar that marched up from the corner of his mouth toward his cheekbone. The upturned chin of smug defiance.

Farley Langhorst, long-lost father extraordinaire. The man she'd given a million chances. And who'd failed a million and one.

"What are you doing here?"

"Now, is that the way you greet your own

blood? I came to see my dying mother. To bond and pay my respects."

"No, you didn't," Gracie said.

A dangerous grin slid across his face and his eyes narrowed. "You sure that's how you wanna play this reunion?"

Gracie swallowed around the lump in her throat. "I'm not playing anything, because it's not a game. And it's not a reunion. Last time we tried to reunite, you robbed my house."

"And you had me thrown in jail. Trust me, I remember."

Vera's voice drifted from the living room. "Gracie? Who's at the door, honey?"

"It's me, Mama. I came to see you!" Farley yelled, his dead eyes and Cheshire cat grin pointed directly at Gracie the whole time. "You gonna let me in?" he asked softly.

No. Never. Not in a billion years. You can keep on marching right back down that road toward wherever it was you slithered out from.

"Farley? Is that really you?" Vera called. "Well, come on in and let me see you."

"Sure," Gracie said, numb as she backed away, opening the door farther to make room for him to step inside. "Come on in."

CHAPTER SIX

"WELL, I'LL BE," Vera said, sitting up straighter. She punched around on the remote until she found the button to mute her TV show. "Are my eyes deceiving me?"

Gracie trailed behind her father, unsure what exactly it was that she was feeling in this moment. Frustration, mistrust, annoyance…but also that same, unnerving excitement laced with the tiniest bit of hope that she'd held on to her entire life. It was the hope that maybe this time would be different. Even if her logical brain told her that it would never be different—*he* would never be different—she just couldn't stop herself from feeling that optimism. It was like it was built into her, and no matter how tough she made herself be, it was still always there, just under the surface.

She hated that about herself.

Farley took off his ball cap and fidgeted with it. "Hi, Mama."

Gracie gritted her teeth. That fidget, that vulnerable *Mama* was calculated, she just knew it.

"Farley Joseph Langhorst, as I live and breathe. Where have you been?"

"Well, as you know, I spent some time *away*," he said, shooting a look at Gracie.

She shrugged. "Do the crime, do the time."

"I never got a chance to explain my side."

"Your side was that you robbed my house while I was at work and stole checks to try to steal from my bank account, too. No explanation needed."

"Doesn't matter where I've been." He tossed his hat on the couch with a familiarity that made Gracie seethe, and went to his mother's side. He leaned down and gave her a kiss. "I'm here now. How are you, Mama?" He sat on the chair where Gracie normally sat and grabbed his mother's hand in both of his. "I wanted to come see you and…you know…well, I've heard things…aren't going so well."

The hope that tickled the back of Gracie's mind popped and vanished like a soap bubble. She knew her father well enough to know what "things" he heard. She narrowed her gaze at him and lowered herself on the couch across from them.

"Well, son, no I'm not doing so well," Vera said. "I'm an old lady. It's to be expected. But

Gracie here is taking such good care of me, I can hardly complain about anything."

"That's what *family* is for," Gracie said, her body so tense, she felt as if a slight breeze might cause her to crack and break into pieces. Farley glanced at her, then glanced away. She wasn't important to his scam right now—an unspoken indictment that only worsened her rigidity. The gall.

"You should have told me, Mama. I'd have come sooner."

"I'm sure you would have," Gracie said.

She could feel the displeasure radiating from him, and the effort that he made to not be distracted by her, not look back at her again. She tried to let it bolster her. Tried to ignore the tremor in her hands, the tingle in her feet, the numbness in her belly. She was no longer an abandoned child. She was a grown woman who had so many bones to pick with Farley Langhorst, she might as well have a whole skeleton.

Vera weakly patted the back of Farley's hand with her free one. "I didn't want to worry you. I'm sure you have a very busy life."

"I'm never too busy for you, Mama. Family is everything. You know that."

"Hah." The noise slipped out of Gracie, but she found she wasn't sad or embarrassed by it. Especially when she saw tension rise in his shoulders. Gracie whisked herself off the couch before she made another noise, or maybe the creaking of her eye-rolls distracted the conversation. *Never too busy. Family is everything.* In all of Gracie's life, Farley had visited his mother only a handful of times. Each and every one of those visits was with an upturned palm extended. And as soon as he got what he'd come after, he was gone again, suddenly too busy for his mother. Not to mention his daughter.

Daughter. Whatever.

Gracie wasn't about to give him a dime, so she wasn't even the tiniest blip on his radar.

"I'm going to check the soup." She walked into the kitchen on stiff legs, unaware of the out-of-control fluttering in her chest until she'd paused to lean against the counter. *Breathe. Just breathe. He's not supposed to be here, and his presence makes everything one thousand times worse. But you can handle it. You can handle anything. As long as you breathe.* Now the tiny voice was making sense. She put her head down and did just that, trying to let go of a lifetime of disappointment, anger and indignation.

She was five when she'd come to live with her grandma Vera permanently, so she had only snippets of memories of living with Farley. She only had vague recollections of being hungry and wanting, but not necessarily hungry and wanting for food. She remembered feeling sorry for her grandma, a young widow all alone on such a big expanse of land, and feeling a kinship with her beyond blood that she couldn't quite understand. Her cravings felt satisfied before she ate a single morsel of food at her grandmother's table, the gnawing in her gut gone before Farley had even left the driveway.

It wasn't until much later that she came to realize that her own vast, empty expanse was within her rather than under her feet, and that was the bond that they truly shared.

When Gracie's mother died, she'd clung to her grandmother's legs at the funeral, refusing to leave the woman's side. Julia, with her crippling addictions that eventually bested her, had hardly been a doting mother, but she was at least a buffer between Farley and Gracie. With her gone, who would save Gracie when Farley flew into one of his rages? Gracie knew better than to be a loud, complaining child, but she begged as hard as she could with her eyes for her grandmother to please save her from being alone with Farley.

She was astonished when her pleas were seemingly heard. Her grandmother suggested letting Gracie come home with her while Farley sorted out his life. By *sort out your life*, Vera had meant to get a handle on the same addiction that had killed Julia. Farley had bristled at first, but then the very next day, without a word, Farley had tossed Gracie and a suitcase into the back seat of his car, and deposited her on her grandmother's farm.

It was only then, in the comfort of her grandmother's arms, that Gracie had allowed herself tears. Vera had shushed and comforted her, likely thinking she was crying over her lost family, her lost home.

But they had been tears of relief. Vera was her family. Vera was her home.

She lifted the lid off the Dutch oven and breathed in the scent of the softly boiling chicken. She let the scent calm her as she stirred it.

"Everything will be okay, Gracie," she told herself. "He will go away again. It's what he does best."

And, she couldn't forget, the clock was ticking. David would be coming over soon, and…

She felt a jolt. David would be coming over soon and would get a front row seat to Farley's shenanigans. She didn't want to care. What was it to her if David witnessed something embarrassing? Why be embarrassed in front of him, anyway? It wasn't like she owed him anything or would ever see him after…well, after.

She hustled back into the living room. Farley remained in her chair. She gritted her teeth and ignored him.

"Grandma, I was thinking maybe we ought to cancel tonight?"

Farley perked up. "Cancel what?"

"Oh, no, honey, I don't see why we should do that," Vera said.

Gracie pointed at Farley's back. "I do."

Farley turned to face her. "What are we canceling?"

"*We* aren't canceling anything, because *you* have nothing to do with this," Gracie said.

"Now, Gracie," Vera reprimanded. She didn't need to say more. Gracie knew exactly what *Now, Gracie* meant. She clapped her mouth shut. To Farley, Vera said, "We're having a dinner guest tonight."

"He'll be here at seven." Gracie checked her watch. "So you'll want to get moving soon."

Farley turned back to his mother. "I was hoping to get more time with you. I thought maybe I'd stay here for a few days. Or, you know, until..."

"Hah," Gracie said again. Apparently, she just couldn't stop that noise from coming out whenever Farley talked.

He whipped around in his chair again. His face was red and creased, as if he wanted to lash out at her, but then he seemed to think better of it, pressed his lips together in sorrowful sympathy, and turned back.

Gracie wanted to cry out, alert her grandmother. What he was doing was purposeful and fake—she had literally just seen it in his face. *Watch out, Grandma! she wanted to shout. Don't fall for it! He hasn't changed in the least.*

But she could feel her grandmother's peace in the air. The look of comfort on her face as she and Farley wrapped hands together. She needed this in her finals days, to believe that her son maybe wasn't a total good-for-nothing after all.

Gracie would just have to grin and bear it, and deal with Farley later.

"I'm sure there's plenty of chicken and dumplings," Vera said, offering a warm smile. "Is there, Gracie?"

Gracie pasted on a smile over teeth gritted so hard she feared they might break and crumble right out of her mouth. She nodded.

"Then why don't you stay on for dinner, too, Farley?" Vera said. "It'll be good to catch up."

Farley's smile looked absolutely reptilian as he turned back to face Gracie once again. She felt his evilness all the way down to her toes.

"Why, thank you for the invitation," he said, pulling out each syllable slowly. "I think I will."

DAVID ENDED UP sitting at his desk in the dark for a solid thirty minutes, waiting for it to be an appropriate time to leave. The afternoon had been raucous and packed, but the problems had been manageable, and in the end, they'd closed up shop ten minutes early.

Renee had poked her head into the office half an hour ago, her purse slung over one shoulder. "Why are you sitting in the dark?"

"Just thinking," David said, although what he was really doing was overthinking, and possibly even working himself into a Ralphie the Screamer type of fit. "Taking a break. You know. Did Leo leave?"

Renee gave him a long, skeptical stare. "Yeah, about ten minutes ago. I'm headed out now. Unless you need something from me?"

He shook his head. "Have a good evening."

"Will you?" she asked, the skeptical look deepening.

"Of course. Why do you ask?"

"Because you're not exactly one to sit in the dark, *thinking*, for no reason."

He smiled. "First time for everything."

"I know what's eating at you, you know," she said, leaning against the doorframe. Renee was five years older than David, and fancied herself an older sister, quite often offering him advice he didn't ask for. But it was advice that he usually ended up taking anyway.

"Oh, yeah? What's that?"

"The practice is getting too big for you to handle alone. You want Leo to join you, but you don't have anything to offer him while we're crammed into this tiny building. You're afraid you won't be able to move us anywhere bigger and stay in Haw Springs. And you're afraid that, by the time you figure it all out, Leo will be long gone and working for someone in Riverside or who knows where. Or, worse, working for himself right here in Haw Springs. How'd I do?"

"Not bad," David said. *Although you forgot the part where, in the middle of all of this, I suddenly have this cute and frustrating redhead who I can't get out of my mind. Try thinking, when every time you shut your eyes, that sweetheart face pops into your head.*

"My dad used to have this saying," Renee said. "A full belly is worth nothing if your mind is starved."

They stared at each other for a beat. "What… does that mean?" David asked.

"Actually, now that I'm saying it aloud," Renee said, "I don't know. I think where I was going with it is that your practice is full, which is a great thing, but you're making yourself crazy, and…well, actually the quote doesn't precisely work. But you got the gist. I tried."

David laughed. "I do now, I suppose. Kind of. Not really. But thank you for trying."

"That's what I'm here for. Well, that and filing and answering phones and holding paws and cleaning up tinkle accidents and giving good, old ear scratches."

"All of which you're amazing at. Thank you, Renee. See you tomorrow."

"Have a good evening." She started to go, but thought better of it and turned back. "You sure that's all that's on your mind?"

David gave a thin smile.

"Ah," she said. "I see. Well. Have a great weekend."

That was the thing about having Renee for a fake big sister. She knew when it was her business to stay out of his business.

At exactly seven o'clock on the dot, David showed up on Vera's doorstep, holding a box of Ellory's cake pops in one hand and a bouquet of flowers in the other.

Gracie opened the door, and his breath caught. Her wild curls were glowing, backlit from the kitchen light shining behind her. She wore a snug, cream-colored T-shirt and a pair of worn jeans. She'd tied an apron around herself, her cheeks were pink and flushed, and she was holding salad tongs in one hand.

"I brought dessert," he said, thrusting the box of cake pops toward her as a greeting.

"Oh. Thank you," she said, taking the box. She stepped back to let him inside. Something was off about her. There was no fire, no fight. Just a *thank-you* and a silent step backwards.

"These are for your grandma," he said, holding out the flowers.

"She's in the living room," Gracie said. She turned on her heel and walked back toward the kitchen.

"Ooo-kay," David said, heading for the living room. At least he knew that Vera would be glad to see him.

But, to his surprise, Vera wasn't alone. There was a man sitting in the chair next to her, a ceramic bowl of walnuts and a silver flask in his lap. He pulled out a walnut, placed it in a cracker and squeezed it until it popped, spilling out its guts into his palm.

"Oh, David, I'm so glad you were able to make it." Vera held out a hand, but she looked small and weak in her chair. It was almost as if she'd shrunk since he last saw her a few days before on the front porch. As if she were withering away to nothing right before his eyes.

He grasped her hand, bent to give it a peck, and then pressed the flowers into it. "I brought these for you."

"Oh my goodness, how beautiful," she exclaimed, taking the bouquet in her shaky hands and holding it to her nose. "I'll make sure Gracie gets them in water right away. By the way,

David, I don't think you've ever met my son, Farley."

The man sitting next to her popped the walnut guts into his mouth, brushed his hands off on his jeans, and held one out to shake. "Hey."

"Pleasure," David said.

"You my daughter's boyfriend or something?" He used his thumb to open the flask and tipped it into his mouth. David could smell whisky in the air.

"Your daughter? Oh, you're Gracie's dad!" David felt very out of place, as if he'd busted in on a family reunion. He didn't remember there being a father around when they were kids—just Gracie and Vera. And, given Gracie's strangeness when she answered the door, her woodenness as she walked back to the kitchen, maybe Farley hadn't been around. And that was the problem. "Ah, no. I'm just a friend of Vera's. Gracie and I aren't dating."

"Although who wouldn't want them to be?" Vera asked. "Smart, handsome veterinarian such as yourself. Smart, beautiful lawyer such as my granddaughter. Both successful as all get-out. And both kindhearted like nobody's ever seen before. They would be a perfect match."

"Grandma." Gracie stood behind David, shaking her head, the two plaintive syllables coming out on a sigh. They briefly locked eyes. David tried to convey that he understood what her grandmother was trying to do, and he wasn't taking any of it seriously. But Gracie was too guarded and weary to notice. "Nobody is dating anybody," she said. "And dinner is ready."

Farley was first up and out of his seat, strolling off toward the dining room without so much as a look back at his mother. Gracie went to her grandma's chair and helped her lower the footrest, extract herself from her blankets, and slowly, slowly pull herself to standing.

The process was gentle and kind and not at all what David was used to seeing in Gracie. She handed him the bouquet of flowers. Then, as her grandmother got her feet under her and began walking toward the dining room, she took them back.

"I'll get these in water if you can help Grandma to the table," she said softly. "Very kind of you to bring these, Doctor McBride."

She padded away.

"Madam, can I escort you to the table?" he asked Vera, crooking one arm out playfully.

Vera cackled and looped her hand through his elbow. "Don't mind if you do, sir. I haven't had this handsome of an escort in a mighty long time. Gosh, it sure smells delicious, doesn't it? Gracie made it all herself. Not a lick of help from me when it comes to anything these days, poor thing."

"It was no big deal," Gracie said, emerging from the kitchen, *sans* flowers. She took over leading her grandmother to the table. "Just some chicken in a pot."

"Well, now you're downplaying yourself," Vera said. "You've been in there all day."

David surveyed the spread on the table, his stomach grumbling. It had been a longer day than he realized, and he was famished. "I think it looks and smells wonderful. I can't wait to dig in. Thank you for inviting me."

Farley, already eating before anyone else sat down, loudly slurped his soup. "No, she's right. Basically just chicken in a pot. You have something against saltshakers, girl?" He cackled, slurped again, and then made a face as he swallowed. "Bland." His eyes were glassy, and David wondered just how much of that flask he'd already put down.

The pink on Gracie's cheeks deepened as she focused on helping her grandmother into her seat. She didn't respond.

"Oh, Gracie is so thoughtful. She seasons that way for me. Don't you, sweetheart?" Vera said, settling in and spreading the napkin on her lap. "I'm afraid I just can't handle spices the way I used to. She keeps plenty of salt on the table, though, so you can season your own bowl."

Gracie gave a fumbling smile as she settled into the chair next to David. Her shoulder brushed up against his, sending a shot of warmth through him. He subtly edged his chair an inch or so away to give her room. He didn't feel the hostility that he normally felt rolling off of her. This version of Gracie seemed leaden, defeated. It was off-putting. He much preferred the Gracie he was used to.

"I would rather salt my own dishes," David said, trying to help out, but realizing that he just sounded strange. "You can always add more, but you can't take it out, right?"

"Well, isn't she just the best, then?" Farley poked his fork into his bowl, fished out a dumpling, and popped it whole into his mouth. Chewing with his mouth open, he said, "Guess I just missed out by not waiting, huh? Didn't know I'd need instructions to eat soup."

David felt Gracie stiffen beside him. Her fists were clenched in her lap. Her jaw was tight. David hadn't even known that Vera had a son until this evening, so he definitely didn't know much about the family dynamic. But it didn't take a genius to understand that this did not feel right. Strange and tense and coiled to strike.

"You can always salt your second bowl, Farley," Vera said. "Right, honey?" She slid a hand across the table. Gracie, offering another meek smile, took it. "Surely it's not that big of a deal."

"It's not," he said simply. He took another nip from the flask. "Just a little friendly criticism is all. Room for improvement. No need to take it personally."

"Please, everyone, help yourselves." Gracie's voice was small and wounded. David wanted more than anything for her to jump up from the table, pick up the shotgun leaning against the wall, and start bellowing about thievery and property and nobody fooling anyone. "You don't want it to get cold."

"Then it would be bland *and* cold." Farley laughed at his own joke while everyone else sat like statues.

Gracie dished a bowl of soup for Vera, who picked up a spoon but never did much more than wave it around in the air and lightly stir and poke at the contents inside the bowl. David noticed that she brought it to her lips only a handful of times.

"Might improve it if it was cold, actually," Farley mumbled, then, feigning surprise, shrugged his shoulders nearly to his ears. "What? It was a joke."

"Ha ha ha," Gracie deadpanned. "You're a riot."

"So, David, how was your day?" Vera asked,

obviously trying to save the dinner party from crashing and burning any further.

David, who thought the soup was perfection, swallowed. "Busy," he said. "Like always. I'll get out to the barn before I leave tonight. Make sure everyone's okay. Didn't have a chance to get by today."

"I fed them," Gracie said.

"I figured you would. Thank you."

"Sure."

"Did you wish Betty and Sam a happy anniversary?" he asked.

Gracie cracked a smile. "I didn't realize."

"Oh, it's a big day for them," David said. "I think they might have even renewed their vows up on the west pasture. That's where they met."

Vera chuckled. "Oh, David, you're such a hoot with those animals."

"What? I can't help it if your alpacas are hopeless romantics."

"Hey, isn't it about time for Haw Games Day?" Vera asked. "We should go. David, will you go?"

"I, uh, wasn't planning on it. I haven't been for years."

"There's a quilting circle I'd love to join that day. What about you, Gracie?"

"I don't like games," Gracie said. "I don't have time for them."

Farley made a noise. "Someone's too good for

farm games, huh? Well, Your Majesty, I'm sure nobody will make you do anything you don't want to do. We would hate for you to break a fingernail."

"David," Vera said. "Have you ever participated in the Games?"

David nodded. "Sure. But it's been a long time."

"Then it's settled," Vera said. "We're going. All of us. I'm sure you'll be gangbusters at those games."

"You said you're a veterinarian?" Farley asked. Gracie's smile instantly evaporated at the sound of her father's voice, as if she'd been trying to forget he was there.

"I am," David answered. "I own the little place down on Main Street in Haw Springs."

Farley gave a low whistle. "Good job, Gracie, landed yourself some money."

"I make my own money," Gracie said. "I have a job. Working is how I *land money*. But I guess that's foreign to you."

Farley shot Gracie a look. "What did you say, girl? You better watch yourself."

Gracie gave an exaggerated shrug, mimicking him. "What? It was a joke."

David cleared his throat. "Um, anyway, so we had a lot of patients today, but at least no emergencies. Kind of a funny story, though. You know the Personett family? The ones who live down on A Highway?"

"That old fart still alive? Geez. I'da thought that nasty geezer woulda croaked by now. Give him my worst wishes." Farley picked up his bowl, took a long gulp, set it down and tossed his spoon into it, then let out a loud belch. The flask reappeared and he took a long drink from it.

"I enjoy Lyle Personett," Vera said, but even her smile began to look taxed. "Good to know he's still getting around."

"He's great," David said. "Their cockatoo was my first bird patient. But, anyway, their dog had puppies."

"Listen, Gracie, I was just giving you some trouble," Farley interrupted, drunkenly leaning across the table. "Dinner wasn't all that bad. Definitely had worse. In prison." He threw his head back and laughed uproariously, slapping at his legs. He wiped his eyes. "But if you're gonna keep your sugar daddy around, you better start using the salt, girlie."

"Puppies," Vera repeated, her jovial interest clearly feigned.

David tried to push forward through his story, though the anger that was radiating off Gracie was starting to prove contagious. He found himself clutching his spoon harder and harder. "Three Dalmatian puppies, if you can imagine.

I don't know if you've ever been around a Dalmatian puppy, but they're energetic, to say the least."

"And Lyle's eighty if he's a day," Vera said.

Farley tapped the table with his flask. "And maybe start taking care of that hair or something. Hot mess curls going every which way. Just like your mama's. I don't miss that hair. I don't miss anything about her, really. Goodbye to bad rubbish."

"So they've got these three puppies..." David trailed off, unable to keep going. The entire room had gone stiff and still around him.

"Farley," Vera chided softly. "She wasn't rubbish. She was sick."

Farley barked out a laugh. "True. Sick in the head." He pointed to his temple. "At least she had the decency to die so I didn't have to put in the effort to leave her. I'm just trying to spare Gracie. She's done hooked herself up to some money, and here she is running around looking just like her no-good mama and serving up paste in a bowl. I'm trying to help her hang on to a good thing." He opened his flask again and winked at David. "Right, doc?"

"I do just fine without your *help*, thank you," Gracie said. "I've done just fine my whole life without it."

"Well, don't look now, but your boyfriend

looks like he'd rather be dead than be sitting next to you. Trust me, I know the look, because I know the feeling."

David set down his spoon. This was spiraling fast. He cleared his throat. "Listen, buddy, maybe you've had enough."

"Who are you to tell me when I've had enough?"

"I think everyone here can see that you've had enough," David said. "I don't want you to say things you'll regret later is all."

"What would you know about my regrets? You don't know me, *buddy*."

"Farley, calm down." Vera had put her spoon down and was reaching across the table toward her son.

"David, it's okay," Gracie said.

"With all due respect, it's not okay," David said. "You went to a lot of work to make this meal. And he shouldn't be talking to you like that regardless."

"And I'm just saying, if you're gonna put all that work into something, it should at least taste good. But now I'm not so sure you want this sanctimonious schoolboy to stick around. *You've had enough*," he mimicked.

"Well, now we've reached your field of expertise, haven't we? You would know better than anyone about not sticking around." Gracie's voice was cold, crackly steel. "And don't pretend for a second that you're trying to help me with anything. You're no help. You never have been and you never could be. You're just a disgusting drunk, rude coward, and a criminal. Nobody cares what you have to say, and nobody wants you here. I wish I'd been able to get you put away for longer."

She pushed her chair back. Everything on the table quivered as her chair leg caught the table leg. David's soup sloshed over the side of the bowl, soaking into the tablecloth that he now noted must have been added for an extra touch. For his benefit.

David wasn't very quick to anger. It took quite a lot to get a rise out of him. But when he got there, he got there. And David was getting there. He didn't know anything about this man, Farley Langhorst, but the picture was becoming quite clear. He was obviously a thorn in Gracie's side, to say the least, and even if he wasn't, his behavior was ruining the evening she'd put so much care into creating.

Even if it wasn't exactly her choice to create it.

Farley stared at the empty flask, as if it held the secrets to all of life's mysteries. "See, now, you're getting yourself all worked up over nothing. Did you have a good life here?" Now he lifted his eyes to Gracie, and David could see where the gray blaze came from. They weren't the same, though. Gracie's eyes spoke of determination and gutsiness, while Farley's shone with selfishness and warning. He raised his voice. "Did you?"

David felt Gracie jump just slightly, but her gaze never left her hands, which were pressed flat against the table. She didn't answer.

"Farley, this is meant to be a nice dinner," Vera said helplessly.

"Did you?" he repeated, ignoring his mother. Then, tiring of waiting, continued on. "That's right. You did. You had a great life here. That, my dear"—he pointed to her with his flask, and then tapped it against his own chest—"was my doing. I did that. You're welcome. Now, what's for dessert?"

Silence fell over the table. David felt the need to do something, but he wasn't sure what, exactly. He didn't want to embarrass Vera or Gracie any more than they already were, and he didn't want to ruin the dinner any more than it already was.

Finally, Gracie straightened. "You're a horrible person who did absolutely nothing for me. I am what I am in spite of you, not because of you. And I'm done listening to you. I'm sorry, Grandma." She spun away from the table and disappeared into the kitchen.

Farley's face was dour, but there was no explosion. "So, no dessert, huh?" he asked.

It was all David could do to keep from launching across the table at him.

Farley picked up his flask, peered into the hole, screwed the cap back on, and tucked it into his shirt pocket. "Well, if there's no dessert, then I'm gonna go grab a smoke. I'll be back, Mama."

He got up and drunkenly made his way out the front door.

"Don't worry," Vera said. "He doesn't have a car. He won't go far. Maybe he'll walk it off a little, huh?"

Gracie timidly came back into the dining room, wringing a dish towel in her hands. "I'm sorry, Grandma. I know this wasn't the dinner you had in mind."

"Oh, honey, that's not your fault. Nobody knew Farley was going to show up. That son of mine…he certainly does struggle."

"He makes everyone else struggle," Gracie said.

"I hope you didn't listen to a word of it," Vera said, clutching her granddaughter's hand. "None of what he has to say is true."

"I know," Gracie said. "I didn't." But she looked sad. No, worse than sad. She looked defeated.

"I think I should go," David said.

If he'd expected arguments from Vera and Gracie, he didn't get them. Instead, they both solemnly nodded.

"We will do this another time," Vera agreed. "After Farley has moved on. Which he will eventually do. I hate to say that about my own son, but the truth's the truth."

Gracie made the tiniest scoffing noise. David was certain that Vera hadn't heard it, but he had. There was something behind that scoff. Gracie knew something, or at least believed something to be true. Something that she didn't necessarily want her grandmother to know.

"Absolutely," he said, pushing away from the table. "Just say the word. I'll check on the animals on my way out." He paused, considered making more Sam and Betty jokes, but decided it was not the time. Gracie was right—Farley did make everyone else struggle. Terrible people usually did.

He could see a shadowy figure standing at the pasture gate long before he got there. The ember of a cigarette bobbed in the twilight as the figure lifted and lowered it. David paused only briefly, and then made his way forward, head down, fists clenched.

"If you're on a death watch, you can go on home," Farley said as David came into clear view.

"Pardon?"

"I said you can leave if you're here to get rich off my mother. This inheritance is mine and I plan to take it." Farley took a long drag off his cigarette and tossed it into the gravel at his feet, but didn't bother to stamp it out. "If you're here for my daughter, then that's whatever. Do what you want. I don't care. But I'll warn you, she's the spitting image of her mother, so you better watch out. That woman was nothing but trouble from day one. I got out while the getting was good, but I won't tell you what to do with your life. You want trouble, go court it. Lord knows nobody else is gonna. Spiteful, that one."

David had listened to just about enough from this guy, no matter who he was. "I know I'm not technically part of this family," he said. "But I've been friends with Vera for a long time, and I'm not here for the reasons you think I am. In all these years of visiting this farm every day, I've never seen you, never heard about you, nothing. Then you show up here, you're rude and insulting, and you're downright mean to Gracie. I never met her mother, but I can tell you that Gracie is someone you oughta be looking up to. She's tough and she's smart and nobody is ever going to push her around. That's pretty admirable, if you ask me."

"Her mom was a junkie." Farley swayed on his feet.

"Based on the condition you're in, I don't know if you should be judging anyone," David said.

"You need to stay away, vet. You're not needed here."

"You'll forgive me if I don't give what you have to say a whole lot of listening. Now, excuse me, I've got work to do."

He tried to edge past Farley, but Farley stood his ground, puffing out his chest and blocking David's path. David knew what this meant and took a deep breath. He didn't want it to come to this, but he wasn't afraid of it. He took one step back.

"Man, you don't want to do this. You're drunk. Just get out of the way, go inside, sober up."

Farley bumped David with his chest. His breath was acrid with smoke and booze. "I'll talk *about* my daughter and *to* my daughter however I see fit. What are you gonna do about it, vet? Nothing, that's what. That's what I thought. Too afraid to back up your threats."

That was enough for David. He reared up on Farley, taking fistfuls of Farley's denim jacket and pulling him in close. The small, drunken man was no match for David, who would have towered over him even if he were in peak form. He kept his face close to Farley's. "I don't care who you are, you don't talk about her like that.

You don't look at her sideways, and you don't say her name. And if I hear that you kept after her when I'm not around, just know that I'm back every single day, and I will deal with you. Got it?" Farley nodded, trying to look nonchalant, but David could see the fear in the man's eyes. "And that goes for Vera, too. Leave her alone, or it's gonna go badly for you."

He let go and Farley stumbled back a couple of steps. He put his hands in the air, as if he were the one who let go of David, and said, "Hey, man, I'm just visiting my mom."

"Right," David said. "Maybe do everyone a favor and make it a short visit. Or at least a silent one. And why don't you sober up a bit before you go back in there." He pushed past Farley and walked into the pasture. "You're embarrassing yourself."

He was halfway to the barn when he heard Farley yell, "You can't tell me what to do!"

David paused, shook his head, and kept walking.

Suddenly Gracie and her shotgun made so much more sense.

CHAPTER SEVEN

DAVID TOSSED AND turned all night, feeling sure that he'd somehow overstepped his bounds. He'd let his temper get away from him and was just glad that he'd hadn't actually hit Farley. That would have been really bad. This was bad enough.

He wondered what might have transpired when Farley returned to the house. If he'd told Vera and Gracie that he'd been attacked by David, or some nonsense.

He barely waited for morning to arrive before giving up on the effort to sleep and going to work.

"You're still here," Renee said, pausing by his office door. "At least you have a light on this time."

"I'm back," David said. "I promise I did go home."

"Hmm. Why do I have a feeling that it's not what we talked about yesterday that's bothering you?"

David smiled and bowed his head. "You got me. I mean, yes, what we talked about is bothering me. But it's not the only thing."

"A world of worries." She leaned against the doorframe, her purse swinging from her arm. "Care to share, or is this one that you have to work through on your own?"

"I'm afraid it's the latter. But, hey, do you know Farley Langhorst?"

Renee pursed her lips and gazed upward, thinking. She shook her head. "I know Vera, of course. And I know the granddaughter that's been coming around. She's full of energy. Or something."

David smiled. "She is definitely full of something. My dad would have called her a spitfire."

"But, no, I can't say I've heard of Farley. Who is he?"

"Gracie's dad. And we almost got into a fistfight last night."

Renee gawked and let out an incredulous croak. "You? A fight?"

"It's not so hard to imagine," he said.

"It's actually impossible to imagine," she said. "You're so gentle and kind. Have you ever seen you with a kitten? Or a hamster? No way can those be fighting hands. That rough-and-tumble stuff is for your brother Decker."

David nodded. "Okay, fair enough. I can see it

when you put it like that. But Decker and I grew up side by side, and these can be fighting hands when they need to be." He held up two fists.

"But?"

"But he was drunk. It doesn't feel right to hit a drunk man, unless he hits me first. That's my dad's doing. Honorability and all that. Also, I held back because of Gracie. I didn't want her to get hurt in the process."

"Like, collateral damage?"

"Something like that. So now I feel like I need to apologize. Make sure she's okay."

Renee pointed at him. "And that's why I'm surprised you almost got into a fight. Who apologizes for *not* hitting someone?"

"No, it's just that Farley is a loose cannon, and I can't say for sure that he didn't go inside and take it out on her."

"You mean beat her up?" She edged into his office and sat in the chair opposite his desk, crossing her legs at the knee and setting her purse on the floor. "Do we need to do something? Call the police?"

"I don't think he would beat her up. Not physically." But even as he said it, in the back of his mind, he wasn't as sure of that as he was making himself out to be. How would he know what Farley would and wouldn't do? He may very well have gone inside and gone on a tirade. For all

David knew, Gracie was hurt and waiting for help. "No," he said aloud, mostly to reassure himself. "He wouldn't." But now the thought was there. And he wouldn't get rid of it until he saw Gracie himself. He gave Renee what he hoped was a reassuring smile. "He had a little too much to drink is all. I'm sure everything is fine this morning."

"Well, I sure hope so," she said, standing up. "You going out there this afternoon?"

"I think I have to."

"Maybe Leo should go with you. Just in case."

"That's not necessary."

"Go where with you?" Leo appeared in the doorway behind Renee. His neck was red from shaving, and his eyes still looked bleary from sleep. "Did I miss something?"

"No," David said, standing and checking his watch. "We should get moving. I want to stay on time today." Because, yes, he needed to get to the Langhorst farm. He would be able to think of little else until he got there.

Renee picked up her purse. "Well, you just let me know if you change your mind about calling someone, okay?" She bustled away to make the coffee and get the computers turned on.

Leo stepped inside the office. "Actually, can I talk to you for a minute?"

David resisted the urge to check his watch again. “Sure. What’s up?”

Leo scratched the back of his neck. Now that David got a good look at him, he could see that it wasn’t sleep bleariness in his eyes, but maybe bleariness from lack of sleep. “I sort of…have an offer?”

David paused. This was not at all what he wanted or needed to hear today. “For me, I hope?”

Leo shook his head. “For me. From The Pup Deck. The lead vet is fixing to retire. Eventually a silent partner situation.”

“Wow,” David said. “That’s a good opportunity.” The words felt sour coming out of his mouth. If only he could offer the same. He was so close. *So close.* “That’s the one up in Kansas City?”

“Yep.”

“That’s three hours away.”

“I know.”

“You haven’t taken your license exam yet.”

“I know.”

“So you’re not ready.”

“Right. It’s a family connection kind of thing. You know. A cousin knows a guy who knows a guy.”

“Ah.” David could hear the clock ticking around him in so many ways, he didn’t know which to address first. He knew this day would come with Leo; he had just been hoping to hold it off until he was able to swoop in with a better offer. He was still standing at his desk, but he dropped into his chair and ran his hand over his face. "So are you going to take it?"

"I would prefer not to. But, I mean, it's an offer." Leo crossed his arms, and then uncrossed them. "Listen, I'm telling you this because I would rather be here. I'm not going to take it if there's a chance that I could stay."

"There's a *but* coming."

"But I need to know soon."

"How soon?"

"I told them I would give them an answer by the end of the month."

"Okay," David said. "Then I have until the end of the month to figure out how I'm going to keep you here. Thanks for letting me know."

The morning went by at a snail's pace. All David could think about was Gracie, Farley, Leo, everything except what he needed to be thinking about. He'd never been so distracted before.

Finally, the afternoon break came, and he grabbed his field gear.

"Going out to check on the animals? Or going out to check on the redhead?" Renee asked as he walked past.

"Yes," he said.

But Gracie wasn't waiting for him in the barn. He went about his chores quickly and silently. He didn't even have time to muse that things had changed and her presence was so normal to him, he expected it now.

No. He craved it.

And, after Farley's behavior the night before, there was no way he was just going to go back to the office without seeing her. Maybe it wasn't his business, but he was making it his business.

He finished up in the barn and headed toward the house.

She answered the door, looking surprised. "You're here." She checked behind her, then opened the screen door and stepped out.

"I'm here every day."

She made sure the door was shut behind her and lowered her voice. "I thought that maybe after last night's…performance…you would never come back."

He wasn't sure if she meant Farley's performance or his. "Sorry to disappoint you."

She gazed up at him. There was something softer in her look. Something more urgent. Normally, she would shoot back a barb to match his, but this time she gave her head a small shake. "I'm not disappointed."

"So you're okay?"

She shrugged. "As okay as I ever am when it comes to Farley."

"He didn't mess with you any more last night?"

"He didn't get a chance to. I got my grandma settled for the night and went on up to my room. Locked my door, put on headphones and got some work done. Even if he'd come up to mess with me, I wouldn't have heard him. By the time I was done, it was quiet downstairs. Grandma was asleep and the guest room door was closed, so I figured he'd passed out for the night."

"He was pretty drunk."

"He's always pretty drunk." She paused, her arms crossed defensively. "I saw what happened."

"Pardon?"

She checked over her shoulder again, and then grabbed his elbow and tugged him off the porch and back toward the pasture. When they'd gotten a good distance from the house, she gave one last glance behind them and slowed her pace. She opened the pasture gate, and they stepped through.

"Last night. I saw you and Farley out here by the gate."

David hung his head. "About that…"

"I heard what you said to him."

"I'm sorry. That's actually why I came to find you. I need to apologize." He wasn't sure how much he could let his guard down with her. How open she would be to vulnerability and honesty. The Gracie he'd seen last night was an artfully buried Gracie, and for all he knew, the real Gracie would pop out at any minute. Still, he had to do it. Because that was who he was. He wasn't good at burying himself like she was. "Well, that's not entirely true. I came because I wanted to make sure you and Vera were okay. And then I wanted to apologize. As soon as I saw that Farley was here, I should have left. I'm afraid my presence made things get a little volatile. Your family business isn't my business. I'm sorry."

The temperature had dropped a few degrees, and the wind, which David hadn't even noticed until now, had picked up. Gracie again stood with her arms crossed. She gazed at the barn, the sunlight bathing her face, making it even more creamy than usual. He had an urge to reach out and brush his fingers along her cheek, just to see if it felt as soft as it looked. But he knew he was already pressing his luck.

"I wish I still had a horse," Gracie said, still not breaking her gaze from the barn. Her voice sounded faraway, dreamy.

Did this mean he was forgiven? David wasn't sure, but he went with it. "I remember your horse. It was black, wasn't it?"

She nodded, then finally came back to reality. "He had a horribly cliché name. Thunderbolt.

But when I was eight, it seemed like the coolest horse name on earth. I was proud of myself for thinking of it. Now, as an adult, I know that literally thousands of people think of it." She turned her face back toward the barn. "I loved him, though. That horse got me through a lot of difficult stuff." Was her chin trembling?

"Hey." He reached out to brush her arm with the backs of his fingers. "Are you okay?"

As if she was coming awake from a deep sleep, she snapped to, shaking her hair out of her face and squaring her shoulders. She stepped away from him. Still, the softer version of her was there, just under the surface. "I'm always okay," she said.

"Last night was not okay."

She shrugged. "It was what it was. Farley is an embarrassment and always will be. It's nothing new. And you have nothing to apologize about."

And that was that. David knew Gracie well enough to know that he shouldn't press her beyond where she was comfortable being pressed. Still, he could feel the tension radiating from her. It wasn't just her arms that were crossed; it was her whole body, shut away, tucked inside, in protection mode.

He had an idea.

A great idea.

A terrible idea.

But it was a great, terrible idea that he was going to go with.

"Come with me." She hesitated, so he reached back and gave her arm a little tug. "Come on."

"Where are we going?"

"Just follow."

She fell in line behind him as he hurried across the pasture and behind the barn, heading north. He'd never come at the fence line where the Langhorst farm and the McBride ranch met from this side, but he'd spent enough time as a young man on the other side of the fence to have a pretty good idea. They wove through a few sparse trees, and then dove into thicker brush, and finally found the blackberry bush where they'd met all those years ago.

"Do you remember?" he asked, plucking a berry off the bush and popping it into his mouth. It was past its time, overripe, and he had possibly eaten an ant in the process, but it still tasted sweet to get one of her coveted berries from her own side of the fence. He smiled while he chewed. "You didn't like sharing them one bit."

"And I still don't. This is what you were in such an all-fire hurry to get to?"

"Do you remember?" he repeated, ducking so that his face was right in hers.

"Of course I remember. You were a thief even then." She grinned.

"I was on my own property."

"Stealing *my* berries." She examined the bush, pulled off a berry, looked it over, and tossed it to the ground. Picky. "I can't believe this is what you wanted me to see. I've seen this a million times." Still, she was bending to gaze at the berries, as if assessing whether or not to pick some to take home.

"It's not. Come on." He moved down the fence line to a spot that looked a little loose. There were always things on any ranch that needed to be fixed, tightened, straightened, redone. And it was Ben's job to do them, but David learned as a child that you couldn't always know when something needed to be fixed. You only knew that if you looked for a way to sneak into or out of a fence line, you would eventually find one.

It didn't take long at all for him to find the spot.

"Here," he said, stepping on a loose bottom strand of smooth wire. "Duck through. Careful now."

"What are you doing?" she asked warily, but she followed instructions. She was small and nimble and fit through easily.

David, on the other hand, was not as small and nimble. He moved to where there was a post and used it as leverage to step up on the middle strand and launch himself over. Thank goodness his brother never agreed to make the fence electric. David had worried about horse thieves, but Decker was more worried about the autistic children in his therapeutic riding program getting shocked. As far as David knew, Decker had never had a student wander this far.

David's fears, on the other hand, were about to be realized.

"I'm getting you a horse," he said.

"What?"

"Not permanently. Just for today." He stopped walking and turned toward her, not realizing how closely she was following. She bumped against him, and then scrambled back a few steps, as if he was on fire. He grinned. "To get you through a tough time."

"You're stealing a horse."

"It's not stealing if it's my brother's," he said, although he was certain that Decker wouldn't see it that way. He would ask for forgiveness later.

"I don't think it works that way."

He started walking again. "It's working that way today."

"If you're wanting me to believe that you're not a thief, this is a terrible way of doing that."

"Well, I wouldn't want to ruin your image of me. I have a reputation to uphold."

He stopped again. This time, she stopped quickly enough not to bump into him, but she was close. Very close. And she didn't back away. He didn't know if this was Gracie showing her fearlessness, or if she wanted to be close to him. Maybe he was just wanting to be close to her, and this was wishful thinking.

"If you really have a problem with it, we can go back," he said. "I don't want to make you uncomfortable. Or…afraid."

She gazed into his eyes for a long time but made no move to turn back. "I'm not afraid of anything."

"That's what I thought," he said, and continued forward. "Let's get over to those trees. We can see the whole ranch from there."

They bent low and ran toward the trees, not because they needed to, but because it made the mission seem more clandestine and daring. There was a danger to Gracie that drew David in a way that he never would have thought possible.

They entered the trees, which swished and rattled with the wind. Leaves had begun to fall over the past week, and one fell onto David's shoulder. He brushed it off while pushing his way through to a good viewing spot. Gracie followed him. They both crouched at the edge of the trees and peered out across the ranch.

"Tango," David said, pointing at Decker's horse, who was tied up, without his saddle, on the outside of the corral fence. He moved his finger to point at the horse tied closest to Tango. "Queenie." There was another horse, Sugar, grazing farther away, and one in the riding pen. David could see Decker's ranch hand, Ben, riding that one. Maybe trying to break a new horse? David couldn't tell. The others must have been in the barn. It didn't matter. They only needed two.

"Tango is a lot of horse." He had no idea why he was whispering. Decker was nowhere to be seen, and Ben was busy in the riding pen, and likely wouldn't be able to hear him well even if he shouted. "You should take Queenie. Do you think you can handle her bareback?"

Gracie narrowed her eyes at him, a determined grin lifting one side of her mouth. "I think you don't know who you're talking to."

And, like that, she was gone, out of the woods and running across the pasture directly toward Tango.

Of course, David thought. Of course she would want Tango. That was who she was.

She slipped through the wooden corral rails and slowed to a walk. David also slowed, watching while she reached up and stroked Tango's side. She talked to him for a minute, then untied him and grabbed his reins. She glanced back at David, her daredevil smile replaced with a smile of real joy, then vaulted herself onto the horse's back with such ease, it almost looked as if an invisible hand had lifted her and placed her onto him. David couldn't move; he was so mesmerized by her gracefulness and athleticism.

"Get your horse," she hissed, propelling David into motion.

David hadn't ridden Queenie a lot, but he had ridden her enough times to know that she could keep up with Tango if she absolutely had to. At the very least, he was familiar to her, so she didn't miss a beat when he untied her and swung himself onto her back. He patted her neck. "Good girl, Queenie. Wanna go for a joy ride?"

"Hey!" They'd been spotted. Ben had gotten off his horse and was coming through the riding pen gate like his pants were on fire. "Stop!"

"Go!" David said, squeezing Queenie with his legs to make her move forward. "Let's go, Queenie, let's go!" She got moving, slowly at first, but picking up speed as he continued to drive his heels into her.

Gracie was doing the same with Tango, and before long, they were cruising through the open field like missiles. Gracie raised one arm and let out a whoop.

Ben stopped running and was watching them with one hand shading his eyes. Decker had rushed out of the barn and was standing with Ben, his cowboy hat in one hand at his side. He shook his head slowly; David was going to get what-for from him later, he was sure.

But as he watched Gracie lead Tango across the field, leaning forward over his neck, her hair flying out behind her, the back of her shirt riding up to reveal creamy skin, he didn't care. He would face a thousand what-fors if that was the price he had to pay to get this moment.

He lifted an arm, pointing to his brother, let out his own whoop, and steered Queenie to fall in line behind Tango. A long string of laughter drew out of him while they rode. It was the lightest and happiest he had felt in as far back as he could remember.

He never wanted it to end.

THE RHYTHM OF Tango's gallop was the most natural motion that Gracie had felt in a long time. She'd forgotten how it felt to ride. It was something akin to swimming and flying all at the same time. At once exhilarating and calming.

How had she built a life in which movement felt like fighting, like trudging, like gutting out the inches, the feet, the miles? Why had she done that to herself?

Thunderbolt. She hadn't thought about him in ages. He had been her touchstone. Her reality. Her goodness.

Yet, she didn't even come home when her

grandma had called with news that he was dying. She didn't have time. She'd simply gone about her day, business as usual, ignoring that one of the very few good childhood connections she'd had was being severed. At bedtime that night, she'd let out a few perfunctory tears that she sensed to be more obligatory than actually felt, then shut herself down and forgot about him.

How could she have forgotten about him?

She and David rode a complete circle around the field, and then stopped in the shade of the trees where they'd started. She was breathless with adrenaline and memories. She felt so free.

"That felt good," she said.

David chuckled. "Did you see the look on my brother's face when we rode past?"

She found herself laughing along. Something else she allowed herself little time for in her real life. "Both of them were looking pretty sour. Can't say I blame them. If you'd been on my land, you'da gotten some buckshot for your troubles."

"Oh, trust me, I know."

Again, their eyes met and lingered, searching each other to make sense of this new…whatever this was.

And in an instant, the freedom evaporated. The breathlessness felt like danger.

Gracie didn't have space for whatever this was

in her life. And she never planned to. So maybe David wasn't the worst man on earth like she thought he might be, but it didn't change the fact that he was a man, and that men were not exactly at the top of her list of priorities. Connecting with a man meant putting your heart on the line, just waiting for the heartbreak to happen.

Connecting with a man might lead to ultimately needing a man, and that was not okay with Gracie. She didn't need anyone. She had herself. That was all she would ever need.

She would never let herself down.

She would never leave herself wanting.

She would always show up for herself.

She. Was. Capable.

She didn't want David to think she was ungrateful for what he was trying to do, but at the same time, she didn't want him to think this was going to lead to him coming around to rescue her over and over again.

She felt herself begin to shut down.

"Are you okay?" he asked.

She pressed her lips together, took a breath. "I should get back."

Without waiting for him to respond, she slid off the horse and handed him the reins. She turned to make her way back to the fence where they'd come in.

"Wait." She heard his feet hit the ground as he let himself free of Queenie. "Gracie. Wait."

She turned. He reached for her. She took a step back. Not that she didn't want him to touch her, but that she wanted it too much. This didn't make sense to her. Didn't compute. She was disappointed in herself for letting it get this far.

"Don't," she said.

He let his arm drop. "I thought you were having fun. I thought the horses were a good thing. Decker won't really be mad. We didn't take them off the ranch."

"It's not that." She found herself having a hard time making eye contact with him. "I just need you to stop."

"Stop what? I don't understand."

"Stop...*this*." She knew that made no sense. "Stop...apologizing and stop defending me and stop getting me a horse to get me through a bad day. And stop delivering kittens in the barn and kissing my grandma on the cheek and...and... stop coming to dinner and being so nice. Okay?"

She felt tears coming on, and if there was one thing that would make her even angrier at herself in this moment, it would be to cry. She would not allow it. No.

Instead, she turned and ran back the way they'd come, until she found the blackberry bushes. She stepped on the loose wire for herself and slipped back under the fence, leaving him behind.

She didn't look back as she ran home. She felt guilty and horrible and…safe.

"There she is," Farley said when she burst through the front door. "About time you graced us with your presence. We're getting hungry."

Gracie ignored him and went to her grandma, who was parked in her chair, as usual. Only Farley held the remote instead. "Grandma? What do you need?"

Her grandmother's face crinkled with worry. "Honey, are you okay?"

"I'm fine. I'm always fine, Grandma. You know that."

"What were you doing out there? Did you see David?"

Gracie nodded. "He's been by, yes." She heard Farley make a disgusted noise behind her and shot him a look. "Everything's good, I promise. Do you need a snack? Want me to start dinner?"

"Honey, I just can't. I was thinking about going back to bed."

"But you didn't eat lunch. Or breakfast." *Or dinner last night.*

You're dying, right in front of my eyes, and I need you. You can't die when I need you.

Her grandma touched her cheek lightly and

gave a smile. "Everything's going to be all right, you know."

Gracie nodded quickly. She couldn't open her mouth to answer. If she did, all the emotions from the entire day—maybe her entire life—would spill right out. She swallowed and swallowed until she had herself under control. "You want me to help you to bed?"

"Farley will do it. You go on and get yourself something to eat. You're practically wasting away."

"I got you, Mama," Farley said, edging in and holding out his hands. *Like he's some model son or something,* Gracie thought bitterly.

Farley pulled Vera out of her chair and walked her back to the bedroom. Gracie heard them murmuring behind the closed bedroom door, and then heard the TV come to life in there, the noise swelling as the door opened, and then quieting as he closed it behind him.

"She may not be hungry, but I am," he said when he came into the room.

"Get it yourself," Gracie snapped. "Preferably somewhere else."

She took the stairs two at a time.

It was only when her own door was closed and locked that she let the tears loose.

CHAPTER EIGHT

It had been days since Gracie visited the barn while David was there. She just didn't know how to face him. She needed time to get past the emotion that she'd felt on their ride. To convince herself that she had been the only one to feel it, or maybe that it wasn't felt at all. That she was making too much out of nothing. That he was just trying to do something kind, because that was what he did.

That he was trying to make it up to her after being in her grandmother's life where he didn't belong.

But it was Haw Games Day, and she'd been invited.

Or, actually, now that she thought of it, just forced.

She stood in front of her bedroom mirror in a pair of jeans, a white long-sleeved shirt, and a denim vest. This was the most cowgirl she'd looked since she left Buck County for college. She was surprised to find the vest still stuffed in the back of her closet and surprised to find that it still fit after all these years.

She felt ridiculous. Like she was playing dress-up.

"Nope," she said aloud. "This isn't me. I can't, I can't, I can't. Grandma will just have to deal. She can go with David without me."

She changed into leggings and ditched the vest for a long cable-knit sweater, and headed downstairs for a cup of coffee.

Her grandma was sitting at the kitchen table all dressed and ready to go.

"Why aren't you dressed?" Vera asked as soon as she saw Gracie.

Gracie looked down at herself. "I am dressed. What do you mean?"

"It's Haw Games Day," her grandma said, as if it was the most obvious thing in the world.

"I wasn't planning to go."

Vera's eyebrows raised. "Nonsense. You have a date."

"What do you mean, a date? It's not a date. Nobody said anything about dating. You invited us to go with you. But I'm not going. David can take you to the quilting circle. I'll be here when you get back."

Vera waved her away. "David isn't going to Haw Games Day with me. He's going with you. He said he'd be here at noon and it's noon, and if David McBride says he'll be somewhere at noon, he'll be there at noon. So you'd better get dressed."

"I don't...you can't..." Gracie sputtered.

"Get dressed, I said." Vera lifted her chin and stared off into the middle distance, which Gracie knew as her signature move to close a case and move on to more interesting topics.

"Where's Farley?" Gracie asked, looking around, hoping for a deflection move of her own.

"He went into town this morning. Said not to wait for him. Now get moving, girl."

"Into town? What for?" Gracie's hackles were up. Of course, when it came to Farley, her hackles were always up.

"I said get moving."

Her grandma was right. David said he was coming, so he would be here.

Dependable. Darn him.

GENERALLY SPEAKING, David was excited. He loved Haw Games Day. Everyone in Haw Springs loved Haw Games Day. It was a celebration of all that was life in Haw Springs: slow, easy, filled with laughter and love, surrounded by the goodness of the earth. A celebration of the few weeks of mild weather they were gifted with each year, before winter bore down on them and blanketed them with cold and snow for four months.

If you weren't there for the games themselves, you were there for the craft booths filled with handmade quilts and painted bread platters and home-canned apple butter. If you weren't there for that, you were there for the apple fritters fried by Scout troop 1276 or banana bread baked by the Haw Springs Chamber of Commerce or the cider squeezed by the mayor himself.

There were stilts to be walked on and hay bales to fall into. There were hoops to roll with sticks, a staple of Haw Games Day since the very first Haw Games Day in 1862. There were bluegrass bands and an archery range and horse challenges and tractor pulls, and the whole thing would end with a town-wide rotten tomato fight.

But mostly it was a chance to sit and chat with friends and family on a cool, early-September evening. Before the frenzy of school and the winter frost that kept everyone indoors.

But, while David was excited, he was also more than a little nervous. Hesitant, even. Considered not going at all.

He was supposed to go with Gracie.

Was it a date? Vera had certainly made it clear that she hoped it would become one. But things had happened, and he and Gracie weren't exactly on speaking terms, much less dating terms.

After his run-in with Farley, followed by the epic failure of borrowing Decker's horses, David did everything he could to avoid running into Gracie. He wasn't sure where he stood with her; he was only sure that it wasn't a good place. He raced to the farm at the end of the day every day, hoping that she would be busy with dinner, and raced through his chores at a breakneck pace. He hardly stopped to talk to Sam and Betty at all, and Henry didn't even have enough time to work up a good warning honk before David was gone again.

He was in and out of the property in minutes, wiping his brow and peering into the rearview mirror while he drove away, both hoping to run into her, and praying he wouldn't.

If he didn't show up today, he was sure that Gracie would be relieved. Happy, even. But it was Vera who'd had her heart set on this outing, and he could hardly let down a dying friend, could he?

He had to go.

He didn't want to go.

But he had to go.

He traded in his usual scrubs for a pair of jeans, a flannel shirt and cowboy boots. He worried that he looked too starched and pressed. Why didn't he wear these things more often, like Decker? Decker practically wore them to bed at night, and always looked so casual and comfortable in them.

David pulled his dusty cowboy hat from the top shelf of his closet, brushed it off and put it on. He stared into the mirror, the years peeling back. Once upon a time, he'd been just as cowboy as Decker. In some ways, he'd been more cowboy than Decker had been. He was much better with the animals than Decker, even the horses. He was a better shot than Decker. He was faster with chores and could toss hay bales like nobody's business.

He could pull this off.

He could.

He grabbed his wallet and keys and headed out, before he had a chance to talk himself out of it.

To his surprise, Vera was sitting on her front porch, a bag in her lap. She looked even more emaciated than she had just a couple of nights ago, and her skin had taken on a yellowish hue that he didn't like one bit. She looked tired on a level that he was certain he had never felt, and her cheeks were gaunt. But her spirits were good. She waved exuberantly as he walked up the drive. Norma, busy weaving around Vera's legs, trotted to him when he reached the porch.

"Good to see you up and about, mama kitty." David stooped to give Norma's ears a good scratch, then climbed the porch steps and gave Vera a peck on the cheek. "And good to see you up and about, too. How you feeling?"

Vera waved him away. "I'm getting along. I'm ready to get quilting. I've got my supplies." She patted the bag on her lap. "I haven't done it in a minute, but it'll be like riding a bicycle, right?"

"Absolutely! Although I think if you fall off a quilt, it's a much softer landing." David paused, bent to pet Norma again, unsure whether or not to ask about Gracie. Had she decided not to go?

As if in answer to his thoughts, the front door opened, and out she stepped, looking radiant—if not equally starched—in cowgirl clothes. She hesitated, misery clouding her face. She put on a wobbly smile and gave a shy wave that made David's heart clench.

"You look amazing," he said. Vera smiled wide, but Gracie pressed her lips in on themselves and brushed the front of her shirt with one hand self-consciously.

"I feel ridiculous."

"But, he's right, you look beautiful, honey," Vera said. "It's good to see you out of those boring old city clothes, all black and gray and stiff material."

"With very serious shoulder pads," David added.

Gracie let out a gasp. "I never wear shoulder pads. And I almost never wear black and gray."

Vera smiled. "Well, at least I know you're still in there somewhere. Good to see that my feisty granddaughter still exists."

David held his hands over his shoulders. "You could sub in for an injured linebacker with those shoulder pads."

Gracie narrowed her eyes at him and placed her hands on her hips. "How many times do I have to tell you that you're not funny?"

"You're right, Vera," he said. "That's Gracie. She's back."

"Can we just go? Before the two of you decide to put on a vaudeville act?"

David and Vera chuckled.

"Come on, Grandma." Gracie held her hands out, and Vera took them, allowed herself to be pulled to standing.

Together, they walked to the car, Vera taking it one very slow, shaky step at a time. David felt the laughter dry up in his throat. It was hard watching Vera like this. He imagined that sitting in one spot at the quilting circle would be about all she could handle. But he could also imagine how happy she would be, holding court with the quilters, the ugliness of cancer forgotten for a few hours.

Gracie helped her grandmother into the front seat and got her buckled in, Vera fussing the whole way that she could take care of herself.

Gracie then deposited herself into the back seat, rebuffing David as he tried to shut the door for her.

Just as David was about to get into the driver's side, a sleek silver car pulled into the driveway and parked. Farley got out of the passenger seat, and another man wearing a silver suit so shiny it all but matched his car, got out of the driver's side. Farley was holding paperwork, which fluttered in the breeze.

David recognized the other man as Lonnie Latham, Haw Springs' seediest lawyer. Haw Springs' only lawyer, which only made him bolder with his seediness. He stood with his hands on his hips and surveyed the farm, nodding as if he approved.

David heard a car door open behind him, and Gracie practically launched into the driveway, as if she'd been spring-loaded.

This was not going to be good.

"What's going on?" she asked. "What are you up to, Farley? Who is this? Who are you, sir? Are those papers what I'm guessing they are?"

"Whoa, woman, take a breath. I can't answer everything at once," Farley said.

David could feel an invisible timer over their heads, ticking down the seconds until Gracie would completely blow. She tapped her foot impatiently on the gravel, hands on hips, forehead creased, a caricature of herself.

"I don't believe he owes anyone an answer to anything," Lonnie said. "Farley, as your lawyer, I advise you not to speak."

"Lawyer?" Gracie said, at the same time that David said, "Really, Lonnie? To his own daughter? You think that's a good idea?"

Lonnie spread his hands, innocently. "I'm just looking out for the best interest of my client. He owes her nothing."

Gracie balked and marched past Lonnie, directly to Farley. "If those papers are what I think they are, then you'll have the fight of your life on your hands. *Dad*."

Farley, who had been steely-faced this entire time, flinched when she said the word *Dad* and turned his icy gaze on her. "I'm not your dad. I'm just a faceless criminal to you. I owe you nothing."

Gracie lowered her voice. "After a lifetime of breaking this woman's heart, you are not getting a single blade of grass from this farm. You understand me? It's not a threat, it's a promise." She turned to Lonnie. "I don't know what kind of so-called lawyer you are, but I can guarantee you that you've never faced an opponent like me. And I will call down my colleagues from Kansas City if I have to."

Lonnie stared at her, amused. "Sweetheart, I'm not afraid of Kansas City lawyers. They don't give two toots about what happens in Haw Springs."

"I'm not your *sweetheart*," Gracie said, her voice going low and dangerous. David didn't know if he should step in or take cover.

Lonnie went from amused to all-out smiling. "My apologies, *ma'am*." He turned as if to walk away, muttering, "Ain't nothing sweet about ya."

All at once, Gracie lunged at Lonnie, fists swinging. David threw himself between them, taking a good, hard hit to the temple in the process. He saw a flash of light and little stars. Gracie had an excellent right hook. He shook his head, wrapped his arms around her waist and pulled her back.

Both Lonnie and Farley were practically doubled over, they were laughing so hard. David had half a mind to let her go, let her wallop both of them. Maybe get in a few good swipes himself.

"Not worth it," he said, dragging her back toward the car. "They're not worth it." Though he had to admit, after that last little comment, landing a solid smack across Farley's always-moving mug would feel pretty good. "Lonnie'll see you put in jail. It'll upset your grandma."

Gracie's swings slowed and then died, but her

body still felt like a live wire in David's arms, twisting and zapping full of energy.

"Get out of here, Farley." She was out of breath. "Go back to wherever you came from. And you!" This was aimed at Lonnie. "You need to get off my property."

Farley and Lonnie exchanged looks and began to laugh again.

"It ain't your property, sweetheart," Lonnie said. "That's what makes this so funny." He mimicked throwing a flurry of soft punches and continued laughing.

"Let's just go," David said. He could feel Gracie tense up as if to propel herself toward Lonnie again. "This guy will sue you for knocking one of his hairs out of place."

"So let him sue me," Gracie said. "I would welcome the fight."

"Your grandma will worry," David said. "She doesn't need that right now." He turned so that he was between Gracie and Lonnie, his arms still holding her around the waist, pulling her into him. She turned her gaze to him and, for a moment, they were the only two people in the world. He felt a zap of electricity that practically doubled him over. He let go and took two steps back. "Let's take her to the Games while she still has energy. Come on."

Gracie searched his face, and then nodded.

She turned and ducked back into the car, breathing heavily.

"Sorry, Grandma," she said. "Let's get out of here."

Lonnie and Farley were walking toward the pasture gate, shoulder to shoulder, Farley pointing at the barn and Lonnie nodding along. They'd moved on so easily, so carelessly, it took everything David had not to rush them and finish the fight.

But he'd meant what he said about Vera. She would worry. She would be upset.

She really wanted to go to the Games.

And this was, for sure, going to be her last chance to go.

CHAPTER NINE

As soon as they parked, Gracie took off to find a golf cart to help get Vera to the quilting circle. This left David and Vera alone in the car.

"How's mama kitty been doing?" he asked, trying to get some small talk going. After the scene in the driveway, the car ride had been grim and silent.

"I know what Farley's up to," Vera said, ignoring his question altogether. "I know Gracie thinks I'm clueless, but I'm not. I know. And Gracie needn't worry."

"I'm sorry about what happened back there. I kind of wish I hadn't stepped in. Would have been fun to see Gracie wallop them."

Vera let out a snort. "And she would have. That girl isn't afraid to wallop anyone. Not even you. Remember that."

"Oh, trust me, I am well aware of her ability to wallop me. Although I think the desire has lessened since Farley rolled into town. What are you going to do?"

Vera stared at her lap for a moment, and then raised her gaze to the windshield. "Farley never belonged here. Here in Haw Springs, you know. He was always the odd one out. Just fought and fought all the time, from the time he was a little boy. Maybe that's where Gracie gets it."

"Don't tell her that."

"Oh, I would never. Eventually, he was fighting me, and then he took on a wife and fought her. He couldn't wait to get out of Haw Springs, and when he left, I thought, *Good. He can stop fighting.* But he only got worse. Once Gracie was born, he started fighting himself." She gazed at David. "And that's the worst person to fight. No matter the outcome, you lose. And he lost. He lost his wife, he lost Gracie, he lost himself. He likes to make it sound like the life he has is the one he wanted, but I know it smarts something fierce to be all alone like that."

David heard the crunch of tires on the gravel parking lot and saw Gracie coming toward them in the golf cart. He unbuckled his seat belt. Vera grabbed his arm, kept him from moving.

"I'm telling you this because I want you to know that I know what Farley is up to. And because I don't want you to fight each other. And, whatever you do, don't fight yourselves. It would break my heart to see either of you end up like

Farley." She patted his arm twice and let go, just as Gracie opened her door.

"You ready?" She had adopted a brighter persona. For her grandmother's benefit, he thought.

They helped Vera into the golf cart, and then Gracie got behind the wheel and David hopped in the back. They dropped her off at the quilting circle, which looked like it was going to be the social event of the year for Vera, then took the cart back to the customer service tent.

All along the way, David studied the curve of Gracie's jaw, the swoop of her neck, the purposefulness of her fingers as they gripped the wheel. Why did they fight each other so much, he wondered? And were they really fighting themselves? He hoped not, but he couldn't say with certainty that they weren't.

Now that Vera was out of the mix, David felt awkward walking with Gracie. Was it him, or did eyes turn to them questioningly? He was hardly a stranger in town—most everyone knew him as the remaining McBride bachelor—so seeing him with a woman was going to be a subject of discussion. He imagined he was going to have a lot of questions to answer come Monday morning at the office.

"Hungry?" he asked. Gracie walked stiff and silent beside him, also awkward.

"Nah," she answered.

"Thirsty?"

"No, thank you."

"There's music up the hill. Want to go listen?"

"I'm good."

David stopped walking, forcing her to stop as well. "Do we need to talk?"

Her cheeks pinkened, and he could tell that she was very aware of the people milling around them, trying to get past them as they stood dead center of the crowd. David was aware, too, but he was more aware of the awkwardness between them, and how much he hated it. "No," she said. "I just…you're so nice to me all the time, David."

"I'm nice to everyone."

"It can't be real."

He held out an arm and pinched it, winced. "Nope, I'm real."

"I'm not saying *you* don't exist. I'm saying the nice thing isn't real. I don't trust it. It's not sustainable."

Given everything he'd seen from Farley over the past few days, David could understand. Gracie was difficult. But David was beginning to wonder if she really meant to be. He was starting to suspect that she didn't, that her difficult nature was simply her being a product of her upbringing. He'd seen her let go on the horse. He'd seen the smile, listened to the breathless laughter. He knew that the real Gracie was in there somewhere, and that she both loved and hated to come out.

But he also knew that he didn't want to spend an entire day with angry, sullen, mistrustful Gracie, no matter how much Vera wanted it.

"Well..." He paused, assessing their choices. "Do you trust my tugging abilities?"

"Huh?"

He pointed to the tug-of-war station, which was just getting going. "Come on, we don't have to be so serious all the time. We're at the Games. We're here for fun. Let's get on a team."

"I don't—" David walked away before she could finish the sentence.

He was pretty sure that Gracie Langhorst couldn't pass up a challenge, so he tossed a little incentive over his shoulder as he walked. "Afraid you'll lose?"

She didn't disappoint. "Not a chance in the world."

Teams were assembling on either side of the rope. David fell in line toward the back of one side, and was surprised—although, not surprised, really—to see Gracie post up toward the front of the opposing side. She held the rope in both hands, eyebrows arched in a dare.

He grinned. *There you are,* he thought. *Good to have you back.*

"Bad move," he shouted.

"For you, maybe," she shouted back.

Teams shuffled into place, and soon the referee, holding the center of the rope in one hand, shouted, "On your marks, get set, tug!" and dropped the rope.

David would like to say his side won handily. But, in fact, the tugging went on forever, each side making ground, and then losing it. David's arms ached and hands burned as he clutched the rope with all that he had.

After what seemed like an eternity, the smaller guys at the front of David's side toppled into the sand pit between them. Like dominoes, they all fell forward. And, like dominoes, the other side fell backward, triumphant.

David watched as Gracie cheered and high-fived her teammates. She was all smiles as she made her way toward him, rubbing her palms together.

"I guess the answer is no," she said. "I don't trust your tugging abilities."

"You know, you could have been on my side," David said. "Did that ever occur to you? We could have teamed up against the other side."

"Literally, no," Gracie said. "Never." The pink in her cheeks was still there, but the embarrassment was gone. This was the same flush he'd seen in her cheeks when they'd ridden horses together.

"Well, we had a weak link," David started, but he was interrupted by someone shouting his name.

They both turned this way and that, looking for the source, and finally saw Morgan, Decker's fiancée, jogging toward them, waving her hands high over her head.

Morgan, too, was a city transplant, returning home after many years away. She had been a hard nut for Decker to crack, but what they had now was beautiful. Morgan was kind and smart and loving. There could be no better fit in the world for Decker than Morgan.

Still, David groaned when he saw her coming.

"What?" Gracie asked.

"Get ready to watch me get scolded," he said. "I still don't have a date for my brother's wedding."

"Hey," Morgan said, breathless. David could see Decker sauntering down the hill toward them in her wake, lazily eating from a telltale grease-stained, powdered-sugar-covered paper sack. Fritters.

"Hey, there, Morgan. Did you see me just whoop Gracie's team in tug-o-war? It was a spectacle to behold. Gracie, this is Morgan, my brother's fiancée."

"Nice to meet you," Morgan said. "Sorry you lost. The McBride brothers aren't exactly known for their gracious victories."

"He didn't win," Gracie argued. "His lies are the true spectacle. Nice to meet you, too. I've heard a lot about you."

David gestured toward the tug-of-war rope. "Want a rematch? Morgan, you can join us."

"No, thanks, Decker and I are headed for the craft tents," Morgan said. "I just came down to see if—"

"He has a date," Gracie said, cutting Morgan off. "To the wedding? He's got a date. Me. He asked last night. Just hasn't had a chance to tell you yet. I'm so excited."

David's mouth fell open. Gracie glanced up at him and winked.

"Oh," Morgan said. "Great. That makes me happy. But I wasn't coming down to ask about that."

Gracie's face fell. "You weren't?" she and David asked at the same time.

Morgan shook her head. "No. I was coming down to tell you that the ranch sorting registration table is open and ask if you were going to do it. If you are, you'll need to get signed up now."

WELL, THAT DIDN'T go the way she'd planned. Gracie couldn't even say, really, why she jumped in to volunteer to go to the wedding with David. Only that she wanted to save him from an awkward conversation. As repayment for what he'd done for her? As a thank-you for standing up for her against Farley? As gratitude for his treatment of Vera?

Or maybe just because you like him and don't hate the idea of spending a romantic evening at a wedding with him. Maybe it's as simple as that.

No. Definitely not that.

Regardless of why she did it, now she was trapped. She would be going to a wedding with David whether she wanted to or not.

Whether he wanted her to or not.

Oh, no. She had invited herself as someone's date to a wedding, without even knowing if he wanted to take her. She was *that* girl now. Mortifying.

Farley's return had jumbled her more than she thought. She barely even recognized herself anymore. Stealing horses, caring what someone else thought of her, inviting herself to weddings, *ugh.* She didn't exactly love this new version of herself.

"Ranch sorting?" she repeated, as Morgan looked on with her giant blue eyes. "I'm afraid I don't know what that is."

The last time Gracie had been to Haw Games Day, she was a teenager. She was there for the food and for wandering around with friends looking cool. She wasn't there for the games, especially anything called a ranch sorting.

"Nah," Decker said, finally catching up with Morgan. He had powdered sugar dust in his scruff. Morgan reached up to wipe it off. "David won't do anything like that. He'd have to go up against me. He's gotten soft since opening his little doggy doctor office. Gotta leave the big animals to the big cowboys, right brother?"

David tipped his head back, his hands stuffed into his pockets. "If I remember correctly, the last time we went head-to-head in ranch sorting, my team won."

"We were on the same team."

"And we won. But, if you'll recall, we won because I bailed you out."

"That's not at all how I remember it."

"Convenient," David said. "Anyway, we don't have horses."

"You can borrow ours," Morgan said. "We've got Tango and Queenie."

"And we know you can ride them," Decker said accusingly. Gracie blushed while David snickered.

"Gracie's never done it. She has no idea what it even is," David said.

"I've never done it before either," Morgan said with a warm smile. "But we've been practicing up at the Newell ranch. They've got some cattle. There's a learning curve. But she'll catch on. Besides, it's fun."

Decker looked into his paper bag, then balled it up, a cloud of powdered sugar dust billowing into the air. "You're basically working with your partner to sort numbered cattle from one pen to another," he said to Gracie. "There'll be one in there that doesn't have a number and has to be left out. It's timed, you only get ninety seconds. When it starts, they call out a number, and that's the number you start on. The team who pens the most cattle in ninety seconds wins. Easy."

"Not easy. She's not a rancher," David said. "She doesn't even own a horse."

"I'll do it," Gracie said, once again surprising herself with the way her mouth just seemed to be forming words and doing things all on its own. "We will, I mean. Unless you don't want to, David?"

He leaned in and whispered, "What are you doing?"

She shrugged. "Sounds like fun."

"Are you sure?"

She nodded, not at all sure, but sure that she didn't like to be underestimated. "I'm not saying we'll win, but..." She shrugged. "How hard can it be?"

"Hard," he said.

She waved him off. "We will need to borrow your horses, though," she said to Morgan. "Again."

Morgan beamed. "Of course! Wow, David, you got yourself a good sport here. First, the wedding. Now, this. I like her!"

Maybe it was only because Gracie had spent

so much time holding David in her sights, but she noticed a slight color change creep up the back of his neck. He was blushing. And no sooner did she notice it than she could feel the same heat creep up the sides of her neck and her cheeks. One thing about being a redhead—she blushed easily and obviously. She dipped her face toward the ground to hide it.

Thankfully, Decker wanted to move on. He clapped his brother on the back. "Looks like you're in, brother. I'll see you in the pen. Hopefully I won't wear Tango out too much with my own speed and agility."

"See you," Morgan said, then, "Ooh, Decker, look at the wedding ring pattern on that quilt over there! Wouldn't it be perfect to hang in the living room? Maybe take care of that draft we keep feeling." And then they were gone.

David looked absolutely tormented. Gracie tried to alleviate the weirdness. "Those two are meant for each other, don't you think?"

"Definitely," David said. "Are you sure you want to do this? You don't have to. I can take my brother's razzing."

"The cattle sort? Absolutely. I'm a quick learner."

"It's one of those things you can't learn by watching," he said. "I'm not even sure if I totally remember how to do it."

"Tango and Queenie already know what to do, and they will have already done it once by the time we get out there. They'll be warmed up."

"Or they'll be tired out."

"David. It's cattle sorting at Haw Games Day. It's not life and death. What happens if we lose?"

"Decker never lets me forget it for the rest of our lives, that's what happens. Worse than death."

"Well, now you're just being dramatic. I thought you could take his razzing. You can blame it all on me." She jostled his shoulder with hers. "It'll be fun. And so will the wedding."

He finally turned to face her dead-on. "What are you doing, exactly? One minute you're declaring me the enemy, and the next you're inviting yourself to my brother's wedding as my date. What gives?"

Gracie squirmed. She knew that nothing she was doing made sense. But she also knew that her grandmother dying right in front of her face wasn't making sense to her. Farley returning wasn't making sense. Nothing about her life at this moment was making sense.

She hadn't realized until that very moment how tired she was. On a bone-deep level. It was the fatigue she'd been ignoring for years, even when her grandma would say, *Are you sleeping enough, honey? You look tired.* She'd always responded with, *All lawyers look tired, Grandma. It's a lot of work.* But even then she knew she was just ignoring the truth. She *was* tired.

And she didn't want to just go back to life as normal after her grandma passed.

Which was looking like it might happen much sooner than she'd anticipated.

"I don't know. I'm helping you out, I guess? You've had to deal with Farley twice now. I'm just returning the favor."

He arched one eyebrow. "Favor." She nodded. He seemed to think it over, and then started walking, the opposite direction of where Decker and Morgan went. "I hope you like the color yellow."

"I love it." She did not love the color yellow and thought it washed her out, but at this point, what did it matter? She was in, and wasn't going to let a color keep her out. They walked in silence for a few minutes, pausing at booths to look over a jalapeño jelly and an array of hand-poured candles. "So, who's the older brother?"

"I am, by fourteen months."

"Yikes, your poor mother."

"Yeah, that's what she thought, too. Come on, let's go look around."

To Gracie's surprise, David grabbed her hand and tugged her toward the craft tents. Even more to her surprise, she let him.

CHAPTER TEN

FORTUNATELY, THE RANCH sorting competition wasn't the big event of the evening. That honor would be given to the tractor pull, which would be happening on the dirt racetrack down the road a clip just after the dinner hour. Most of the crowd had wandered to the track to settle in with their hot dogs and popcorn, so they could get the best seats, leaving some of the Haw Games contests a little sparse.

This meant that the only spectators at the sorting were the old-timers, who didn't care for all that dust and noise and loud music and emceeing that took place at the pull. The smaller crowd calmed Gracie's nerves as she studied the teams before her, including Decker and Morgan, who appeared to be in the lead by penning eight of the ten cows in their ninety seconds.

"Okay, so to me it looks like the strategy is to push a cow along the pen so it naturally goes in through the gate. Then you chase it the rest of the way in and I'll go get one and do the same.

We switch like that, back and forth, back and forth. Yes?"

"Generally, yes," David said. "Every team develops their own strategy, but that sounds like a solid one, as long as you're good at cutting one from the herd."

"I'm equally good at cutting one from the herd as I am at chasing one through the gate," she said.

"Changing your mind?"

"Nope. I'm just trying to figure out the strategy."

"Well, if it makes you feel any better, I'm not great at cutting a cow from the herd, either. I haven't done this since my dad died and we got rid of all the cattle. And Decker was right—he was the one who carried us to victory back then, not me."

"You didn't mention that part before I volunteered us to do this," she said.

"You didn't give me a chance."

"Fair enough," she said. "Regardless, that doesn't change our need for a strategy. Switching off seemed to work for Decker and Morgan. And the horses are accustomed to it."

"I think that plan is as good as any."

"Final contenders… Langhorst and McBride…you are on deck…" The announcer's voice echoed through the little arena.

David gave Gracie a smile. "This is your last chance to exercise good sense."

"I think you mean my chance to win," Gracie said, standing. She held out a hand. David took it and stood up. "Come on, partner. We've got this."

THEY, IN FACT, did not *have this*.

They were terrible.

Not for lack of trying. Tango raced around the ring like saving their dignity was his job. But David was as bad at cutting a cow from the herd as he remembered himself to be. Maybe worse. *Rusty*, he thought, over and again. *You've gotten rusty.*

And still he was one hundred percent better at it than Gracie was.

On top of that, Queenie wasn't so into it at all. She mostly seemed to want to stand in one place and watch the cows stream past her, as if she were the host of a dinner party and they were her guests.

Gracie gave it her all, leaning far over Queenie's withers and shouting nonsensical noises, in hopes that one would work to make the horse go in the right direction. David could hear the low rumbling of laughter in the audience. His face burned. He was the veterinarian in this town. The number of times he was going to hear about this would be staggering. He wondered if he would ever outlive this moment, or if he would forever be the vet who got bested by tired cows.

The very thought made him laugh. And the bewildered look on Gracie's face, as if she just couldn't understand why the cows wouldn't just count themselves off and walk inside the correct pen single file, made him laugh harder.

She caught his eye and the crease in her forehead melted away. She started to laugh, too.

"This was a terrible idea," she shouted. "Whose idea was it?"

Thank goodness it was only a minute and a half, because it was the longest minute and a half of his life. At the last second, one cow sauntered into the new pen. It just happened to be the cow wearing the correct number. The crowd cheered, and Gracie threw her arms into the air in victory. "One!"

There was something about her exuberance that drew David. Seeing her on that horse with her arms up, he forgot about the humiliation as well as the certainty that the humiliation would carry over into his office. He could only gaze at her, take her in, wonder at what it must be like to live life with all that energy.

He couldn't decide if it would be exhilarating

or exhausting. Maybe a little of both. After all, simply being in her presence was a little of both.

"That was not at all what I thought it would be," she confessed as they walked away from the ring. "Why didn't you warn me?"

David raised his eyebrows. "I tried. You're maybe just the tiniest bit hardheaded." He used one knuckle to knock lightly against the top of her head.

"I thought, *how difficult can this be*, you know? It's cows. Turns out it can be difficult. Like, really, really difficult."

"Well, fortunately, only half the town took in that spectacle. Not the entire town."

Decker and Morgan came at them from the other direction. Decker was wiping the corners of his eyes from laughing so hard.

"Congratulations, champ," David said, holding out one hand.

Decker shook it. "Look at it this way—you almost won in reverse. If the challenge had been to keep all the cows out, you had everyone beat."

"Okay, okay, get it out of your system."

Morgan stepped in for a brief hug. "It's hard," she said, conciliatory. She turned and gave Gracie a hug, too. "If it weren't for Decker, I don't know if I would have gotten a single cow. And Queenie has no idea what's going on. You did great."

"Did you hear that?" Decker said to his brother. "I basically did it by myself."

Morgan swatted at him. "I did not say that."

"Well, I hate to cut off such a good time," David said, "but we need to eat. Congrats again, see you later." He grabbed Gracie's hand and pulled her away.

Once out of the arena, they headed for the strip of food trucks lined up near the parking lot. David let go of Gracie's hand; his hand instantly felt cold without it.

"I don't know about you, but I'm feeling the need to take the edge off the humiliation with some really greasy fries," he said.

"Just what the doctor ordered," Gracie agreed.

Ten minutes later, they were sitting side by side at a picnic table, each of them with grease-slicked fingers as they picked through massive mounds of loaded french fries. For quite a while, they ate in silence.

Gracie finished hers and wiped the corners of her mouth with a paper napkin. "You and Decker seem close."

"We are," he said. "Always have been. He's my best friend."

"Your parents still alive?"

He shook his head. "Dad died a few years ago, and our mom…well, she could be dead, for all we know, but we haven't heard anything if she is."

"She lives somewhere else?"

"She left Buck County when we were kids. We never saw hide nor hair of her again." He caught the look on her face and grinned. "And here you thought you were the only one with a sketchy parent situation."

"One dead and one might as well be. Sounds like we have some experiences in common."

"I don't know," David said. "My mom was okay when she was there. Nothing like Farley. Maybe we were just being kids and not noticing that there was anything wrong, but she seemed happy and fun for the most part. And then she was gone. And she stayed gone. Which is bad and good, right? None of this coming back to make everyone's lives miserable thing that Farley seems to like to do. Her leaving us alone to grieve and figure out how to do life without her isn't all bad when you look at it that way."

"Making everyone miserable is Farley's pastime. Well, that and scamming people out of money. Which is why I want him gone. I know he's come back right now to try to bully my grandma into leaving him everything. That's why he brought that lawyer. He wants to con her into signing something while she's weak."

"Do you think he'll succeed?"

She shrugged and pushed the empty fry basket away from her. "She's his mom, you know? I don't know what that bond is like, because my mom died when I was still really young, and I don't even remember her, really. But I don't have to experience it to know that a mother's bond with her child is going to be pretty strong."

"Stronger than her bond with the granddaughter she raised, though?"

"Maybe not stronger, but possibly equal. And all Farley needs is an inch. He won't hesitate to turn that into a mile. It's what he's best at."

"Vera's smart, though," David said, stuffing the last fry into his mouth.

Gracie paused, and David could feel her eyeing him. Could sense her trying to size him up.

"Can I ask you a question?"

He stopped eating. "Sure."

"Why are you always at my grandma's farm, really?"

"What do you mean?"

"At first, I thought you were there to do exactly what Farley is doing. Little old lady, all alone, maybe doesn't have any family at all. Try to get into her good graces in hopes that you'll come into some cash, or land, or maybe both, real soon."

"Do you still think that?"

She studied him so hard he could feel it down to his toes. "I don't think so."

"Don't think so? You're not sure? Is it so outlandish to think I'm there as a friend?"

"Kind of. People don't just go doing things out of the kindness of their hearts. That's just not the way life works."

"Your grandma sure did."

"How so?"

He swallowed the last of his fries. "She came running to Decker's ranch one day. Her black horse—"

"Thunderbolt."

"Thunderbolt, yes. He was sick. She came running to the ranch, and I just happened to be there. My dad wasn't very neighborly, so we knew who she was, but we didn't really know her. Same as I knew you lived there, but I didn't know you. Anyway, she came to Decker's ranch for help, so I went over right away, and the very next Monday, she showed up at my office with Fannie for a checkup. Fannie didn't need a checkup. She was healthy as—well, probably healthy as a horse isn't the best phrase in this particular story—but she was in fine shape. Vera brought her in just because she knew I was just getting started and needed clients. She was my very first official client. She's been a loyal client ever since. And over the years, we became friends. And, so, when she's needed extra help, I've been first in line."

"What was wrong? With Thunderbolt? I never knew this happened. When she called to tell me he'd died, it was the first time I'd ever heard of anything going wrong with him at all. It was a shock."

"Parasites," David said. "It wasn't what killed him. That happened a few years later. This time, he was just having some belly issues, and it turned out he had parasites. We treated him and he was right as rain. And I had a dedicated client and new friend. That's why I'm there, Gracie. I don't want anything from her. I believe she deserves something from me for all those years of dedication. I'm there to give, not take. And I care about those animals now. Kind of like they're my own. I want to make sure they're getting the care that they need. That's all there is to it. Nothing shady, I promise."

She paused for a long time, and then said, "I believe you."

"Thank you. I'm glad." They gazed into each other's eyes for a long moment. David could barely feel himself breathing. The intensity threatened to bowl him over. He checked his watch. "Do you think Vera's getting hungry?"

Gracie shook her head. "She's never hungry

anymore, but I do think we should ask. But first, there's one more game I saw that we didn't do."

"What's that?"

She pointed across the fairgrounds to a dirt strip surrounded by a loose crowd of people. She grinned. "The pedal pull."

"Nah," David said. "I'll pass."

"I wasn't talking about for you," she said, standing up and brushing crumbs off her hands.

"You know they put a weighted sled on the end of that thing, right?" David asked.

She cocked one hip to the side. "You think I'm afraid of that?"

"I don't think there's anything in this world that could scare you, Gracie Langhorst," David said, surprised at the warmth that spread through his chest when he said it. When had this begun happening, exactly? When did the daredevil gleam in her eyes make him feel off-balance in a good way?

He didn't know. He only knew that he kind of liked it.

And he definitely didn't like that.

CHAPTER ELEVEN

DAVID HAD TAKEN only one step in the door before Ellory literally threw her oven mitts across the counter and came running at him, arms open wide.

"Shut up, David. You did not!"

Smiling, he held the squirming kitten toward her, one hand clutching the animal around the chest, the other hand holding its wiggly bottom. It mewed in protest. "Well, not me, really. Vera Langhorst did. Eight weeks today, and ready to become a coffee shop cat."

"He's so cute!" she cooed, taking him out of David's hand. The kitten mewed again but seemed to wiggle less in Ellory's clutches. She held him up to look directly into his eyes and touched her nose against his. "Hey, there, little Latte. Aren't you just as sweet as your name?"

David, and all of The Dreamy Bean, may as well have disappeared altogether in that moment. It was just Ellory and her kitten, and a bunch of background noise, of which David was a small part.

Ellory took a pause from cooing at the kitten and flung her free arm around David's neck. "Thank you, thank you, thank you. This place gets so quiet at night. Latte and I will have plenty of opportunities to get to know each other. Won't we, little Latte? Oh, he's just the best. And so are you, David McBride."

He ducked his head. "I'm glad you're happy. If you should change your mind, I'm sure Vera would take him back into the barn. She needs mousers, and his siblings could very well run off the first chance they get."

"Well, that's just so sad, isn't it? You won't be running off, because you will have the sweetest life right here in our coffee shop. I'll make sure of it. No drafty barns for you. No mice, either." She stage-whispered, "But if you see one, you can go ahead and do your kitty thing, okay?"

David was starting to feel like a third wheel. "I'll leave you to your bonding," he said, turning for the door.

"Wait. Were you going to say hi to Morgan? She's in the back."

David turned, and sure enough, there was Decker's fiancée sitting on a cloud chair in the back of the store, reading a book and sipping a coffee with Annie, who was sitting right next to her, staring at an iPad screen. David started to sneak away, but Annie saw him and called out.

"Doctor McBride! Hi! Over here!"

David wasn't exactly feeling sociable at that moment. His mind was playing the events of Haw Games on a loop, and his heart felt heavy with thoughts of Gracie.

But Morgan looked up from her book, smiled and waved him over. He had no choice but to be sociable. He would just exchange niceties and go back to his rumination. He plastered on a smile and walked through The Dreamy Bean.

He was never very good at hiding emotions. He knew this. But it was obvious from the way Morgan's face fell and grew into a look of concern that he was doing an especially poor job of it today.

"Uh-oh, what's wrong?" She pushed an empty chair toward him with her foot.

He sat. How did he always make it so obvious? "Not a thing," he said, still trying to keep up the ruse.

"It's not about the ranch sorting thing, is it?" Morgan asked. She closed her book, using her thumb to keep her place. "You know Decker and I were just ribbing y'all, right?"

"Oh, I know," he said.

Annie giggled. "I saw it. You weren't very good."

David smiled. "Thanks, Annie."

"Next year, Ben and I are going to try it, because we know we won't be in last place if you and Gracie are going to do it again."

"I can't make any promises," he said. "I wasn't exactly planning to do it this time."

"Well, now you can make plans," Annie said. "Because you have a whole year."

"It's not the ranch sorting thing," Morgan said, still studying him. "It's Gracie. That's what's bothering you, isn't it? What happened?"

"Nothing," he said. "No. I…how do you do that?"

"Do what?" Annie asked.

Morgan gave him a sympathetic look. "It's a gift. What's going on?"

David hadn't come into The Dreamy Bean planning to spill his guts about what was going on inside of him regarding Gracie, but then again it seemed like these days he was doing all sorts of things he wasn't planning on doing.

It was maddening.

But suddenly he wanted nothing more than to talk about his feelings.

"Nothing is going on," he said. "Absolutely nothing. Until there is. And then it's just the tiniest glimmer that something possibly could go on. And still, nothing."

"And that's the problem," she said. "You want there to be, and she doesn't?"

"Not exactly," he said. "She doesn't and I don't. But I do. And I think so does she."

Morgan blinked. "Oh. Wait. I'm confused."

"Join the club," he said.

Now she shut her book entirely and set it to the side, then stretched back in her chair. "Let's start from the beginning."

He took a deep breath. *Might as well get it out there, because it's tearing you up on the inside.* He let the breath out and started talking. "I've worked too hard for too long, just to have someone come in and distract me now. I've always had my plan, you know? Go to school, start a practice, grow my practice, pick up another partner and keep growing. Once everything is up and running and feels…right…then maybe start looking at finding a wife, having some kids, I don't know. That part of my plan has never been formed, because I haven't achieved the steps I need to achieve in order to get there."

"But suddenly it's coming into the picture because you like Gracie," Morgan said. "Now I get it."

"I don't," Annie said. "If you love her, just love her. And if she loves you, just let her love you. And if she doesn't love you, then sorry, Charlie, you're out of luck, Chuck."

Morgan put a hand on Annie's arm and gave

her head a quick shake. Annie pressed her lips together and went back to her iPad.

"Do you remember when I first came around, Decker and I fought like cats and dogs trying to ignore our feelings for each other?"

David nodded. "It was frustrating for the rest of us who could see that you two belonged together."

Morgan nodded. "And you wanted us to be happy."

"Of course."

"Maybe you should want that for yourself as much as you wanted it for us."

"It's not the right time."

"Who's to say when the time is right?" Morgan asked.

"I am," he said. "Listen, I should go. I didn't mean to interrupt your reading." He stood. "Good to see you, Annie."

"Bye," Annie said without looking up from her iPad, already absorbed in something else.

"Don't get in your own way, David," Morgan said. "Don't try to fool yourself like Decker and I did. We wasted so much time telling ourselves that it wasn't right, we actually missed the fact that it was perfect and staring us in the face."

"That's not what's happening," David said. "I've worked too hard for too long just to get derailed now."

He left The Dreamy Bean as briskly as he could, repeating to himself, *It's not the right time, it's not the right time, it's not the right time...*

VERA SLEPT SO long the morning after Haw Games Day, Gracie feared the worst had happened. When noon came and went, she knocked softly on her grandma's bedroom door and pushed it open.

Vera was just waking, smiling, but looking completely sapped of energy.

Gracie rushed to her bedside. "Are you okay? I should have come in sooner."

Vera shushed her and rubbed her eyes. "I've been in and out for a few hours now. Just so tired."

"Should I call someone? A doctor?"

Vera took Gracie's hand in hers and patted it with her other hand. "Sweetie, I had such a good time yesterday. I'm tired, that's all."

"Do you want something to eat? A drink, maybe?"

"A few sips of orange juice might be okay."

But Gracie knew that it wouldn't be okay. Orange juice was one of the things that her grandmother repeatedly asked for, only to take a few sips and declare it too acidic for her stomach. Gracie hated that such a simple pleasure was out of the question now for her grandma. What must it be like to want something that is literally at your beck and call, and not be able to have it?

She went to the kitchen and poured a glass of juice. She was just taking it back to the bedroom when she bumped into Farley coming down the stairs from his bedroom.

"About time she woke up," he grumbled.

"She's still waking up, so leave her alone," Gracie said. "She's tired, and she doesn't need nonsense from you."

"Don't tell me what to do. You're still my kid, no matter how old you are."

Gracie squared up. "I was never your kid. You don't get to claim that."

He rolled his eyes. He stank like old booze and sweat and had the bloodshot eyes of someone who was up way too late doing things he shouldn't have been doing. He let out a rattly cough and shoved her shoulder to move her out of the way.

"Let it rest already. And get out of my way. I've got things to do."

She couldn't help noticing that he was carrying what looked like the same pack of papers he was carrying when he was with his lawyer.

"What is that?" she asked, swiping for them and missing. He held them up high, out of her reach. "It's what I think it is, isn't it?"

"It's none of your business," he said.

"If it's what I think it is, it's absolutely my business." She made another grab for it, but missed, the orange juice slipping over the side of the glass and dripping down her hand. "You can give it a try, but just know that I will fight it with everything I've got."

His eyes bugged comically. "Oooh, I'm so skeered."

"If you had any sense, you would be scared. Remember what happened last time you underestimated me. But it doesn't matter. Scared or not, I will beat you at your own game."

"Funny that you think of it as a game. I think of it as taking care of my mother in her final days. I think of it as a birthright."

"Don't get lofty." His face was blank. "Oh, sorry," she said, "you probably don't know what that means."

"Why do you want this place, anyway?" he asked, arching one eyebrow. "It's not like you're going to live here."

"It's not like you are, either. And, besides, what makes you so sure I won't live here?"

"Fancy-pants lawyers like you don't want to be in the sticks. That's how I know. Unless…oh, wait a minute, it's that dentist, isn't it?"

"What?"

"It's that doctor you've got. He's holding you here. That won't last anyway. He'll see you as the big nothing that you are and walk away like a smart man."

"First of all, he's a veterinarian, not a dentist."

"Whatever, I just knew he wasn't a real doctor."

"Well, secondly, he most definitely *is* a real doctor. Third, I'm not going to bother to dignify that last part. And fourth, I don't *have him*. I don't even know what that means."

But she did know what it meant, and it was something she'd been thinking about all night. She didn't have him, that part was true. But she was starting to wonder what it would look like to have him. She had some trust issues, for obvious reasons, but she'd started to entertain the idea that maybe she could put her trust in David.

And she absolutely hated that Farley could see that in her.

"Wow, you can count to four. Good job." Farley looked at his nonexistent watch. "Ope. Look. It's *I don't care* thirty. Live your life. I'm living mine." His face lit up. "Hey! When I own this place, I'll rent it out to you and your dentist for a real reasonable price. How about that?"

She glared at his back as he disappeared down the hallway and into Vera's room.

"Good morning, Mama!" he crowed. "Rise and shine!"

Gracie's hand caused the juice inside the glass

to tremble. She didn't know what exactly she was feeling—fear, fury, or a little of both—but she knew that the less alone time Farley had with her grandma, the better for everyone. She followed him in.

He had already pulled the soft chair that normally sat in the corner of the room up to her bedside, and was leaning across the mattress, a fake look of concern etched on his face. Gracie thought she maybe even saw a forced tear begin to squeeze out of the corner of his eye. What a faker.

Everything about Farley was false and disgusting, and she hated that it was his blood that coursed through her.

"I brought your juice." She set it on the nightstand and tried to help her grandma into a seated position to drink it, but Vera waved her away.

"I'll get some later, honey," she said.

"But you need to drink something," Gracie said. "You can't just..." She trailed off, unable to finish the sentence aloud. *You can't just give up and let yourself die.*

"I will. Just not now."

"Okay," Gracie said. "How about I help you to your chair?"

"Not today, sweetie." Vera closed her eyes and pressed her head deeper into the pillow. "I'm quite comfortable right here."

"Do you want me to turn on one of your TV shows?" Gracie asked.

"Maybe in a while." Vera still hadn't opened her eyes.

Gracie stood awkwardly for a few seconds, trying to think of what to do.

"You can go. I've got her right now," Farley said, his voice syrupy sweet and completely fake.

Gracie gave him an equally fake smile. "I can take over. I'm sure you have a lot to do today. You'll be moving on now, correct?"

"Incorrect," he said. "I'm here for my mother. Right, Mama?" He reached out and grabbed one frail hand, rubbed his thumbs over the back of it, as if he were giving her a massage.

Vera offered a thin smile, but still didn't open her eyes.

Gracie didn't want to start an argument right here by her grandma's bedside, so she only pressed her lips together harder, the smile growing thinner, and tried to convey her conviction to get rid of Farley with a steely glare in her eyes.

"Go ahead, Gracie," Farley said, his voice so gentle it made Gracie want to scream. "I'm sure your doctor friend will be here soon. He may need assistance out there in the barn."

Vera opened her eyes. "Oh. Please tell David I said hello."

"I will, Grandma," Gracie said.

"And tell him thank-you for taking me to the Games yesterday. I had the best time."

"I will," Gracie repeated.

Vera's eyes slipped closed again, but the smile remained on her lips.

Gracie snuck out of the room and, unsure of what exactly to do, went into the kitchen. She stood at the sink, deep in thought, and then started washing dishes that had already been washed.

For most of the day, she puttered around the house, cleaning things that were already clean, just because they were close to a window that faced the pasture and the barn. But David didn't come and didn't come. Lately, he wasn't so much like clockwork. He arrived at all hours of the day, and sometimes into the evening. He would arrive, harried and mumbling about how busy the office was. Looked like today was going to be another one of those days.

They hadn't even talked about the wedding. She wasn't even sure if they were still going.

Her phone rang just as she was in the middle of dusting the coffee table for the third time. It was Jem, her boss back in Kansas City.

This couldn't be good.

"Hey, Jem. Working on a Sunday?"

"Well, you're still alive. Good to know."

"I emailed you two days ago. You know I'm on leave."

"I also know that we've got new cases coming out of our ears, and we're down one associate. When are you coming back? Are you ever coming back? It's been two months."

Gracie rolled her eyes and flopped down onto the couch. "Andrew can't handle the workload? It's almost like I've been telling you that for years now."

"You're on speaker," Jem said, at the very same time that Gracie heard Andrew's voice say, "I'm right here."

"That's just great," Gracie said. "Thank you for the warning, Jem. A little heads-up might have been nice."

"Or maybe not trying to sabotage me behind my back would have been nice," Andrew countered. Gracie supposed she couldn't blame him for being angry. "Especially since I'm bailing you out while you lounge about in the boonies."

"I'm not trying to sabotage you. But it's not beneath you to try to push me out, so if I was sabotaging you, would you really blame me?" Gracie pressed her thumb into one eye and then the other. This conversation brought on a weary feeling that she hadn't had since she came back to Buck County. The scrapping, fighting, maneuvering, posturing…it was all so exhausting. She didn't miss it. "Plus, I'm hardly just *lounging about*, as you put it. Have some empathy, man."

"Anyway," Jem said. "Andrew is handling it just fine. But he's one human, and we could use another human so we don't have to come in on Sundays. How's your grandfather?"

"Dead for like forty years. It's my grandmother I'm here for."

"You know who I meant."

"If you mean, is she dead yet, the answer is no." *But she's not getting out of bed today, and that's not exactly a positive step forward.*

"Gracie. I'm not so heartless, you know," Jem said softly. It was her hurt voice, and Gracie knew her just well enough to know that it was a voice that she put on when she needed to get results. She wasn't so sure that Jem could actually be hurt. Cyborgs didn't have feelings. "I'm not waiting for her to die so you can come back. I have true concern."

"Thank you for your true concern," Gracie said, putting on an equally fake earnestness. "She is doing as well as expected. As am I."

"That's good, that's good." Well-placed pause. And then, "Do you think you could pick up some remote work? Just a little research. No client interaction. At least not yet."

Gracie sighed. Why bother fighting it? "Sure," she said. "Send me the files."

A few more pretend niceties passed between them, and then she hung up and dropped her phone on the couch next to her. She let her head fall back against the cushion and did a little deep breathing to calm herself.

How dare Jem be so impatient? How dare Andrew be so incompetent? Her grandma had warned her about making the choice to work for a cutthroat firm. She'd been right, as always. Fine. She would look at their stupid files. She would do some research. But only a little. What she missed, Andrew would just have to catch. Or Jem would herself.

Or maybe they'll bring in someone else and when you come back, you'll be stuck with all the boring cases no one else wants.

When I come back. How about if?

Vera's door opened and Farley emerged. "She needs to go to the bathroom. That's your duty, not mine."

Gracie sat forward. Vera had asked for help getting out of her chair a few times, but once she was up, she was able to get to the toilet all by herself and take care of her own business. This was a new, awful development. She jumped up and brushed past Farley without a word.

"You okay?" she asked as she went to her grandma's bedside. "Farley says you need help?"

"I just can't seem to find any energy today,"

Vera complained, as Gracie slid one arm behind her back and helped push her to a seated position. She then removed the blankets and helped Vera swing her sticklike legs over the side of the bed. She knew her grandma had taken off some weight, but she didn't realize how skin-and-bones she had become.

"You need some calories in you," Gracie said.

She wrapped her arms around Vera's waist and pulled her to standing. Vera wrapped her hand through Gracie's arm and held on tight. "Honey, I'm afraid that ship has sailed."

"Don't say that. You're having an off morning is all. You'll feel hungry later." She said it, even though she knew it wasn't the truth, and the time to call the phone number the oncology nurse had given her was rapidly approaching. She didn't want to bring hospice here. Hospice meant the hope was gone.

Gracie walked her grandma to the bathroom, and paced, biting her thumbnail, outside the door. When Vera called for her, she went in and helped her up, and then back to bed again.

"What can I get for you?" she asked as she smoothed the blankets around the frail old lady.

"Why don't you sit down so we can talk?" Vera gestured toward the chair that Farley had pulled to the bedside. Gracie paused, not wanting any of this to be true. Maybe if she just refused to follow orders, it wouldn't be. "Sit," Vera repeated.

Gracie sat.

"You're such a good girl," Vera said, gazing at her granddaughter.

No. No, no, no, I refuse. Gracie fought the urge to squeeze her eyes tight and run out of the room.

Vera reached for her hand. Gracie took it. She could feel her chin begin to wobble. She could feel the tears begin to rise in her throat. "Tell me about how things went with David at Haw Games."

Gracie blinked, her tears stilling in her throat. "What?"

"When you two came to pick me up from the quilting bee, you were both on cloud nine. Tell me about your day."

Gracie let out a laugh. This was not at all what she thought the conversation was going to be. It didn't change the fact that her grandma was getting sicker and sicker, and that Gracie would have to face the idea of calling hospice soon, but it was a reprieve, and she would gladly take those for as long as she was given them.

"We had a good time," she admitted. "We were awful at the ranch sorting. But he was surprisingly good at the pedal tractor pull." She blushed at the memory of how she couldn't tear her eyes away from him as he muscled the sled weight through the dirt, his leg and back muscles solid and bulging. It was hard to see how muscular he really was when he was wearing scrubs all the time. "He didn't win, but he didn't lose, either. And he beat his brother, so he was really happy."

"I'm not talking about the tractor pull," Vera chided.

"What are you talking about, then?" Gracie asked. "That's really all we did, other than eat a lot of unhealthy food. I felt absolutely sick by the end of the night."

"Lovesick?"

"Grandma!"

"Well?"

Gracie felt a telltale blush coming on and ducked her head to hide her face. "I don't know if I would say lovesick exactly."

"But?"

"But I like him. It was easy being with him."

"Do you want to see him again?"

"Grandma, where is this all coming from?" Gracie couldn't quit smiling. "I mean, sure I want to see him again. And I'm sure I will see him again, since he's here every day. And we have the wedding to go to."

Vera got a dreamy look on her face. "Weddings are so romantic. It'll be a perfect time to tell him."

"Tell him what?"

"That you like him and want to continue seeing him."

Gracie's eyes flew open wide. Her heart panged at the very thought of it. "No way!"

"Well, for goodness' sake, why not?"

As if on cue, Farley belched in the doorway, interrupting them. *How's that for why not?* Gracie wanted to say. *Farley Langhorst is Why Not Personified.*

"I've got to run to the store," he said.

"Nobody cares," Gracie said without turning around. "In fact, you should keep going once you reach it. Don't stop until you're out of Haw Springs for good."

"Can I borrow your car?" he asked, ignoring Gracie's barbs. "I'm sick of walking all that way. Takes all day."

Gracie finally turned around. "No. I don't want your germs infesting my upholstery."

"I wasn't asking you, so shut your trap," he said.

"Yes, of course you can," Vera said. "The keys are in the bowl on the hall table by the front door."

"Thanks, Ma. You're a peach."

He bounded away, and soon they heard the

front door open and close, followed by the rev of an engine.

"Grandma, you know you don't have to let him borrow your car. Or anything else." She tried to convey with the seriousness of her tone what exactly she meant by *anything else*.

"I know. But what am I going to do with it? I can barely walk, much less drive. It's not like I'll be going anywhere that I'll need a car to get to."

"You shouldn't say that."

"Oh, honey, it's true. I know you've been thinking about hospice. It's probably a good idea."

Gracie wanted to respond but found that she couldn't. Her lips wouldn't part. Her eyes wouldn't lift. Her vocal cords were paralyzed.

"I also think you should tell David how you feel. Life is short. Take it from someone who is at the end of theirs. You will regret every second that went by that you didn't tell him you love him. Truth be told, I can't wait to get to heaven and reunite with your grandfather. I've missed him so much."

"I'll think about it, Grandma. But I can't make any promises. I don't really know how I feel."

"And, while you're at it…" Vera touched Gracie's chin; Gracie lifted her eyes at last. "I think you should forgive Farley."

"No. Absolutely not. Not in a billion years."

"It's not good for you to foster such hatred. It isn't hurting him. It's hurting you."

"Farley Langhorst can't hurt me," Gracie said, but her voice sounded tiny, like a child's, and she wondered how true that was. She didn't know anything for sure anymore. If her sense of betrayal from Farley wasn't a given, what was?

"He's not hurting you. *You're* hurting you. He's just being Farley."

Gracie stood, pushing her chair with the backs of her knees. "Do you think you might want to try some broth?"

"Honey…"

"Maybe some crackers with butter? Or yogurt?"

"Gracie, sit." Vera's tone was firm, with a snap to it that Gracie hadn't heard since she was a teenager acting out. She sat. "Now, I'm going to die soon. We both know it, and we can't continue to dance around the subject like it's not happening. I know it hurts you to think about it, but you have to. I'll be gone, and you'll be left alone here on the farm without me. I don't know much about your life in Kansas City, but I know I've never heard you talk about dating or being in love or anything even close to it. I don't want you to be lonely in life, and I'm afraid you've walled yourself off. Break down those walls. Forgive your father, and let David in. Take it from an old, dying woman. You will never regret opening your heart."

Gracie's eyes were swimmy, and a teardrop landed on the thigh of her jeans. Vera's words felt like punches. She was right about one thing—Gracie didn't want to face the truth. About any of this.

"I don't want to hurt you, honey," Vera said, stroking Gracie's hand again. "I love you and want you to be happy in life."

"I am happy," Gracie said, her tiny voice now barely more than a whisper. But even she didn't believe herself. She wasn't happy. She hated her job. She hated the isolation of the city.

She hated being alone.

And she hated admitting those things, even just to herself.

"Okay, so be it. Then I want you to be happier," Vera said, choosing not to argue. "Now, I think I'm going to take a nap."

But you just woke up, Gracie wanted to say. But she withheld. This was a long time coming. *And, besides,* Gracie thought irrationally, *maybe she'll get rested up and be spry as ever when she wakes up.*

But Vera didn't wake up for hours. The light in the house shifted from window to window as the sun rose until it began to fall. Farley came home, drunk as ever, missing crashing Vera's car into the side of the house by mere inches.

Gracie escaped to the barn to wait for David. Fannie, who normally followed her to the barn every chance she got, instead stayed in Vera's bedroom, sleeping on the floor next to the bed, occasionally emitting sorrowful doggy sighs. *Not good,* Gracie thought as she walked to the barn without her canine companion. *Fannie knows. Dogs are good at sensing when the end is near for someone.*

When she arrived at the barn, she realized that David had already been and gone, and she had missed him. Still, she slipped inside the barn and sat on a hay bale. Norma appeared out of her hiding place and twined her way around Gracie's legs. Gracie reached down and began stroking the cat's head. Finally, the tears started in earnest.

"What am I going to do, Norma?" she said. "What will I do without her?" Vera had been Gracie's backbone for so long, Gracie wasn't sure she could so much as stand without her. She let herself cry, wiping her face with the sleeve of her shirt. Norma jumped up onto the hay bale beside her, then curled up to sleep, pushing her neck into Gracie's leg. Gracie continued to stroke the cat's fur. "I'm not ready for this," she confided. "Any of this. I can't let her go, and

I can't forgive Farley, and I can't tell David how I feel about him."

A kitten appeared, mewing for its mother. Norma opened one weary eye, as if to say, *I can never get any rest around here.*

Gracie chuckled and gave Norma one last stroke down the length of her body. "I totally understand, mama kitty. I sure do."

She got up and walked back to the house, the late afternoon sun shining through the trees and speckling her skin. She could hear Farley's voice all the way outside.

She paused, sighed, then kept walking.

CHAPTER TWELVE

GRACIE PACED THE length of her living room nervously, as if she were the waiting bride. Her stomach was in knots.

She hadn't spoken to David all week and had begun to worry that maybe he wouldn't show up at all. On top of that, after a small rallying effort on Monday and Tuesday, during which a little bit of chicken noodle soup and even a sliver of cheesecake was consumed, her grandma had taken to bed again, no longer interested in *I Love Lucy*, and dozing round the clock.

Gracie had a feeling that her grandma wouldn't leave that bed again. And the very thought made her afraid to leave the house. She didn't want to miss Vera's final breath.

More than that, she didn't want to leave Vera alone with Farley for that breath.

Gracie was only going to the wedding because Vera had made her promise that she would go and had insisted on seeing her in her dress before she left. But when Gracie had stepped into her grandma's bedroom, feeling pretty in her dress, the bodice hugging her waist perfectly, the skirt flaring out and making her want to spin like a child, her grandma was asleep.

"I'll tell you all about it when I get back," she whispered and kissed her grandma, leaving a dot of candy-apple-red lipstick on her cheek.

And then the pacing began. She felt as if she was on the clock.

What if he didn't show? She'd never been stood up before. Would she just go without him? Show up anyway so he could see what he was missing? But she wasn't exactly invited. She didn't even really know Morgan and Decker all that well.

Ugh, why did I volunteer for this? she thought.

She picked up her phone, started to call David to cancel on him before he could stand her up. But she stopped herself, chewed her fingernail and stared at the phone.

No. That was what the old Gracie would do. Old Gracie would jump to take control of the situation. Old Gracie would rob him of the chance to be a good date. Old Gracie would make assumptions and shut him out.

She didn't exactly think of herself as *New Gracie*, but she was under orders to start to open herself up. Dying wishes, actually. She couldn't go against dying wishes. As much as she wanted to.

She groaned, turned off her phone, and stuffed

it into her handbag. "Why did I volunteer for this?" she said aloud this time. "I don't even like him. I don't. I don't have to tell him that I like him, because I don't like him. At best he's… meh." She could practically hear her grandma's voice in the back of her mind: *Keep telling yourself that, and maybe it'll come true.*

The clock ticked. She paced.

And just as she was about to give up and go to her room to change out of the dress, there was a soft knock on the door.

David was on the other side. He'd traded his scrubs for a suit and tie, his hair carefully combed, his face soft from a fresh shave, the dimple in his chin showing through. She felt a sudden urge to press her finger into that dimple. He smiled, and her breath caught. She felt numb as she grabbed her purse and pushed open the screen door to step outside.

"You look…whoa," he said.

She froze. "I look whoa? Is that a good thing or a bad thing?"

"It's a great thing. Marlee is wrong about yellow not being anyone's color. You're absolutely stunning, Gracie."

She forced herself to relax and smile. "Thank you. You clean up pretty well yourself."

They walked side by side to the car and headed out silently. Gracie hadn't felt this awkward since the seventh-grade spring dance. She could sense the same angst radiating off him that she felt inside. It was nerves and anticipation all rolled into a giant lump of tension that was both electric and agonizing. She wanted to break it, but she didn't know how. All she could think was that she really wanted to reach over and hold his hand. She wanted to sit by him and eat wedding cake. She wanted to dance with him.

She wanted to feel his arms around her.

She wanted to kiss him.

She wanted him to want those same things.

But she also didn't.

After what seemed like forever, they finally arrived at the wedding venue, which looked like a glittering yellow wonderland, as if the sun had decided to set right there inside the event barn as a special favor to Morgan and Decker. As they got out of David's car and walked toward the door, Gracie could see inside. There were practically fields of yellow flowers, with tiny purple and white accent flowers. There were string lights wrapped around every square inch of the room, giving the atmosphere a pulsating sense, as if it were alive.

"It's beautiful," she said.

Ben met them at the door, dressed identically to David, but adorned with a cowboy hat. He tipped his hat as they arrived.

"Doctor McBride. Ma'am."

"Whoo-wee, looking sharp, Ben. Annie's gonna get some big ideas at this wedding. You're gonna be the next one getting hitched."

Ben gave a nod to the floor, but didn't respond. To Gracie, it seemed that he was working out a riddle in his mind.

David gave Ben's shoulder a pat. "I'm just joking with you, Ben. You look very nice. I'm sure Annie does, too."

"Annie is very pleasing to look at tonight," Ben agreed. "I'm supposed to let you know that you have to go on to the groom's room." He turned to Gracie. "And I'm supposed to show you to your seat, Miss…um…"

"You can just call me Gracie," she said. "And I would love a chaperone, thank you."

He tipped his hat again. "Yes, ma'am, you're welcome." He crooked one elbow for her to take.

"Okay, I guess that's my cue to start best-manning. Before I go, do you have everything?" David asked.

Gracie nodded.

He frowned. "Are you sure?"

She patted her skirt where pockets would normally be, out of habit. "Positive. Why?"

"I just don't know how you managed to fit it in that tiny purse is all."

She held up her purse—a gold-beaded handbag she'd unearthed from a box pushed to the back of her closet—and gazed at it, confused. "Fit what?"

"Your shotgun, of course."

Now she could see him holding back a smile, his eyes glimmering with mischief in the halo of wedding sparkle.

She swatted at his arm, unable to contain her own giggle. "That's how it's going to be tonight, huh, McBride? Get back there and make yourself useful. I'm here to see a wedding."

"Yes, ma'am."

David disappeared, and Ben walked Gracie to the rows of white plastic folding chairs that had been carefully lined up on the dance floor for the ceremony. A smattering of people were already seated, excitedly chatting. The room buzzed with anticipation.

"I have been informed that there is no longer a bride's side and groom's side at weddings, but if you would like to sit near where you can clearly see Doctor McBride, I would say you should sit on the right-hand side," Ben said.

"I would like that very much," Gracie said, choosing to ignore that only a couple of months ago, she would have rather been hog-tied than have anything to do with David McBride. Now, she wanted nothing more than to sit close to where he would be standing.

"It's about time," Decker grumbled when David walked into the groom's room. "I was starting to think you weren't going to show."

"Nah, what kind of brother would do that? I got slowed down by a little bit of nerves, but I'm here now."

"Nerves? I'm the one getting married. Why are you nervous?"

David shrugged. He'd been nervous about his date with Gracie, but didn't want to burden his brother with that on his wedding day. "I want everything to be perfect for you and Morgan is all," he said. It wasn't a lie. His brother deserved a fine day.

"I need help with this thing," Decker said, handing David an untied bow tie. "You're not the only nervous one. I have a heck of a time with these when I'm not shaking like a leaf on a tree."

David took the tie and maneuvered himself behind his brother, so he could look in the mirror while he tied the tie. "Everything's going to be great. You and Morgan are perfect for each other."

"I know we are. I don't know why I'm on edge. I spent an awfully long time avoiding getting married. I guess I'm just hoping that I'm not going to ruin everything."

"You're not going to ruin anything. You love Morgan and she loves you. And you have Archer, who also loves you. You've got the good life, brother. Reach out and grab it."

He finished tying the tie, and turned Decker so that they were face-to-face so he could straighten it.

"I just don't want her to run out like Mom did," Decker said. "You know what I mean?"

David did know what Decker meant. He'd been thinking a lot about his mom lately, too, which was strange. Usually, he didn't give her a second thought. He'd tried telling himself that it was the impending loss of Vera that brought his mother to his mind, but he suspected it was something else.

He suspected it was his brain trying to force him to confront what could really be holding him back from getting too close to Gracie.

But now, seeing the fear in his brother's eyes, he realized how silly it was for either of them to deprive themselves of love just because she deprived them of it a million years ago.

He put his hands on his brother's shoulders and looked him in the eyes. "Dad would be so proud of you right now, Decker," he said. "He would be doing that thing where he pretends he's got something in his eye so nobody knows that he's getting misty-eyed. Dad would tell you that marrying this woman is the right thing to do because you're made for each other. And because he wouldn't want either one of us to be alone when our perfect person is right there in front of us."

Decker gave a weak smile, but David could feel his shoulders relax the tiniest bit. "Yeah," he said. "Thanks, man."

The door opened, and Ben peeked his head inside. "The guests have arrived and so has the minister. Annie wanted me to tell you that you have two minutes, and you cannot be late."

"Got it," Decker said. "I wouldn't dream of being late. I've got the best girl in the world to marry in two minutes."

Morgan's sister Marlee burst into the room, a flurry of yellow and sequins and orders issued in a firm tone. She expertly pinned a boutonniere onto David's lapel and shooed Decker into the chapel where he waited with the minister for the ceremony to get started.

They lined up behind Annie, Ben and Archer. David felt something tugging at him as the music began to swell inside the church.

"Everybody remember, this isn't a foot race," Marlee hissed.

Ben gave Annie a confused look. She leaned in and whispered, "Walk slow." He nodded in understanding.

The doors opened, and Annie and Ben stepped out, Annie holding Archer's hand. They inched their way down the aisle. Next thing David knew,

Marlee was squeezing his bicep—his signal to start moving.

As soon as they stepped out, the music enveloped him, something somber and sweet and romantic and important. He lifted his eyes and locked onto Gracie without even trying. She smiled up at him shyly, and he forgot to breathe.

He heard his own words echoing through his head: *He wouldn't want either one of us to be alone when our perfect person is right there in front of us.*

THERE WERE YELLOW flowers printed on the plates and wrapped around the napkins. At each setting was an edible flower lollipop, with a note wrapped around its stick: *Love is Sweet. Thank you for celebrating ours. Decker & Morgan.* Gracie slipped one into her handbag to show her grandma later. Vera would get a kick out of a flower suspended in candy.

"Is this seat taken?"

David stood next to Gracie, his hand on the back of the chair next to her. "It is now," she said, indicating that he could take it. "All done taking pictures?"

He sat. "They are tired of this ugly mug ruining their photographs, that is correct."

"Hardly an ugly mug," Gracie said. "I doubt you ruined a single thing. Although…"

His eyebrows crooked up. "Although?"

"I mean, nobody is going to outdo Morgan tonight. I didn't know they made wedding dresses that beautiful. I didn't know they made humans that beautiful."

"I don't know," he said. "I can think of one person who's at least giving her a run for her money." He gazed at Gracie. She felt herself swoon, but forced herself not to pull away or even look away. Her heart gave two big thumps in protest. She wasn't used to being so open with her feelings. She chalked it up to the contagious nature of wedding romance. "Don't tell her I said that."

"Thank you," she said. "And I won't."

He leaned in. "I want to dance with you tonight."

Now the thumps in her chest were revving into a galloping herd. She could hardly open her mouth to say, "Then I think you should ask me to dance."

An hour later, after the bride and groom had been announced, the dinner served and eaten, and the traditions out of the way, he did just that.

The DJ cued up "Celebration," and David scooted his chair back, stood, and held out one hand. "Would you like to dance?"

She took his hand and let him pull her up out of her chair and lead her to the dance floor.

It took her a minute to warm up—it had

been so long since the last time she danced, she couldn't really remember when it was—but once they got going, there was no stopping them. She felt so free as he took her hand and twirled her, just as she imagined herself doing in her grandma's room. All that existed were the twinkling lights and the fabric brushing her calves and the warmth of David's hand in hers.

There was no Farley.

There was no death.

Two songs later, they were sweaty and out of breath. The DJ switched to a slow song, one that Gracie knew from when she was a teenager who still might have believed in swoony romance. David caught her around the waist and pulled her in, wrapping his other hand around hers, and leaning down so close, his nose was nearly touching hers.

"Is this okay?" he asked.

She nodded, self-consciously, as the exhilaration from dancing combined with the delight of being in his arms. There was comfort there, but at the same time, she felt off-balance, reeling. He pulled her in tighter and she let herself be pulled.

"This night has been perfect," she said. She could feel him staring at her lips as she talked. She could practically feel his heart beating against her. Her cheeks hurt from smiling so much. "Thank you for inviting me."

He took two big steps, whirling them both across the dance floor, pulling a delighted giggle out of her, and then drew her in again. "Technically," he said, "you invited yourself."

She threw her head back and laughed. "You're the worst, David McBride."

The song ended and the DJ switched back to party music. But David didn't let go of her waist. Instead, he let go of her hand and ran his thumb down the length of her jaw. "Ah, but I kind of think you're the best, Gracie Langhorst."

She swallowed past the lump in her throat. "Only kind of?"

He leaned in so he was whispering in her ear, his cheek brushing up against hers, sending goose bumps down the length of her body. "I mean, you did try to shoot me."

She threw her head back and laughed. He flung her out to arm's length and pulled her back in again, joining her laughter, as they went back to dancing.

They danced until Gracie's feet throbbed. Even then, she shucked off her heels under the table and they danced some more. Every song was better than the one before. For a moment, Gracie lost herself in time and place. This was the life she chose for herself, and she was happy. She wanted it to never end, even while she knew that it had to.

At the end of the night, they said their goodbyes to the wedding party, and sank into David's car and into a comfortable silence. Gracie rode with her head thrown back and her eyes closed.

Which was a mistake.

The farther away from the wedding they drove, the more reality set in. She began to worry about her grandma again, and about what kind of havoc Farley might have wreaked while she was gone. Her thoughts turned to Jem and Andrew and the dread of all the things coming for her over the next few weeks.

She would have to plan and attend a funeral.

She would have to take on Farley and his lawyer.

She would have to try to untangle the mess she left behind at her job.

She would have to do it all while grieving.

She didn't want to do any of it.

Nowhere in any of those situations was there any room for David. How would she possibly be able to attend to a new relationship while unraveling the terrible, tangled knot of her life? How would she be able to work out her own mess of emotions?

For the first time in maybe her entire life, Gracie felt an overwhelming sense of incapability. Even if she walked into the next few months of her life with confidence, it would only be window dressing. The real confidence would not be there.

She opened her eyes and stared, steely and silent, through the windshield, her feet throbbing in the enclosed cases of their shoes.

"Everything okay?" David asked.

Her jaw felt creaky as she talked. "I don't want to lead you on."

"Pardon?"

"Tonight," she said, still staring through the windshield, afraid to face him. Afraid that she would lose her nerve if she saw herself hurting him. "Tonight was amazing. But I don't want you to think that just because we danced tonight and…felt things…that it's going to lead to anything…more."

"Okay." She could feel him stiffen beside her, his arms taut as he gripped the steering wheel. "Gotcha. Just a dance. I didn't expect anything more. I wasn't going to propose or anything, don't worry."

"It's just that I have a lot going on, and the last thing I have time for is…" She didn't know how to finish the sentence.

"Oh, trust me, you're not the only one. I have way too much on my plate to begin something new," he said.

"It's not that I'm not appreciative." *Apprecia-*

tive? Like he did you a favor? Come on, Gracie, stop talking while you're ahead.

"Totally," he said. "Me, too. But, you know, one dance with feelings doesn't mean anything. We haven't had the best relationship."

Ouch. Okay. Deserved, I guess. "Exactly."

"I don't usually date girls who are so…" It was his turn to trail off.

A lump formed in Gracie's throat. She bristled. "So…what?"

He shook his head. "I didn't mean… I shouldn't have said that."

"But you did. So…what? What am I, that you don't usually date?" She felt herself slipping into lawyer mode, not wanting to hurt him, but her desire to win taking over. "It's not like I just throw myself at guys like you, you know."

He glanced at her, one eyebrow arched. "What's that supposed to mean?"

"You tell me first," she said. "Since I'm just *sooo* something."

"You're exaggerating things now," he said.

"And you're being avoidant."

"Fine. I don't usually date girls who are so cynical, okay? You're jaded and you're paranoid and you think everyone is out to get you all the time. And you react by throwing punches at any target that might get in your way. You're…aggressive. That's not usually my type."

She laughed but felt no mirth behind it. "If I had a nickel for every time someone called me *aggressive*," she said. "In my line of work, that's a compliment."

David paused just briefly, then aimed another glance at her. "But you're not working, are you?" he said softly.

Gracie glared at him, her jaw clenched. She felt tears prickle the backs of her eyes. This had not gone the way she'd intended it to go. At all.

His shoulders slumped as he pulled into Vera's driveway. He let out a sigh. "I'm sorry. I shouldn't have said all that."

She reached for the door handle. "It's okay. You said what you feel. There's nothing wrong with that."

"Come on. Let's talk it out," he said. "I didn't mean…"

She pulled the door open. "I don't need to talk anything out. I'm fine. It's all fine."

"Gracie. I'm sorry. Don't leave it like this."

"There's nothing to leave. We're just not each other's type," she said stoically.

She saw the realization fall over him, like a heavy, hot liquid. He drooped and fell, top to bottom. "I couldn't agree more," he said, his voice robotic, injured. "Good night."

She paused, gave him one last, sad look. "Goodbye, David."

CHAPTER THIRTEEN

SOMEHOW, DAVID HAD managed to avoid Gracie every time he came to the farm. Ever since the wedding, she'd been conspicuously absent. Or maybe he'd been coming at odd hours. Or maybe something had happened with Vera. No, surely Gracie would have told him if that happened.

She would have, wouldn't she?

Why didn't he exactly trust that she would?

No, no. She would. She would. He had to believe that.

He was glad to be avoiding her. Out of sight, out of mind and all that.

Unfortunately, what made for a great little phrase didn't always work in practice. He couldn't get her out of his mind, no matter how hard he tried. *Out of sight, on your mind* didn't exactly have the same ring to it.

But he needed her to be out of his mind. He needed to stop thinking about her every second of the day, before he became tempted to turn thinking about her into seeing her, into…well, into something else.

He'd even rehearsed in his head what he would say to her when he inevitably bumped into her at the farm.

Listen, I don't like the way we left things, and I want to clear the air. I think you're great. You're so smart and you're fearless and you can be sweet when you want to be, regardless of how hard you try not to be. You're also incredibly beautiful, and I don't even think you know it, which seems impossible, but you're so effortless with it, it has to be true. And you're funny. I can't forget funny. And the most genuine human I've ever met. But the timing between us is just not right. If I'm being honest, it will never be right. I have to focus on my work. It's the only thing I've ever really focused on, and I can't drop the ball now. Because you're all those things I previously listed, you are also a distraction. So I'm afraid I'm going to need you to stay away.

When he practiced it, though, it sounded so harsh. Also, it was such a bait and switch. It started like a marriage proposal, and then wham, hit her with the bad news.

Of course, he was only assuming it was bad news. For all he knew, she would laugh in his face and tell him he didn't need to worry about having her for a distraction, because she wanted nothing to do with him.

When David and Decker's mother had walked out on their father, they'd both taken it hard, but in their own way. Decker swore off love and trust and dedicated his life to their father and their land. David, on the other hand, was left adrift. He didn't remember his mom being a huge help on the farm, but once she left, their dad was forever swimming, swimming, swimming, just trying to find the shallow end so he could stand up. David felt swooped along for the ride, and he hated that feeling.

He'd sworn that he wouldn't ever let himself feel that tide sweep him away again. Head down, work hard, one step ahead all the time. No time for love and marriage. Who wanted that, anyway? It didn't last. Hard work lasted.

He'd gone to school, but that wasn't enough. He'd opened his own practice, but that wasn't enough. He'd gotten out from under the ranch so he could concentrate on his business, but even that wasn't enough.

He needed to stretch, to expand.

Whether that was enough, he wasn't sure. At some point, he began to fear that he would never reach the *enough* stage. And now he began to fear that maybe he would never reach the enough stage because he was afraid of love.

Sure, there were women everywhere.

But was his perfect match somewhere?

He wasn't sure he could allow himself to be vulnerable enough to find out.

And that was the real problem, wasn't it? You could call an apple an orange for the longest time—maybe even your whole life. You could maybe even make yourself believe that when you picked up an apple you were picking up an orange. But, in the end, when you bit into that apple…it would be an apple, each and every time. No oranges anywhere to be found. Even if oranges were much easier for you to bite into.

Lately, he'd taken to waiting until after work before going to the farm. The excuse? He was just flat-out too busy in the office to take a break. And, actually, that wasn't an excuse. It was the truth. He'd felt guilty leaving things to Leo, knowing that Leo's time at the clinic was about to end. And Renee was already maxed out on what she could do. And soon Leo would leave and he and Renee would be doing it all again. Renee stretched herself as far as she could, but facts were facts, and the fact was Renee was an administrative assistant, not a vet assistant. She was great with spreadsheets and a wiz with calendars and could talk down a difficult client like nobody's business. But there were things she couldn't do, and those things were crucial to being a vet assistant.

Even as busy as he was, he knew that the real reason he'd been waiting to head to the Langhorst farm was that he envisioned it to be dinnertime inside and he knew that Gracie had her hands full with her father in town and her grandmother being sick. She was less likely to come outside.

But today was an exception. He arrived and parked at the pasture gate, then let himself in, just like always.

Betty came running toward him; Sam continued to graze by the barn.

"Good evening, Betty." He reached out and scratched the alpaca behind her ears. He knew that it was only the shape of her face, but he could swear that Betty smiled at him when he gave her ear scratches. It was one of his favorite things about Betty, that smile. "Look. I have a treat for you. Sam's going to wish he hadn't chosen grass by the barn."

He opened his bag and pulled out a Ziploc filled with fresh broccoli florets. Betty's favorite. He opened the bag and tipped it so that the florets fell to the ground. Betty immediately bent to start munching.

"Sam! You better get a move-on before your wife eats it all!" he yelled, but Sam ignored him.

"Well, Betty, I guess this is what's meant by you snooze, you lose?"

"You wouldn't catch me snoozing," he heard behind him. "I love broccoli. I'd give Betty a run for her money."

Startled, David whirled around. Gracie stood behind him, looking fragile and cold, but also content in some way. She wore a long pink sweatshirt over a pair of leggings with fuzzy socks pulled up over the hems, and stark white tennis shoes. She looked comfortable and cozy, like she was ready to settle in for the evening by a roaring fire with a good, thick novel. But here she was, standing in the pasture, not out of sight. And, especially, not out of mind.

"I expected you to be eating dinner right now," David said.

Her serene look faltered just a bit. He saw her visibly fight to put it back in place. "We don't have those anymore. Grandma is basically just staying in bed."

He wrinkled his nose. "That bad?"

She nodded, and again he could see her struggle against emotions that wanted to emerge. "We brought in hospice. She's getting really weak, really fast."

"I'm so sorry, Gracie. Should I come visit?"

She shrugged. "She's probably asleep, but I'm

sure she'd love to see you. Since you're her favorite subject and all."

David opened his mouth to ask what that meant, but his phone rang, interrupting him. He recognized the number as belonging to the owner of one of his favorite patients—Kevin the black Lab.

He didn't even get a word out before Misti, Kevin's owner, was crying into his ear.

"Doctor McBride? Doctor McBride!"

"Hello? Misti? What's going on?" He had already begun walking toward the pasture gate. His gut told him whatever was going on, it wasn't good, and he was going to have to go back to the office, and in a hurry.

"It's Kevin. He ate chocolate."

"Okay," he said. "Take a couple breaths, Misti. It'll be okay. It's not ideal, but most dogs have a little gastric distress and then–"

"He ate a lot," she said. "A whole bag. He's having seizures. I'm at your office but nobody's here. It's locked up."

David had begun walking quicker, but now he'd quickened to a trot. He got about a dozen chocolate calls every year, and most of the time it was mild. But theobromine toxicosis could absolutely be lethal, and he'd lost a few dogs over the years to it. All of them had been in a state of seizures when they got to him. This wasn't good, and he needed to hurry.

The nearest emergency vet was an hour away in Riverside. David was the only line of defense for poor Kevin.

"I'll meet you there in fifteen minutes," he said, jumping into his car.

"Please hurry," Misti cried on the other end. "Oh, no. Kevin!"

He hung up and put the car into Reverse. He'd only barely let his foot off the brake when the passenger door opened and Gracie dropped in.

"Go," she said. She didn't ask questions. She didn't need an explanation. She seemed to only need to know that it was urgent, and the more hands on deck, the better.

David hadn't thought it through yet, but if he was going to be counting on Misti to assist in the absence of Leo, he was going to have a time of it. But he had a feeling that Gracie would be steady and reliable, no matter what he asked her to do.

So he went.

He tried to brief her as best he could during the drive into town, but he was concentrating on his driving, trying not to think about the possibilities of what could happen when they arrived. It could be too late. Kevin could be gone before they even got there.

They screeched into a spot right in front of

the office, double-parked, but David didn't care. He was barely aware of taking the key out of the ignition, and may have forgotten it if he hadn't needed his keys to get into the office.

As expected, Misti was a mess, sitting on the sidewalk clutching a weak and shaking Kevin. David rushed to her, Gracie at his heels, and unlocked the door. He turned and picked up Kevin and carried him through the door. Gracie had silently wrapped her arms around Misti—someone she didn't know from Adam—and was leading her inside behind him.

"I'm going to need you," he said over his shoulder.

"What do I do? Where do I go?" Misti asked.

"Have a seat out here," he heard Gracie murmur. "I promise I'll come out as soon as we have him settled and have started treatment."

"What will you do?" Misti asked.

"He's in good hands," Gracie said, her voice growing closer to David's back as she left Misti on a chair. "I promise, Doctor McBride will do his absolute best for him."

She came through the door right behind him, all business, as he set Kevin on the floor. Kevin rolled to his side, panting. David crouched and quickly checked his vitals.

"What do I do?" Gracie asked.

"First, we're going to give him a benzodiazepine to help control the seizures. Just sit next to him while I grab what I need, please."

Gracie sat, cross-legged, stroking Kevin's side, and David rushed out to grab his supplies. Normally, Leo would have already beaten him to it, knowing exactly what treatment Kevin would need. He felt a pang of desperation that Leo could not take this new job he'd been offered. David needed him—that was the long and the short of it.

He returned to the room, his arms loaded. Kevin was standing, a small puddle of brown vomit between his front paws. Gracie was unrolling paper towels to clean it up.

"Good," David said. "As long as the vomiting isn't uncontrollable, it's good for him to get it out of his system."

Gracie crouched and wiped up the vomit wordlessly while David drew the medicine into a syringe and screwed on an aerosolizer. Gracie had thrown away the towels and was waiting for him expectantly.

"Here," he said. "Hold this. Let's go ahead and get him on an exam table." Gracie took the syringe, and David picked up Kevin, whose tail wagged, slow and low, a sign that he trusted David, and thought he was in some kind of trouble. "It's okay, buddy. We're going to help you feel better now."

He set Kevin on the table, and Gracie immediately moved to the back side of the dog, her instincts good. She handed David the syringe, which he quickly pushed into Kevin's nostril and squirted. Kevin flinched, but otherwise didn't fight him.

"Good job, buddy," David said, giving the top of Kevin's head a quick stroke. "That'll control the seizures." He glanced up at Gracie, who continued to calmly stroke the dog's back. "You good?"

She gave a quick, confident nod. "Just let me know what I need to do."

"I'm going to put in an IV," he said. "I'm going to need you to hold him. Stand next to him just like you're doing, but more over here." She moved to Kevin's side, her calm warmth empowering. "Great. Now you're going to hold his head with one arm like this." She moved her arm. "No, more like this." He maneuvered himself behind her and moved her arm. Always a live wire, she let herself go soft and movable, and in that moment, David nearly lost his concentration. He was so close to her. His face was nearly buried in her hair, and he had a momentary longing to run his hands up the back of her neck and bury his fingers in her hair, too. He regained himself as he maneuvered her other arm. "Now loop this arm through and hold his leg right…there. Yes. That's right. Hold it good and tight. I've got to shave him, and the noise of the clippers sometimes freaks them out. I also don't want him to jerk while I'm putting the line in. Steady and tight will help calm him."

When David was in vet school, he excelled in emergency care situations. This was the stuff that made him want to become a vet. He loved his regulars and would happily clip toenails and remove ticks and treat bad breath all day long if he had to, but urgent situations like the one gripping Kevin were the tasks that made him feel like he was really making a difference.

He got out his clippers and watched Gracie's grip tighten around Kevin's leg just slightly as he zipped off a patch of fur. Kevin was a good boy—or maybe just a wildly sick boy—and didn't flinch in the slightest. Gracie remained silent and steadfast as David prepared the IV line and then slipped it into the bulging vein on Kevin's leg, then taped it up.

"Okay," he said. "Let's get him to a kennel where he can rest while we work on flushing out his system."

Wordlessly, she followed as he carried Kevin to the kennel room. He placed the weary dog inside a kennel and shut the door. Kevin laid down with a sigh. "Welcome to Hotel McBride, Kev.

Make yourself comfortable. You'll be our guest tonight. I'll go talk to Misti."

Misti was much calmer than he'd expected, which actually ratcheted up his nerves a bit. *I trust you completely, Doctor McBride.* On the one hand, it was great to have the trust of your clients, and that trust was part of why his practice had grown by leaps and bounds. On the other hand, it added even more heft to the weightiness of a life-and-death situation and made him feel very weary.

When he returned to the boarding room, he was almost surprised to find Gracie still there, sitting on the floor next to Kevin's kennel, slowly stroking the fur between his eyes with one finger through the bars. So much had happened so quickly, he half forgot that she'd been alongside him the whole way. At the same time, he had the thought, *Of course she's still here.* Gracie's presence by his side at this moment was just right. The way things were supposed to be.

He sank to the floor facing her, their knees touching. He would have liked to have not noticed the zap of warmth that coursed through him when they made contact, but he noticed. It thrilled and concerned him. He clearly needed to rein in whatever was going on with him right now. Whatever feelings he was fooling himself into thinking he was feeling. Whatever lies he was trying to tell himself about being with Gracie.

But it was so hard to get things under control when she was right there next to him.

"Thank you," he said. "That would have been so much harder by myself. Maybe impossible."

She shook her head, but didn't tear her eyes away from Kevin. "It wouldn't have been impossible. You're amazing. First, kittens in a barn, and now this. You didn't even have to stop to think. You can do anything."

"I don't know about that," he said. "Trust me, I stop to think all the time. I've just been doing this for a few years, and I've run across my share of chocolate poisoning. Dogs and their chocolate."

"It was scary." She turned her eyes toward him. They were large and wet, the intense glowing silver he had grown accustomed to now more of a dull gray. This was yet another side of Gracie Langhorst that David hadn't seen. How many sides of her were there? "Is Kevin going to be okay?"

He reached in and stroked the dog's fur, his fingers brushing up against hers. "Time will tell. But I sure think so. He seems calmer now. The vomiting has stopped. The seizures have stopped. He's resting." They continued to pet Kevin. David hooked her finger with his. "You okay? That was a lot. And you were a champ. Strong as a rock."

She jutted her chin in the air the way he'd seen her do a million times, her jaw square and tight. But then her chin began to wobble and tears spilled over her bottom lids and skipped down her cheeks.

"Hey," he whispered. "Hey. It's going to be okay. You were amazing. Whatever happens from here, you helped save him in the moment."

"It's not just about him," she whispered through the tears. She didn't need to continue for him to know what was happening.

He let go of her finger and shifted so that he was next to her, closer to her. He pulled her into his chest. He didn't know what to say, so he said nothing. He just held her, resting his chin lightly on the top of her head, his eyes closed, trying to remember what it was about loving her that he couldn't do.

GRACIE HESITATED JUST the tiniest bit before letting herself be pulled into David's chest. The way she'd been feeling lately, she knew that it would be dangerous to allow herself to become physically close to him.

He felt warm and safe and strong and all the things she wanted him to be. All the things she normally needed to be for herself.

Gracie didn't mind being her own safe harbor in the least. In fact, she thrived on it. She wanted it. She'd worked her whole life to become it.

But it was nice to rest in the safety of someone else's arms in this moment. And she knew that not just anyone would make her feel this way. Others had tried and failed. David was different.

He'd been so confident while rescuing that dog. So calm and sure and knowledgeable. A hero.

She couldn't help wishing he would be able to swoop in and save her grandma with the same self-assuredness. *She needs a hero, too,* she thought, while stroking Kevin's fur. *Where's her hero? Where's mine? And when did I start allowing myself to believe that I need one?*

And then when David had sat down next to her, his knees touching hers, flooding her with warmth and security, and when his fingers brushed against hers, buried in the fur of Kevin's nose, she'd been overcome with the unfairness of it all.

Her grandma was dying. That was unfair.

Farley was lurking around, probably talking her grandma into leaving him the things that were most precious to Gracie. Not the house and the money and the farm, but the memories and the tradition and the only roots that Gracie had ever been given in life. That was also unfair.

And she'd gone and fallen in love, despite herself and her best efforts to stay unattached and untrusting. And she was pretty sure David loved her, too. But she was too proud to find out for certain. She pushed him away and pushed him away, just like she always did with everyone in her life. And he'd pushed back. And that had hurt. But it still felt safe. And she hated that about herself.

After Vera was gone, she would leave, and go back to fighting Andrew for assignments that she—if she was being honest with herself—didn't really care about, so that she could continue to live a bitter and lonely life.

And that was the most unfair of all.

The only person who'd ever loved her unconditionally and fully was about to die. And Gracie had dropped the ball on the job of filling her heart. She could feel it now, Vera's desire and need for Gracie to not just be successful in business and in life. She needed for her heart to be filled. She needed to know that Gracie wouldn't be alone and lonely.

And now, even if Gracie cultivated this feeling she had with David into something more, it was too late. Vera would still die never knowing that Gracie had fallen in love. Because Gracie had waited too long. She'd been standing rigidly upright for so long, she'd forgotten to allow herself to fall.

When David pulled her against him, she buried her face in his chest and let the tears flow in earnest. It was the first time she'd truly let go, maybe ever. In some ways, she was grieving not only the loss of her grandma, but also the loss of her mother, and the loss of Farley, which, at some point in her life, must have hurt, even if she couldn't remember it. Somewhere deep inside, her soul remembered.

Finally, when she felt all cried out, she pulled her head away from his chest. The sun had lowered, and the kennel was filled with gray shadows. Kevin was fast asleep, much calmer and more comfortable than he had been when he arrived.

"I'm sorry," she whispered, her face entirely too close to David's chest. She studied the lines of his collarbone, the swell of his Adam's apple. She couldn't make herself lift her eyes to his.

"Don't be." He didn't make any move to pull away. She felt little puffs of breath on the top of her head when he talked. "It's okay to let your guard down sometimes."

She pulled away from him completely, severing the connection between them. She pushed her hair out of her face, where strands wanted to stick. She was trying to collect herself, to tamp down the need inside of her, which was pulsing so strongly through her veins, she was afraid he could see it.

"I'm good. I'm good," she said. "I'm sorry. That won't happen again."

"Stop," he said, using one finger to help her smooth a strand of hair away from her forehead. Even that tiny gesture melted her. She was in a bad way and needed to get herself collected, before she did something completely rash like kiss him. "You don't need to always be a rock."

"I need to be better than this, though," she said. "I can't go around crying on every chest that comes into view just because it's there."

He looked a little stung, and she wanted to reassure him, but she couldn't make herself do it. She'd already shown too much vulnerability.

The walls between them were too high and too carefully constructed.

"I didn't mean..." she started.

"It's okay," he said, but she could tell by the chill on the edges of his words that it wasn't okay. "You don't have to... I probably shouldn't have pulled you in like that. I apologize."

It took everything she had to break contact between them, but she pulled away from him, their knees and hands and beating hearts distancing. She felt cold and alone immediately. She stood.

"It's okay. I should go back and make sure my grandma doesn't need anything," she said.

"Gracie, don't do this." David stood. "We should talk."

"It's really okay," she said. "I had a minute. I'm sure it was just me getting carried away."

"No," he said. "It wasn't."

"David." She looked into his eyes earnestly. "It isn't about you. I'm fine. Really. Don't force yourself somewhere that you don't belong. I've got this."

She regretted every word, even as it came out of her mouth.

"Understood," he said, taking two steps backward, looking down at the ground, as if he were ashamed. *If you were even a halfway decent person, Gracie Langhorst, you would reach out to him,* she thought. But she couldn't make herself move in his direction. *Guess I'm not a halfway decent person.* The thought struck her to the core.

Some truths were cruel to digest, even when you served them to yourself.

"I should get home," she said.

"Yeah," he said. "Please tell Vera I'm thinking of her. Should I come see her?"

"I don't know," Gracie said. "She's…well, Farley…"

They were in a partial-sentence mode, each partial sentence more awkward than the one before.

"Of course. I understand. She should be with family right now."

"She is."

"Good, good."

"Let me know how Kevin comes out?"

"Yes, of course I will."

Before she knew it, she was out. Free. Walking down the sidewalk, away from the discomfort of whatever had transpired between them.

But she didn't get far before he was chasing her down.

"Hey," he said, car keys jingling as he ran. "You rode here with me."

"Oh. Yeah. Um…"

"It's okay. I'll take you home. I'll only be away from Kevin for a few minutes. I'll come right back to him."

"Okay," she said, wishing more than anything else that she could think of a single excuse to get her out of riding home with him. She couldn't. "Sure. Of course."

But the entire ride home was silent.

Awkwardly silent, as each of them tried to figure out exactly what was going on between them.

And how to make it stop.

CHAPTER FOURTEEN

GRACIE WAS THE only one awake when the doorbell rang the next morning. Farley had yet to make his presence known and her grandma was sleeping peacefully, contentment etched across her face. The hospice nurse had started her on a ritual of drugs for the pain that she would encounter as the cancer grew and overtook her. Gracie tried not to think about it, and only focus on the slight grin on her sleeping grandmother's face, wondering if she'd finally started packing for that long trip in her dreams.

Ben and Annie were standing on her porch. Annie held up something wrapped in plastic wrap.

"For your struggles," she said, very formally.

"I'm sorry?"

"It is tradition to bring food to a family when a loved one is dead or dying," Ben explained. "And Vera Langhorst is dying, so we are honoring tradition."

"It's a zucchini loaf," Annie said, her eyes

lighting up excitedly. "We grew the zucchinis in the garden behind Ben's house. We have a lot of zucchinis, so we can share and still have some left for ourselves."

"Annie stayed up very late baking many loaves of zucchini bread, because she had to wait until the session was over to get started. And we are both very tired, because the doctor-recommended hours of sleep are eight to ten, and we only got five hours and thirty-seven minutes. Which is far short of what is recommended. Next time, she will have to bake the bread at her own house, so I can go to bed."

Annie lifted the bread higher. "Go on. Take it."

"Oh. Thank you so much." Gracie was beginning to see why Annie and Ben were the town sweethearts. They were adorable separately and together, their relationship innocent and sweet. *If only it were always that easy,* she thought, and then immediately felt bad for assuming their lives were easy. Maybe it was harder for them, being on the spectrum. Who was she to assume that she knew? "Do you want to come in? I just put on coffee. It should be ready by now."

Annie was through the door before Gracie even finished her sentence. Ben seemed to have conflicting thoughts, but went with it, removing his hat and giving her a curt nod as he, too, crossed the threshold into the house.

"Would you like some bread?" Gracie asked as they followed her into the kitchen.

"No, thank you, ma'am," Ben said. "We made it for you. It would be rude for us to eat our own gift."

"The gift is your company," Gracie said, pulling two coffee cups down from the cabinets. "I'm happy to share."

"Plus, we ate a whole bunch of it before coming over," Annie said, sinking down into a seat at the kitchen table. "We're full."

Ben sat on the other side of Annie, putting himself in the corner. Gracie could tell this wasn't his idea of a good time at all; his efforts warmed her heart and made her like him all the more. She slid two cups of coffee in front of them. He peered into his cup, a look of distaste on his face, so she slid the sugar jar closer to him and retrieved the carton of milk from the fridge before sitting down, a cup of coffee between her hands.

Gracie wasn't great at awkward silence. Usually, when she was sitting in silence, it was to break down an opposing counsel and their client into seeing things her way and giving in. She had grown so accustomed to her entire life revolving around fighting that she didn't even know it until she'd come back to Buck County. Here, she was growing used to contemplative silences, even in the presence of another person. In the city, it was talk, talk, talk, all the time. Everyone yapping without ever really communicating and thinking that was somehow superior.

She and her grandma had spent so much time in silence since she came home that it now felt second nature to her in some ways.

But Ben did not look at all comfortable. He kept glancing at Annie, who grinned over her mug, visibly searching for things to say.

"This reminds me of Latte the cat," she finally blurted. "I think you should know that your cat is happy."

"Huh?"

"Your cat that is now Ellory's cat. Latte. He's happy. Isn't he, Ben?"

"I have not been to The Dreamy Bean. I don't like coff..." He trailed off, staring down into his cup. "I have not visited."

"Latte the cat has the cutest little bed. It looks like a coffee cup. Ellory made it. He curls up in it and he's a little latte, just like his name says. Ellory is very clever, don't you think?"

Gracie nodded, feeling a little guilty that she had not yet made any real attempt to befriend Ellory DeCloud. Everyone seemed to love her. But, as usual, Gracie had been too guarded and too mired in her own misery to reach out. If ever she needed a sign that how she was living her life wasn't working, her time back in Buck County might very well be it. At the very least, she should check on the kitten for herself, make sure he was doing okay. *Grandma Vera would like that report*, she thought.

As if reading Gracie's mind, Annie leaned forward, her neck nearly resting on her steaming coffee cup. "I'll go with you if you ever want to visit Latte."

"Thank you," Gracie said. "I'll probably take you up on that offer. I'd like to see his little coffee cup bed."

Annie grinned, her nose crinkling. Her joy was adorable. "It's so cute!"

Ben took a sip of his drink, made a face, and inched the cup away from him. Gracie held back a smile. There was something endearing about Ben and the way he tried so hard.

"You don't have to drink that if you don't like it, Ben," she said. "Coffee isn't for everyone."

"Technically, ma'am, you are correct. Many people are unable to drink coffee due to its high caffeine content, and for others it may cause too much acid in the stomach. That would make it quite literally not for everyone. But, also, I think you meant to say that coffee does not appeal to all tastes. And that is also correct. It would be impossible to find any food or beverage that appealed to every single person, as we all have different taste buds and experience flavors differently. You are also correct in identifying me as someone who does not enjoy the flavor, so thank you, ma'am. I'll stop drinking it now."

"Ben works really hard not to hurt anyone's feelings," Annie stage-whispered. She picked up her cup and took a big slurp, then let out a loud breath, as if she were refreshed. "I love coffee though. And not just the little kitten." She pushed herself away from the table as she set the mug back on the table. "Well, we should probably get going. We just wanted to bring you the zucchini bread. We don't really have anything else to talk about. Besides the kitten, that is."

Ben followed Annie's suit and stood, visibly relieved to be distancing himself from the coffee.

"Well, thank you for the bread," Gracie said, following them to the front door. "I'll be sure to have a piece tonight before bed. With lots of butter." Her mouth watered just thinking about it.

"Oh, and Miss Langhorst?" Annie stopped short. Ben went on without her and was standing in the driveway next to his truck.

"Yes?"

"You're a really good dancer. You and David were the talk of the wedding with all of your dance moves. Miss Marlee said that. *The talk of the wedding.* Maybe sometime you could teach me some dance moves? Um…*after your grandma dies*?" She whispered the last bit.

Gracie smiled. "Of course. I would love to do that."

"And maybe David can teach Ben? I want to go dancing in some of the big places in Riverside, and I want us to be the talk of those places."

"I don't know. But I'll ask him. I'm sure he'll say yes."

Annie flung her arms around Gracie's neck, surprising her. She blinked a few times, and then wrapped her arms around Annie, too. If only she could be more like Annie—trusting and exuberant and full of love and honesty. "Thank you, thank you!" Annie said, and pulled away.

Gracie kept her smile for a long time after Ben and Annie left. They'd been such welcome positivity, even Farley's reappearance couldn't ruin Gracie's smile.

"What are you walking around looking so dippy like that for?" he asked, passing her in the hallway.

"What? What kind of sentence was that?" she asked.

"It was the kind of sentence where you look stupid, that's what kind."

She shook her head, careful to keep her smile. Farley had stolen so much from her over the years, this was one thing she could make sure he wouldn't take away. "You make no sense." She began to walk on.

"You know what doesn't make sense?" he said to her back. "You being here. That's what doesn't make sense. I'm here. Mama doesn't need you anymore."

She stopped. "I'm here because I care about her. And I want to see her through her final days. Can you say the same?" She waited, her smile starting to feel a little pasted on. "I didn't think so."

"When she's gone, you go, too," he said, his eyes narrowing, looking dangerous. She felt the corners of her mouth tug and droop. "I'm not asking, I'm telling. I'll get you out myself if I have to."

"What?"

"When she dies, you need to leave. Skedaddle back to Kansas City. I'll take care of business here."

"I guess you'll have to make me leave, then, because I'm not going anywhere until I'm good and ready to go," Gracie said. But now that he'd said it aloud, she was cold with worry and fear. What would he do to her grandma's farm? What would he do with the animals? With Fannie? "You don't have any business to take care of here."

Now it was his turn to grin, but it was a wicked

grin. "That's what you think. She says otherwise."

Not if she's in her right mind, she wouldn't be, Gracie thought, and she knew that this would be the approach she would use in court, if it came down to it.

And why would it come down to court? the little voice inside her head argued. *Are you being just like him? Greedy? Do you want the farm so you can sell it instead of him?*

No. No way. She wanted to be the one to settle Vera's estate because she knew that she would do right by her grandma. She knew she would keep her grandfather's old work boots, simply because Vera had kept them by her bedside all these years. She knew that she would care for the animals as long as she possibly could, and then would find the perfect home for them. Not just good, but perfect. She knew that she would take Fannie and Norma with her back to Kansas City, if it came down to that.

If. Since when did returning to Kansas City become an if*?*

Now her head hurt. She felt tossed and bumped and jostled. How had she so quickly gone from the contagion of Annie's easy smile to wondering if she would return to Kansas City? How had she gone from despising the very thought of

David McBride to thinking maybe she couldn't move far away from him?

"I need air," she said, turning on her heel and hurrying outside, barely hearing Farley's laugh follow her.

"That's right," he hollered. "Just keep going until you see that old sign that says *Leaving Haw Springs.* And then go some more."

SO MUCH HAD happened over the past few days, David didn't know where he stood. Sometimes literally. He would blink and find himself standing at the reception desk, staring blankly down at an open folder, Renee having just asked him a question he didn't hear. Or he would find himself holding a coffee mug in his kitchen and have no earthly idea how he got there or where the mug came from. He lived in some sort of alternate reality now.

A reality where almost nothing existed except for Gracie's smile, Gracie's laugh, Gracie's fire, the feel of Gracie against his chest.

Lately, he'd been questioning his resolve.

Maybe he could make this work. Maybe he didn't need to have his business all settled and sorted. Maybe Gracie could be a fine partner for helping him grow.

Maybe he was looking at everything wrong, if he was thinking he would count on her to help him grow. What would he help her with? She deserved a man who helped himself.

His dad relied on his mom too much and look what happened. She helped herself right out of existence.

Distraction, distraction, distraction.

He shook his head, trying to clear it, as he gathered his things to go to the Langhorst farm.

"Need help?"

Leo had adopted even more confidence since his job offer. He seemed like a partner already. Someone loyal, who would always have David's back. David knew, without a shadow of a doubt, that if he asked Leo to go to the Langhorst farm in his place, he would go without a second thought. And he would do a darn fine job of it.

"Nah." He eyed Leo. "When did you say your last day here was going to be?"

"Looking to get rid of me?"

David let out a laugh. "Quite the opposite. Pinpointing the date I'm dreading. I'm assuming you've given your decision to The Pup Deck by now?"

"I have. I'm staying here until after I pass this test," Leo said. "And maybe give myself a couple weeks of downtime to pack. Give my mom a couple weeks to beg me to stay."

"So, December."

"I'll probably wait until January, honestly. He said the offer stands and he can be flexible."

"Do me a favor," David said. "Can you write down what kind of salary and benefits would keep you here?"

Leo raised his eyebrows. "You got something going on that I don't know about, Doc?"

"No, but I would like to. Or at least I would like to know what it will take to lure you back to Haw Springs when I do have something going on."

"I would be more than happy to come back," Leo said. "And my mother would be twice as happy."

"Not thrilled with the move?"

"Not in the least." Leo followed him to the door. "You sure I can't help?"

"Nope. I have something personal I need to do while I'm at it," David said.

Leo winced. "Sounds heavy."

"I hope not, but maybe," David said.

He thought about that wince all the way to the Langhorst farm. He thought about the way Gracie leaned into him, crying. He thought about the woman he met when she first showed up on this farm, and the woman she'd become. Soft, trusting. Vulnerable.

And he thought about what a gift vulnerability was to give to someone else, and that he wasn't sure if he was worthy of that gift. He was pretty sure that Gracie didn't know quite what to do with this new development between them, either. She didn't seem the kind to dole out vulnerability like candy at a parade. If nothing else, she was incredibly defensive, incredibly tucked away, deep inside, behind a mask of toughness.

Gracie was sitting on a hay bale when he entered the barn. He froze when he saw her.

"Hey," she said.

"Hey." Weird how two words spoke volumes between them. "I wasn't expecting to see you here. How's Vera?"

She shook her head sadly. "Not good. I wouldn't give it much longer at all."

He walked into the barn to check on Norma's food and water. "Why are you out here, then? I promise I won't take this opportunity to steal from you. That would be about as low down as someone could get, stealing from a dying lady."

She made a *psssh* noise.

"What does that mean?" He saw the look on her face, and understanding dawned on him. "Oh. Farley."

"Yeah. Farley." She hopped off the hay bale and began following him. "But to answer your question directly, I'm out here because Farley is in there, and he's doing everything in his power to start a fight with me and I'm not having it.

Not at my grandma's deathbed. I figured I would come out here, get a breath of fresh air, and then go back in and deal with him clear-headed."

"That bad, huh?"

"Always that bad. How's Kevin?"

"Good as gold. Went home the next day, if you can believe it. I want to thank you again for your help that day."

She waved him away. "You don't need to."

"You were amazing. Ever think about working at a veterinary clinic?"

"You trying to hire me?"

He let out a laugh. "No. I'm still trying to figure out how I can hire Leo."

"Ah. So, you're trying to get rid of me. Get me to go work somewhere else, preferably not in Haw Springs or Buck County. Don't worry, I have a job back home."

He stopped and faced her. "Believe it or not, I'm just trying to compliment you."

"Oh. Well, thank you."

He captured Norma and gathered her into his arms. She yowled, but didn't fight. He scratched her ears as he gave her a quick once-over, checking her belly to make sure everything had healed fine, giving the insides of her ears a quick look, feeling along her legs, her spine, her tail. He wasn't fooling himself in the least. He knew that Norma didn't need a checkup. He was stalling, to spend more time near Gracie. When he let Norma go, she darted in between two hay bales, and he turned to find himself close enough to Gracie to feel his heart begin to race.

Keep it together, McBride. Don't fall for her. Don't do it. Remember your speech.

"Annie came over," she said. "With Ben. Apparently, we were the talk of the wedding with all the dancing. She and Ben want us to teach them to dance."

He took a breath. This was as good as any segue he was going to get. "Listen, Gracie, about the wedding."

A slight frown dipped between Gracie's eyes, and she leaned away from him, as if studying him for the first time. "We don't need to talk about it."

"I kind of need to. Because I feel like it just keeps coming up again and again. And, well…" He took a breath, trying to remember his speech. "Listen, I want to clear the air. I think you're great."

"You can't be seriously saying this right now."

"I am. Just give me a second. You're smart and beautiful and…"

"Oh, boy. I know where this goes. *It's not you, Gracie, it's me, I swear.* Well, you can save the speech. Dancing is fun, and Annie wants to have some fun. That's all."

"Right. But you and I are not fun. You know, historically." *Except when we stole Decker's horses. That was fun. And Haw Games Day. That was definitely fun. And the wedding was the most fun I've had in ages.* She stood with her head tossed to one side, her eyes narrowed in thought, and he could practically hear her thoughts so loud, he wasn't sure if those were his own, or hers. "I mean. I know we've had some fun. But…"

"But…" she said. Her fists found their way to her hips. He wanted to find her infuriating the way he had when she first arrived, but he only found her feistiness endearing. He forced himself to look away.

"But…" He let out a frustrated sigh. "Listen, Gracie. Things are getting too close between us."

"So this is about me crying. I knew it. I'm sorry for having emotions."

"No, it's not about that at all." Except it was, a little. Holding her had felt too good, and he couldn't get it out of his mind. "I was thinking I needed to say this before the whole Kevin thing happened."

"It's because you're scared that the wedding might have been contagious, and now I have expectations of you? I thought I made it clear that's not the case."

"It's not that, either. It's not about you at all."

She tipped her head back and let out a laugh that bounced off the metal ceiling and back at them. "You did not just do that. You did not just say exactly what I predicted you'd say a couple of sentences ago."

This was not going the way David wanted at all. He'd hoped to let her down easy. Make her understand.

But how was he going to do that when he didn't totally understand himself?

"That's not what I was saying."

"That's what it sounded like."

"Gracie, it's just not the right time for me to get involved with anyone."

She raised one eyebrow. "*Get involved.* We danced at a wedding, David. You *got involved* with half the town, if that's the case. Everyone was there and everyone was dancing."

"But you're not everyone."

She let out a sniff, but didn't say anything.

"Gracie, come on. You know you're misconstruing this. You're going to make me spell it out? Fine. I like you," he said gently. "And I think I could like you a lot. But I have a lot going on with the practice, and it just won't work." Her expression was a mix of haughtiness and confusion, with a dash of amused skepticism thrown in. "I think I need to explain. For as long as I can remember, I've had one goal in mind. To be a veterinarian."

"And you are one. Congratulations, goal accomplished."

"No, I mean, it's the *only* goal I had. I didn't know how to create other goals. I didn't want to. And I still don't know if I want to."

"Well, that's sad and lonely, but it's your life. And I don't know why you're giving me your life history when we already agreed that there is nothing between us." This was the Gracie he remembered. But also the Gracie he knew well enough to know that she was reacting out of hurt. And he was the one doing the hurting.

He reached out for her, but she moved away from him, and he ended up lightly touching her elbows, feeling silly, while also wanting to feel that connection between them. This wasn't going how he wanted it to go. But it was also going exactly like he meant for it to go. "You confuse me. You're the first woman who ever has. The first person who ever distracted me from my vision of my future. I want to be with you. I think about you all the time. Day and night. It's messing with me. I have to get back to who I am. To focus on my work."

He swallowed, unsure of where to go from there. He felt like he'd said everything and nothing. And from the look on her face, he'd said everything wrong.

"Are you finished?" she finally asked. Without waiting for him to answer, she crossed her arms and leaned forward over them. He waited to be devoured by her rage. "You overthink things. You're taking this way too seriously." She threw up her hands in exasperation. "You don't have to go through all this song and dance. I'm not some smitten teenager. Excuses, and pretending that you're just oh-so-conflicted…it's just insulting."

"It's not a song and dance. I really am conflicted when it comes to you."

"Well, let me help you out then. I'm not conflicted when it comes to you. I thought it would be fun to play dress-up and go dance at a wedding. That's all. I never thought I would be walking down the aisle with you, so you can put your little head down and go back to work. Save the chocolate-eating dogs. I don't need a savior. I'll save myself, thank you."

"I never said anything about saving you."

But she had already gone and was hurrying across the pasture. He watched her go, wondering how he had gotten it all so wrong when he'd really been trying to do the right thing. Her head was held high, her hair flying out behind her, and she walked at a good clip, loose arms, long strides, and overflowing with confidence.

Maybe he had read things between them completely wrong. Maybe he was the only one with feelings, and she was laughing herself silly at the thought that he'd tried to break off something that never was.

I SHOULD HAVE *KNOWN. I should have known. I should have known.*

That sentence was all Gracie could think as she hightailed it across the pasture. Her pride was stung, and she felt embarrassed, sure that he could see past her bluster and right through her.

She should have known. And she never should have let her guard down.

David McBride was a good guy. He was nice. He was very generous. She may even have been inclined to call him heroic. But, make no mistake, he was still a man, and, in Gracie's steadfast belief, men would let you down every single time. Period. Men would never miss a chance to serve themselves first. Men didn't understand heartbreak.

But actually, as she thought about it, people in general were that way. Men had no corner on letting her down. Starting with her mother, who chose Farley, had let Gracie down and broken Gracie's heart when she died.

It just seemed like anyone not named Vera Langhorst was, in the end, not to be trusted.

She paused at the pasture gate, grief punching her in the gut, leaving her doubled over in pain. She couldn't lose her grandma. Not now. How was this anywhere close to fair?

She chanced a glance back over her shoulder. David stood in the barn doorway, watching her. With great effort, she pulled herself up tall and continued through the gate, determined that he wouldn't see her falter, lest he think it was about him.

You're not that important, she wanted to yell. *You don't want to be with me? Fine. That does nothing to me.*

But that was a lie, and she knew it.

It hurt.

It felt like loss.

Because as much as she had tried to keep David McBride out of her heart, he had somehow wormed his way in. When she wasn't busy fending off the world, she wanted romance, and she'd been horribly wrong, apparently, because she thought that with David McBride she could possibly have it.

He didn't need to know that she was so mad and so sad, she was shaking as she walked into the house. It was all about appearance. Fake it 'til you make it, and all that.

The house was dark and silent.

Farley had apparently gone out for the night.

Gracie crept down the hall to her grandma's room and pushed the door open a crack. A table lamp had been left on, and the soft glow illuminated Vera's face. She looked peaceful and happy in her sleep, and Gracie couldn't help but be washed with alternating waves of gratitude and bitterness.

She tiptoed into the room to turn off the lamp. Her grandma stirred and gave a weak smile.

Sorry, Gracie mouthed, continuing to try to be stealthy, but Vera wouldn't have it. She tried to work her way to sitting but failed. Sinking back into her pillow, she held out one skeletal hand.

"Come here, honey."

Grateful, chin trembling, Gracie sat in the chair Farley had been occupying and grasped her grandma's hand.

"Something's wrong," Vera said. "I can tell. You always tried to hide it from me when you were upset, but I always knew. I can feel it." She tapped her bony chest. "In here."

Gracie shook her head, unable to look her grandma in the eye, but even avoiding eye contact, it was too much for her. She hiccupped, then let out a sob. Tears streamed down her cheeks. She felt so silly, crying again. It was as if her entire personality were crumbling apart. She wasn't sure who she even was anymore.

"I'm sorry," she said, wiping her face with

her free hand. "I'm okay. Really." She gave a defiant sniff.

"Anyone can see that's not true," her grandma said. "Even me, and I'm dying."

Gracie let out another sob.

"Ah. So that's it. You're mourning me before I'm even gone, huh?"

"I'll mourn you for the rest of my life. I don't want you to go."

Vera let out a weak cough that turned into a hard wince. "You make it sound like I'm taking a trip overseas."

"You made a face. Are you in pain? Do you need more meds?"

Vera waved her free hand weakly. "I'm barely awake for any amount of time as it is. A little pain won't do me in. Not yet. And, besides, we're not talking about me. We're talking about you, and you're trying to change the subject."

"I'm not."

Her grandma shushed her. "Sweetheart. One of the best things I ever did in my whole life was love you. Used to be when people would say it was good of me to take you in, being a young widow myself, I'd tell them it was you who took me in. Gracie, look at me. Listen. It won't be much longer for me. But I've had a good amount of time to think about my life. I have regrets, sure. Everyone does. But the one thing I have never regretted is loving someone. I loved my mother and father. I loved both of my sisters. I loved all my nieces and nephews. I loved your grandfather more than words can even convey. And I loved you even more than that."

"I love you, too, Grandma. I'm sorry I moved away." Tears flowed faster as Gracie's words broke on the word *away*. "If I could go back, I would never have gone. I would have stayed here with you."

Vera raised her eyebrows. "Is that what this is about? You feel guilty for living a life that makes me so proud?" She shook Gracie's hand a little to get her attention. "You listen to me here. I've never been anything but proud of you. You did exactly what I wanted you to do. You went out and made something of yourself, despite the hand you were dealt in life. It's a wonderful thing that you did."

"It doesn't feel wonderful right now," Gracie said.

"You're grieving right now. It'll come back. But there's something else I want you to do."

"I know what you're going to say, and I'm telling you, he doesn't like me like that," Gracie said.

"Who? David?" Vera chuckled. "Oh, yes, he does. Trust me. I've known that young man for a minute or two. I've never seen him look at anyone the way he looks at you. You scare him."

"He says I confuse him."

"Scared and confused." Vera smiled. "That's a good thing."

"Doesn't feel like a good thing right now."

"Love never feels like a good thing until it does." Vera yawned. "Besides, I wasn't going to say a word about David. All I was going to say is that I want you to open yourself to the possibility that not everyone in this world is bad. Love and let yourself be loved, that's all. You deserve it. You just don't believe that you deserve it."

Gracie nodded. She had no argument against this. "Grandma, what about Farley?"

"What about him? I suppose it's not the worst thing in the world to have my only son at my side while I die."

"Yeah, but he's—"

"Remember, your relationship with Farley is much different than mine, honey. You only know the man who abandoned you and stole from you and went to jail. And those were awful things, I know, and there is no taking away that awfulness. But I know him as the baby I cradled. The little boy whose boo-boos I kissed and triumphs I celebrated. Once upon a time, he was a good boy. My boy." Her voice had gotten soft, and her eyes began to droop. She let out another yawn and seemed to sink deeper into her pillow. Her hand went limp in Gracie's. "There goes that medicine, kicking in again."

Gracie didn't know what to say. Her grandma was right about Farley. Gracie didn't know any good things about him, but her grandma had different memories. How could Gracie begrudge her his visits while she was dying? Worse, how could Gracie break it to her that he was only here to solidify his inheritance? No, she couldn't do that to her grandma. She would just have to face Farley after the fact.

Gracie let go of her grandma's hand and stood. "Can I get you anything?"

"No," Vera said, her eyes drooping almost closed. "I just need to sleep. I'm glad we had this talk."

"Me, too," Gracie said. "Get some rest now. We'll talk again later."

But her grandma's eyes had completely closed and she was gone again.

CHAPTER FIFTEEN

DAVID AND DECKER stood side by side, arms identically crossed, as they looked over the landscape of the empty building, David in his blue scrubs and sneakers and Decker in his cowboy hat and blue jeans and dusty black boots. What was once a thriving supermarket was now a gutted building for lease, as more and more Haw Springs residents took their business to the new mega superstore off the highway just ten or so miles out of town. This old store, owned and run by a couple of Oklahoma transplants, couldn't keep up, and almost overnight, the owners had abandoned it and continued on north to Kansas City, where they perceived their fortune to lie.

"I don't know. It seems big," David said.

"Isn't that the point?" Decker challenged. "Aren't you specifically looking to grow? The last place was too small."

"Yes, but this is just a big, empty box." David gestured. "What about a big, empty box says hometown veterinarian to you?"

"You're thinking too small," Decker said. "Not hometown veterinarian. You've got that where you currently are. Think Veterinarian Hospital. This place screams that, don't you think? Haw Springs doesn't have an emergency vet."

"Yes, they do. Me."

Decker made a fist and knocked on his brother's head. "Hello! That's the point. But it could be you in this much-bigger space."

"That's a lot of build-out."

"We can build it out ourselves. Most of it, anyway. It'll take time. I'll get Ben on board, if you want. He can build almost anything."

It was true. If they all put their backs into it, they could turn the space into what he needed. He tried to imagine what he would do with all this space. Tried to picture two waiting rooms—one for cats and one for dogs—some exam rooms, a surgical area, lots of boarding space. He could keep Leo and hire a second receptionist so Renee could take some time off without feeling guilty. He could expand his cat room. Hire in a groomer and make the entire back of the store a spa. Doggy day care. Obedience school. The possibilities jumbled around in his head, and still, he couldn't make himself quite get there.

"I don't know," he said again. "It's pretty echoey. Can you imagine ten dogs barking in here? It would get earsplitting pretty fast."

Decker let his arms drop, as they walked toward the Realtor, who was waiting for them just inside the sliding doors.

"The last one was too small. The place before that was too narrow. Before that, too far out of town. Now it's too big. You're like the Goldilocks of veterinary medicine."

David didn't respond, mostly because he knew that Decker was right. He couldn't find the perfect place. Almost as if that place didn't exist.

"Maybe you're stalling," Decker said to David's back.

David stopped, turned. "What do you mean?"

Decker shrugged. "Maybe part of you doesn't want to expand and be settled, because you know that once you do, you'll have no excuses for your personal life anymore."

"What is that supposed to mean, *no excuses for my personal life*? What kind of excuses? My personal life is just fine, thank you."

Decker held up his hands. "Don't get mad. I'm just saying that as long as you focus on building your practice, getting bigger, getting established, whatever you want to call it on any given day, you aren't focusing on moving forward in your personal life. And maybe that works for you on some level. Or maybe it scares you and you're avoiding it. Been there, done that."

"I have no idea what you're talking about."

But he knew exactly what Decker was saying. He'd thought about it himself. Now that he'd made the decision to start looking for a place to expand, and had a plan for really buckling down and making things happen, he was suddenly dragging his feet. He could feel it.

"I think you do. You're afraid to make a move, probably because you know that this is the wrong thing you should be moving on."

"I should never have brought you along today," David said, continuing his journey toward the Realtor. She looked up from her phone and smiled expectantly. "It's perfect. Let's get some paperwork moving."

Her eyes flew wide. Every eye in town would fly wide when it became known that the old Cotton's Supermarket was about to be filled with a veterinary complex. Was that the right word? Complex? No, maybe not. But it could be.

Decker caught up with him and clapped him on the back. "I didn't think you'd ever pull the trigger, brother. Congratulations. This is big. What you've talked about wanting since you were what, seven years old? Finally making it happen."

David nodded as the Realtor excitedly tapped something into her phone. "Yeah. Something like that." Decker was right. This was what

David had dreamed of his whole life, finally becoming a reality.

So why couldn't he feel excited? Why did he only feel dread?

And why did he have a sinking feeling that the answers to those questions had red hair and steely gray eyes and an attitude bigger than all of Buck County?

GRACIE CHECKED HER WATCH. Forty-seven hours.

It had been forty-seven hours since her grandma last opened her eyes. Longer than that since she last spoke. Longer still since she'd eaten a bite or drank a sip.

"It won't be long now, honey," the hospice nurse had said, and in the grand scheme of things, Gracie supposed she had been right. A couple of days was a drop in the bucket over the span of a lifetime. But every second by that bedside felt like an eternity.

The hospice nurse had helped her drag Vera's recliner into the bedroom after that. Gracie had purposely been clumsy about it, bumping and scraping into the room, with the wild hope that the noise would wake up her grandma, but even then, she remained in the faraway place that her dreams were taking her to. Gracie tried to be happy that maybe her grandma was at last taking the trip she so longed for, but she couldn't be happy when she was so full of grief.

She had rarely left the recliner, except for a quick bite or to use the bathroom, or when Farley came around.

Rather than sit at Vera's bedside, Farley seemed to hover about the room, a ghoul, impatiently checking his watch and typing into his phone. He wasn't there for comfort or support or even for his own grief. Because there wasn't any. Farley, typical in his selfishness, was waiting for his own mother to die, so he could go about the business of getting his. *There's no limit to your self-absorption*, Gracie thought. *No limit to how pathetic and disgusting you are.*

She didn't speak when he was in the room.

And, normally, neither did he.

Until now.

Gracie was just nodding off, curled up in her chair, when he bounded into the room.

"Get out," he said.

Gracie jerked awake, her body jolted to high alert, her heart pounding. "What?"

"I said get out." He barged farther into the room and pawed the light switch. The overhead light felt harsh and garish, burning her tired eyes. She hated the way her grandma looked under that light—pale and drawn with a slightly bluish tint beneath, as if she were already gone.

"Turn that off," she said.

"No. She needs to wake up. Mama. Up and at 'em."

Only then did Gracie realize that there was someone else with Farley. The lawyer who'd been with him before. And Farley was carrying that fistful of papers again.

"Stop." She got out of her chair and drew herself to full height, holding one hand out as if she were directing traffic. "No. Farley, no. You're not coming in here like this. Not now." The lawyer backed out of the room, hands up at his shoulders, face to the floor.

"Come on, Mama. I know you're in there somewhere. Let's go. Mama? Mama!" He was bent over the old woman, practically shouting in her face. He reached down to shake Vera's shoulder. Vera's eyes fluttered, and rather than be relieved to know that her grandma was still in there somewhere, Gracie was appalled and enraged...and a little bit frightened.

"Leave her alone," she said, coming at Farley with her arms outstretched. "She doesn't owe you anything. She deserves to die in peace." She felt a vague pang of shock that she'd finally said the word "die" aloud. She grabbed hold of Farley's shoulder and clutched at his shirt, pulling at him, only vaguely realizing that this was the only recollection she had of ever touching her father.

He felt feverish and sweaty and coiled, like he had just finished fighting the world. Her hands wanted to jerk away, but she wanted him out of her grandma's room even more, so she hung on.

"Get off me," he growled, shrugging his shoulder away from her, but she held tight. "Mama, wake up. You've got work to do."

Vera's eyelids fluttered again.

"Stop it. You're harassing her." Gracie tugged hard, and felt stitches break in his shirt.

Farley turned with a burst of energy that seemed to fill the entire room and reared up on Gracie, grabbing both of her wrists and twisting them as he leaned into her face. "You don't listen. Just like your mother, you always gotta be the one bossing everybody around. Let go of me and get out." On the last two words, he shoved.

Gracie flew backward several steps, catching her hip on her grandma's footboard and hitting the floor hard. She let out a cry of anger, surprise and pain.

He lurched toward her and leaned over her. She could smell the alcohol on his breath all the way from the floor.

"You would do yourself a favor to get out of here. Next time I won't be as soft. Got it?" He stomped back to Vera's bedside. "She's my mother and I have every right to say goodbye in my own way. You're the granddaughter. You have no rights."

She knew that wasn't even close to true. But she was too stunned to argue. Too afraid of Farley.

She grabbed onto the footboard and pulled herself up. Her hip was throbbing, and the skin of her wrists burned. She cupped her hand around one and rubbed the skin as she made her way toward the door. The attorney still stood there, but he looked a lot less certain than he looked the first time she saw him.

"How can you just stand there and watch him?" she asked. "Just so you know, whatever you've got him doing right now, I'll fight until the day I die, if I have to. But I doubt I'll have to. The signature of a dying woman so heavily dosed on morphine she can't open her eyes may not be the soundest signature in the world. And if you were even a little bit not a fraud, you would have already called him off from this ridiculous plan."

"I don't know how many times I gotta say it," Farley growled. Gracie turned just in time to see him launch himself away from Vera's bed and across the room toward her. "Guess I gotta *make* you leave."

Gracie backed up quickly, bumping into and

then through the lawyer. She spilled out into the hallway, landing on her backside. She pushed herself backward with her feet, never losing eye contact with Farley, who looked half-crazed as he chased her down.

Panic welled up inside her as she realized that while she had always presumed there to be an element of danger to Farley, she didn't exactly know how dangerous he truly could be. She prided herself on being tough and unafraid, but at this particular moment, she was neither of those things. She was scared and was very aware of her own vulnerability.

"I'm going, I'm going," she said as she scrambled to her feet. She held her hands out as if to stop him. "Just please don't…"

She didn't need to finish, because he reached the threshold of the door, but didn't pass through it. Instead, he slammed it shut, leaving Gracie panting on the other side.

The lawyer, also now stuck in the hallway with Gracie, stared at her, his eyes big, his Adam's apple shifting as he swallowed uncomfortably.

"You have no idea what you're doing," she said.

"He's the next of kin," he said weakly.

"That's what you're telling yourself," she said. "But you know that it's wrong for him to be in there trying to wake a dying woman to put the squeeze on her."

The door opened and Farley poked his head out. "Come on. She's awake," he said. Gracie shrank back, trying to disappear so he wouldn't see that she was still there. But he was so focused on finishing the task he'd come for, he didn't even look her way.

The lawyer gave her one last wary glance, then followed Farley inside and shut the door.

Alone, Gracie wasn't sure where to go or what to do. She stood in the middle of the hallway, the shock of being pushed settling in on her. She felt her breath quicken, her heart rate speed up and her knees bend at the ready. She had to get out of there.

She grabbed her car keys off the hook by the front door and left.

It wasn't until she was halfway into town before she realized where she was going.

The only place that made sense.

With her hip throbbing with pain, the sting of her wrists singing bright and constant, she pulled into a parking space.

And walked into McBride Veterinary Center.

CHAPTER SIXTEEN

RENEE TOOK ONE look at Gracie and rushed to the back to retrieve David. Gracie stood at the counter, listening as Renee mumbled something and David mumbled back. She wasn't sure, but it seemed like maybe the receptionist was afraid of her. She supposed she couldn't blame her. But after her run-in with Farley, this stung. Even though she'd spent most of her life being proud of her intimidation factor and the way it made people hesitate to mess with her, now any whiff of sharing this trait with him was too repugnant for her to stand.

She wanted to be better than him.

She wanted to be better, period.

Sarah, the office cat, lumbered along the countertop and instead of flopping down on Gracie, chose to affectionately rub against her shoulder repeatedly. Gracie was in no mood for cute animal antics, but in this moment, she wanted to bury her face into Sarah's soft side and cry. Somehow, she thought the cat might be okay with this. Instead, she pushed her fingers into the fur. Sarah made a warbling noise and closed her eyes, light purrs emitting from her.

"I wish I could be as happy as you right now," Gracie said. "And I wish I could just plop down and go to sleep like you, too." She blinked, trying to keep herself together.

David came around the corner, drying his hands on a paper towel. A look of guarded, cold concern was etched across his face, but after taking one look at her, the crease between his eyebrows deepened, and he hurried to the counter. "Is it your grandma?"

Gracie nodded, then shook her head, then nodded again, unable to keep the tears at bay any longer. His eyes drifted to her wrist, which she hadn't realized she'd gone back to holding.

"Is she…gone?"

"No, not yet," she said. "But I don't think it will be much longer."

"Why aren't you there?" he said. "You could have just called me."

"Farley."

His eyes flicked to her wrist again, and understanding seemed to dawn on him. "Did he hurt you?"

"I'm not hurt."

"But he got physical with you?"

She nodded. "He pushed me down. I don't

know if he really meant to, but he did really want me out of the room when he did it."

David's face had grown harder and more shut down with every word she spoke. "I don't care what he meant to do. It's about what he did. Are you okay?"

"I'm fine." She paused, trying again to keep the tears from restarting, even though she knew it was a failed effort. *Come on, Gracie, there's losing your edge and there's turning into a sobbing mess.* "I just didn't know where else to go."

"Where is he now?" David asked.

Renee, who had followed him back out to the lobby, said, "I'll close up here."

She'd barely finished her sentence before David was around the counter, digging his keys out of his pocket. "He's at the house?"

"He was when I left." Gracie followed him, unsure what she had just set into motion, and unsure if she even wanted it. But also totally sure that it was happening, whether she wanted it or not. "I don't need you to save me. That's not why I came here."

He paused, one arm halfway in the sleeve of his jacket. She'd left so quickly, she hadn't even thought to bring a jacket. Nor had she noticed the cold. "Then why did you come here?"

"I don't know." She felt sheepish. "I didn't

know where else to go. This was the only place I thought of. You were the only person."

He considered this, then continued to wind his way into his jacket. "Well, you're not the only person in that house I care about. If he's there alone with Vera, who knows what exactly he's up to? I only know that it can't be good. So I'm going."

When he put it that way, bringing Vera into it, Gracie couldn't exactly argue. After all, she too was worried about what Farley could be doing to her poor grandma. She didn't think he would be enough of a monster to actually hurt a dying woman, but she also hadn't realized he was the kind of man who would twist his own daughter's wrists and shove her to the ground for no reason.

"I'm coming, too," she said. "Let's go."

DAVID DIDN'T WANT to care.

The entire drive to Vera's house, he tried to convince himself that he didn't care.

This is not my family. Gracie is not my family. Vera is just a friend. Farley isn't my problem. I don't have to get involved. I can turn around and just go home. Leave Gracie and Vera to deal with Farley themselves. He is their family to deal with.

He was not convincing himself. Some things

were just out of his control. He cared about Vera. He cared about Gracie.

And he wanted Farley gone.

He gripped the steering wheel so tightly, he could hear the squeak of faux leather beneath his hands. He checked the rearview mirror. Gracie was behind him, her face grim and serious. It was more than just that Farley had forced her out of the house; he had rattled her, and that meant something dangerous had transpired.

His thoughts searched back to that first day when she held a shotgun on him, steady as a rock, after he delivered the kittens. Something had happened to her over these past few months. She'd gotten softer, lightened up. But there would always be that hard shell that she wrapped herself in like an invisible armor.

And Farley had chipped through that armor.

In fact, he had shattered it into pieces.

They arrived at the farm and pulled up to the house just as the front door opened and Farley stepped through it behind his lawyer.

David barely even waited for his car to come to a complete stop. He threw it into Park and launched himself out into the driveway, the gravel skittering away under his feet.

Farley came at him. "You comin' at me, vet? Let's go," he shouted as he lowered his shoulder and launched into David, driving straight into his gut.

But David was ready. He absorbed the blow and then squared his own shoulder, driving Farley backward until they met the side of the house. Farley hit the wall with an *oomph* but stayed on his feet. David pinned him in place with a forearm, leaning in so that their faces were nearly touching.

He was aware of the lawyer shouting, "Hey-hey-hey!" and of Gracie's footsteps in the gravel.

But she didn't say a word. Didn't tell him to lay off or leave Farley alone or stand down, back off, nothing. She simply ran past him and into the house to check on her grandma.

"I told you to leave her alone, didn't I?" David growled. Farley's nostrils flared, and his breathing was heavy, but he didn't respond. David pushed harder. "Didn't I?"

"What are you, her bodyguard?" Farley said between breaths.

"Hey, man, ease up," the lawyer said, but it was clear that he wasn't coming to Farley's aid.

Good, David thought. *I can make my point crystal clear*. He pushed his forearm harder into Farley's chest and leaned in another inch.

"I spent a lot of time in prison with much better fighters than you," Farley said, panting. "I'm not afraid." But the sweat that had formed on his upper lip told a different story.

"We're leaving," the lawyer said. "Just let him go."

"He's had a warning," David said. "And he still put his hands on her. This is your last chance. Leave and don't come back. If I see your face again, it won't be good for you. You won't get another warning from me."

"That a threat?" Farley's alcohol breath wafted in David's face. As angry as David was in that moment, he could still see that Farley was a sick man who needed help, not a beating. Plus, David was here for Gracie and Vera, not for Farley. And he sure wasn't about to waste time cooling his jets in jail because he couldn't hold his fists around Farley Langhorst.

"It's a promise." David backed off, letting go of Farley, who was an instant stream of red-faced, vein-bulging profanity. Every word that came out of Farley's mouth further convinced David that nothing he could physically do to this man would do anything to change him.

"Don't worry, we won't be coming back," the lawyer said, getting into the driver's seat of his car. The tight, annoyed look on his face told David that he'd had enough of Farley's nonsense for one day. "There's nothing for us here."

"Smart move." David turned his back on Farley and strode into the house. Farley continued to bluster behind him, but he didn't care.

The house was dark and quiet, with a dim glow coming from a bedroom down the hall. He could hear hiccupping sobs coming from the open doorway. Gracie. He hurried toward the room, jaw tensed at the possibility of what he might find that Farley had done.

But when he rounded the corner into the room, he found Gracie standing by her grandma's bedside, not just crying, but laughing, too. She held a sheaf of papers in her hand.

"Everything okay?" he asked

She turned, tears streaming down her face and handed the papers to him.

It took a minute for what he was seeing to sink in.

"He tried to get her to sign some crazy will," Gracie said. "Basically giving him everything."

"Do you think she knew what was going on?"

Gracie's laughter began anew as she nodded. "Turn to the back page."

David leafed to the back page, where Vera had shakily scrawled on the signature line.

Not on your life.

"That's why they were in such a hurry to get out of here," David said, a smile creeping on his lips. "They were defeated and headed off to lick their wounds."

Gracie held the page at arm's length and sucked air through her teeth. "I mean, ouch. Not just no, but *not on your life*. That's about as definitive as you can get."

David reached down and patted Vera's hand. "Way to go, old friend. Looking out for yourself until the bitter end."

"Looking out for me." Gracie turned the paper over. On the back, in the same shaky letters, was *4 Gracie.*

David hadn't really given it any thought, but it made total sense for Gracie to take the land she grew up on.

"That'll be a nice paycheck," he mused.

"Yeah," Gracie said, but her face clouded over while she said it.

Only then did the realization that they were at the bedside of his dying friend really sink in on him. He gazed at Vera, his heart tugging. The mirthful, rosy cheeks had given way to pallid, loose skin. Her eyes, bright crescent moons when she smiled, were closed. Still, she wore a hint of amusement, as if she, too, could appreciate the humor in what happened with Farley. He felt awash with warmth and friendship.

Gracie must have followed his gaze because her laughter, too, had dried up. She'd let the papers drift into the garbage can next to the dresser. "You want to sit a while?" she asked.

"Sure."

Gracie left the room and came back with a wooden chair from the kitchen table. David took it and positioned it next to the bed. Fannie, snoozing on the floor on that side of the bed, opened her eyes and lazily thumped her tail against the floor in greeting. He reached down and stroked her head. "How are you, girl?" he asked softly. "You doing okay? This is a lot for you, too, I would imagine."

"I never thought about that," Gracie said from the recliner on the other side of the bed. "This is going to be a big change for Fannie. And for Norma, too. She comes in for lunch with Grandma just about every day. Just not…lately. Are they going to grieve?"

Fannie stood, and David's fingers moved down the back of her neck. He nodded. "Probably. But they're resilient, like people. It'll eventually get easier for all of you. But you may need each other to get through it. It'll just take time."

"How much time…do you think?"

"Oh. You'll go home. I didn't even think about that. What are your plans?"

She sank back into the recliner miserably. "Honestly, I thought I would have longer here to figure all this out, but I've been avoiding it. I don't know. She has the house and the land and all these animals. I can sell the house and land, no problem. But…"

"She loved her animals," David said.

"Yeah. And I live in an apartment in the city. It's going to be a lot to even have a dog, much less an alpaca."

"Two, actually. Sam doesn't go anywhere without Betty."

"Right. Two."

There was a beat of silence, while David tried to think of the logistics of how he could make two alpacas, two geese, a barn cat and kittens, and a hound dog work in his small house just off of Haw Springs' square, but he quickly realized that he couldn't logistic this out.

And it didn't matter.

Vera had been a loyal friend. And Gracie was…well, she was something else entirely that intrigued and terrified him. There was only one action that made sense.

"I'll take them," he said.

"What?"

"I'll take them," he repeated.

"David, you don't have to do that."

"I'm not doing it because I have to," he said. "I'm doing it because I want to. Because it's the right thing. And because Vera would do it for me."

"Where will you keep them?"

"I'll ask Decker to take in the livestock. Annie will be thrilled about the alpacas. And I'll take Fannie. She can come to work with me every day. We'll let Norma decide for herself if she wants to chase mice in Decker's barn or live the good life like Sarah, getting loads of ear scratches and treats every day, but also having to listen to a whole lot of barking in the process."

"And sitting on people's car keys," Gracie said.

David grinned. "And sitting on people's car keys, yes."

Gracie was silent as she gazed at her grandma. Finally, she turned her gaze back to him. "Thank you, David. Truly. For everything. I don't know how I ever could have doubted you. I'm sorry."

Her eyes were shiny. He wanted nothing more than to gather her into his arms, sink his fingers into her hair, console and reassure her.

"Of course." He stood, kissed Vera's forehead, and whispered, "Don't you worry about a thing, my friend. I will make sure everyone is taken care of. You can just rest now."

Maybe he was imagining it, but he could have sworn she let out a soft sigh. And he wasn't imagining that her breathing began to slow in that moment. He gave her hand a soft squeeze.

"I should go," he said. He started to make his way around Fannie.

"No. Stay. Please?" Gracie asked. "I don't want to be alone."

David had a million reasons to say no. But they all melted away in that moment. He lowered back into his chair. "Of course."

For the longest time, they sat in silence, listening only to Vera's soft, slow breaths. David idly stroked Fannie's head and neck, feeling a visceral loss laced with gratitude at having known Vera, and the first real peace he had enjoyed in as far back as he could remember.

After a while, he found himself simply watching Gracie, who seemed to be deep in a world of her own, and, despite himself, imagining himself in that world with her.

CHAPTER SEVENTEEN

GRACIE HAD NOT expected him to still be there in the morning.

But to be fair, she hadn't expected herself to ask him to stay in the first place. It had just popped out. And she certainly hadn't expected it to feel so comfortable between them. They didn't speak. They didn't cry. They simply existed in Vera's final hours.

At some point, Gracie had fallen asleep, curled up in the recliner. She slept deeply and long, longer than she'd slept since she arrived back in Buck County. It was as if her body finally felt that it would be safe to let her guard down.

When she woke, David was softly snoring, his fist propping up one side of his face, elbow resting on the arm of his chair, Fannie sleeping on his feet. Gracie blinked twice, unsure that he was really in the room with her. Had he actually stayed just because she'd asked him to? Was it possible that he was just that kind?

Yes, of course it was. She already knew that about him.

In that fuzzy moment of just-awake dreaminess, Gracie could make out a hazy future, one where waking up next to David was normal and expected. Where they would spend their early mornings discussing their plans for the week over steaming, sweetened cups of coffee. Where they would keep their voices hushed to let the children sleep in.

Mornings filled with love and trust and hope and excitement.

Mornings surrounded by the lightly smoky scent of Buck County fall air, filled with the familiar honks of Henry and Henrietta, silhouettes of Sam and Betty dipping their heads to graze against the pink-orange sunrise.

Gracie hugged herself, savoring this fantasy, knowing that it was only that—a fantasy.

In reality, what awaited her was months of paperwork while she tried to grin and bear the idea of someone else living that life—*her* life—in her grandma's house. Someone else baking cookies in her grandma's kitchen. Someone else riding a horse to the blackberry bushes.

Someone else loving David and building a life with him.

And for her efforts, she would be afforded the opportunity to work tireless, unforgiving hours in a job that no longer brought her passion. Fighting for the chance to fight, arguing for the opportunity to argue. Her life was built on so much opposition. So much animosity.

So much shoveling a microwaved dinner into her mouth while standing over the kitchen sink at nine o'clock, still wearing her court clothes, her feet throbbing from being squeezed by impractical shoes.

All the while she would be telling herself that she wanted this, that she did everything right, that this was the life she was supposed to have.

So why did it suddenly feel like the life she was supposed to have was snoring in the chair directly across from her? Why did it suddenly feel like she'd done everything wrong, followed the wrong path, if the path didn't end at David?

She let her eyes drift closed while she imagined herself quitting the firm, buying out her lease, and taking over the Langhorst farm.

I could do it, she thought. *I could walk away and never look back. This way could be the right way, too. Right?*

She opened her eyes, only to find herself staring into the open eyes of her grandma. Startled, she sat forward and grabbed her grandma's hand.

"Hey," she whispered. "Are you okay?"

Her grandma gazed at her, and in that moment, Gracie felt so much love wash over her.

She'd never had a parent, but she didn't need one, as long as this woman existed. She knew that she owed everything she had and everything she was to her grandma and the love that was emanating from those eyes at this very moment.

She knew that she was who she was because of Vera Langhorst.

And she knew that her grandma was trying to impart a message to her in her own way. She just wasn't sure what the message was.

"Grandma?" she said, only it came out soft and tiny, squashed by tears.

Vera squeezed her hand, surprisingly strong and steady, but let go quickly and drifted back to sleep with a serene smile.

"Grandma?"

She felt a hand on her back and turned to find David there, his face still puffy with sleep.

She stood and came around the chair, folded herself into his arms, and cried until she was weak and tired.

As the day wore on, he brought her tea and sandwiches, and he made dinner and fed the animals and did all the things she needed without her asking. The shadows grew longer, and Vera's breathing grew shallower and slower, and David went home to take a shower and tend to his boarded animals, with promises that he would be back in time to make breakfast in the morning.

Gracie was alone in the silent, still house, the room lit by only a dim night-light. Her back ached. Her eyes felt like they'd been stuffed with sand. Her head throbbed. Her stomach growled. And yet she sat vigil, only drifting in and out of a fitful sleep, then waking with a start to make sure she didn't miss another lucid event with her grandma.

But in the night, the hours stretched long by the dark and still, as Gracie's head flopped to one side, finally falling into a deep sleep, Vera took her final breath, let it out, and died.

DAVID DIDN'T COME back in the morning as promised. Gracie had texted him just as he was getting out of the shower.

She's gone. The ambulance is coming now.

I'll meet you at the hospital, David had texted back.

No, you've done enough, Gracie responded. More than enough actually. Thank you for everything, but I've got it from here. Get some sleep.

David sat on the edge of his bed, so tired he felt as if he were looking at the world from the end of a long, narrow tunnel, his hair dripping cold water down his spine. He wasn't sure what to do next. He only knew that the thought of not being with Gracie now felt foreign and cold and alone.

I'll stop by for the animals this afternoon, he said.

It took quite a long while for Gracie to respond, the text bubbles appearing and disappearing, as if she didn't know quite what to say. Finally, No need. I've got that, too.

You sure? You're going to be very busy for a while now.

I'm going to be very alone, she responded. Then, after another long while of text bubbles appearing and disappearing, That's the way I prefer it. Thanks again.

David stretched back on his bed, his phone cradled against his chest, and stared at the ceiling until he began to see designs move and twist. He fell asleep that way.

Alone.

With Gracie on his mind.

And, unlike her, not preferring it that way at all.

CHAPTER EIGHTEEN

THE PARKING LOT, overflow parking lot, and street parking for Obendorfer Funeral Home were all full by the time David arrived. He ended up parking in his own small lot and walking down the length of Main Street. Vera was loved, but also Haw Springs was loved. When someone died or got married or had a baby or moved in, the town showed up, and that was the long and the short of it. They celebrated together, and they grieved together.

The tiny chapel inside the funeral home was similarly packed, the receiving line snaking all the way from the front door, through the lobby and up to Gracie, who stood like a tiny sentry next to the casket. Checking the time, David decided to forgo the long line and instead slid into a seat next to Decker and Morgan.

"You okay?" Morgan asked, giving him a side hug.

He nodded. "She went peacefully, and she wasn't alone."

Morgan lifted one eyebrow. "Well, that didn't answer my question at all. Are *you* okay?"

David opened his mouth to answer but was saved by a swell of music. The funeral director swooped in to usher Gracie to her seat, as the line dispersed, people lighting wherever they could land. David was grateful for the timing. He didn't know how to answer Morgan's question.

Was he okay?

Yes, and no.

Losing Vera hurt, but he knew she'd lived a good, long life, and he knew that she had been with someone who loved her more than anything at the end, and he knew that she was at peace now. So, yes, he was okay.

But he hadn't spoken to Gracie since Vera passed. Hadn't checked on the animals with her at his heels, snarking at him, making suggestions, asking questions, informing him of everything he was doing incorrectly.

He missed Gracie more than he missed Vera, and he felt terrible about that.

So, no, he was not okay.

Gracie would tie things up at the farm and go back to Kansas City, and he was just going to have to accept that. The thing was, he wasn't sure he could.

It wasn't a long funeral. Gracie sat all alone in the front pew of the chapel, chin up and head held high. She was a rock, only dabbing her eyes with a tissue once or twice. David kept an eye out for Farley, ready to pounce and quietly and quickly escort him away if he should show. But he never did, his sudden dedication to his mother gone as quickly as it had arrived.

The service ended and they all stood and shuffled outside to caravan to the gravesite. Gracie, who was being directed to a car, found David and made eye contact for the first time. Instead of following the flow, she turned and spoke a few words to the man leading her, and then made a sharp turn toward David instead. His heart flipped as he watched her come toward him.

"Hey," he said. "How are you holding up?"

There was a guardedness about her. Not the hands-on-hips hauteur he'd grown used to, but a crossed-arm blankness, as if she were desperately trying to feel nothing. She nodded, staring at his feet. "As expected, I suppose. I don't think it's really sunk in. I miss her already."

"I'm sorry for your loss."

"Thank you." She finally made eye contact. Hers were red rimmed and bloodshot. "I wish *sorry* could bring her back. I've gotten so much *sorry*."

"I know. Do you need anything?"

"I don't think so."

"I can come help with the animals, of course."

She reached out as if to grab his arm but thought better of it and crossed her arms across her chest again. "Listen. David. I need you to know. I'm selling the farm. I've already listed it."

"I see. The animals?"

"I'll find a place for them. It's not your responsibility."

"I wasn't offering out of responsibility. I care about them."

"I believe that completely." Her eyes swam with tears as she looked up at him. Clouds floated by in her gray irises. "I think it's cleaner this way."

"What's cleaner?"

"You and me," she said. "Or…or maybe I'm just imagining it, I don't know. I've been all over the place. You know I have to go back to Kansas City." Her eyes lingered over his, and for a moment he thought maybe she wanted him to ask her to stay, or to at least confirm her feelings about the two of them. And for a moment, he really wanted to. But he didn't.

He heard Decker's voice in the back of his mind. If he'd said it once, he'd said it a thousand times: *Brother, you are always so worried about what's down the road, you miss all the best pit stops.* The thing was, he didn't know if Gracie was a pit stop or what was waiting down the road. The destination.

Or maybe she was on a different road altogether.

Maybe being with her didn't fit into his plan, because his plan was wrong. He didn't know how to know.

She glanced over her shoulder. "I should get going."

"Okay. Yeah. Of course."

"Thank you for being here. And, well, for everything. I won't forget all that you did for us, I can promise you that."

"It was my pleasure."

She launched at him with a quick, awkward hug, and was walking away before he could even hug her back.

"Gracie," he said, unsure what else to say, only that he wanted to say something. He didn't want her to go. He wanted to be by her side, hold her hand at the gravesite. Go home with her tonight. Make her some dinner. Just sit and hold her before beginning the packing process tomorrow.

But when she turned, all that came out was, "Best of luck to you." She nodded and kept going, quickly ducking into the car that was still waiting for her.

Best of luck to you?

Best of luck?

He walked to his car, disappointed in himself in every possible way. What did it matter what road she was on, if he was too in his own way to take a road at all?

TRINKETS. SO MANY TRINKETS. *Why do we live our lives in cheap pieces of porcelain and scraps of felt and glittery plastic?* Gracie wondered.

In the end, she'd decided to have an estate sale. As much as she wanted to hang on to her grandma, she just couldn't take in all these trinkets.

Growing up, she'd always found estate sales unsettling, picking through someone's life, offering a dollar for a platter that once served Christmas turkey, ten for a blanket that soothed a sick child, a quarter for a snow globe that was originally procured in hopes of capturing a vacation memory. It all seemed so morbid, trivializing someone's life, their best moments and favorite memories, into literal nickels and dimes.

But now that she was faced with a house full of someone's life, an estate sale seemed like the only answer. And wouldn't Vera love for her Christmas platter to be used to create beautiful memories for someone else?

There were just so many trinkets.

Gracie had been going through closets for weeks, and she was finally on her last one.

She wasn't eager to get back to her life, but she was eager to leave this one behind. So full of disappointment and sadness. She felt an urge to get back to normal, even if her version of normal was not much better in the disappointment and sadness department. The enemy you know, and all that.

Shoved high up on a shelf of her childhood bedroom closet, tucked behind a tub filled with spools of thread and jars of buttons and enough paper patterns to outfit all of Haw Springs, was an old metal cookie tin. She drew in a breath and pulled it down.

She'd forgotten all about this tin.

For the longest moment, she simply clutched it in front of her. Almost as if she didn't believe it really existed.

She opened the lid and let out the breath she'd been holding. Inside the tin were mementos of her mother's—movie and concert ticket stubs, random earrings, a tiny, plastic baby doll, a button that read *I Refuse to Grow Up*, the little knit newborn cap that Gracie had been wearing when they'd brought her from the hospital for this first time. Somehow, Vera had gotten hold of these things when Gracie's mother died and had brought them home for her. As a child, when Gracie was sick or sad, she would get the tin out and sift through the items inside. They were comforting to her, even though she couldn't remember her mother at all.

Now there was a folded piece of paper lying

on top of the keepsakes. Gracie certainly didn't remember a piece of paper being in the tin before. And the paper looked newish, not yellowed with age.

She picked it up and unfolded it. It was a letter from her grandma.

A small cry escaped Gracie, and she found herself hugging the paper to her chest rather than reading it right away. She missed her grandma so much, her grief was almost like another person in the room with her at all times. Her hands shook as she read it:

Dear Gracie,

You just left for college and I'm sitting on the sofa wondering where all the time went. When your grandpa Jack died, I didn't have any idea what I was going to do with myself. I was young still, and had so much responsibility, and I knew I couldn't count on Farley to come around and help out.

But then, instead of Farley coming around, you came around. We had an instant connection, didn't we? It sure seemed to me like we did. You would grab my finger with your tiny hand and just squeeze the dickens out of it. I looked forward to your visits more than you know.

I didn't want your mama to die. She was a lovely girl, really. She had her problems, of course, but inside she was kind and soft and caring. She loved you so much it overwhelmed her. I think she knew that she would never be able to truly do right by you. She never said it aloud, but I could see it in her eyes. I always wanted to help her, but I just didn't know how.

Anyway, I didn't want her to die, but she did, and in a horrible, selfish way, that was my good fortune. You and I were meant to be roomies and partners. You brought life back into this house and back into my soul. Thank you, sweet girl, for being you.

Which brings me to why I'm writing this letter. If you're reading it, I know you're going through a tough time. You only get this tin out when you need it. Heck, for all I know, you're reading it because I'm dead! Hahaha! Just kidding. Maybe.

So I'm going to tell you three things.

1. I'm so proud of you. You've been strong and good and hardworking, and you've always been there for me. You've always done what's expected of you. And because of this, I know you're going to be a success in life.

2. At the same time... You've been strong and good and hardworking, and you've always been there for me. You've always done what's expected of you. And because of this, I worry that you'll never be there for yourself. Be there for yourself sometimes, Gracie. Maybe even right now. Maybe you're looking through this box because you need to be there for yourself. Do things because you like to do them. Be with people because you want to be with them. Love yourself. Accept love from others. Sometimes you'll need to make a big statement. So, make it. Sometimes you'll need to cry. So, cry. But also laugh, because the same toughness that keeps you from crying also keeps you from laughing.

3. I love you, and I'm always here for you. That will never change. Not even when I'm gone.

One more thing. If I'm dead, know that I'm thrilled beyond capacity to finally be reunited with my Jack. There's something about that lifetime-and-beyond love that is just special. I hope you find that for yourself, too, Gracie. It's worth it to try.

Now that's all I have to say, so go ahead and go through your mama's things and reminisce and think about what might have been and what was and what's to come. Dream a little. Keep those dreams close to your heart or let them out. You'll know which one is the right one. And don't forget, you can follow more than one dream at a time.

You've always done the right thing. This moment will be no different.

I love you.
Grandma Vera

Gracie pushed herself back against the headboard and pressed the letter against her chest.

Keep those dreams close to your heart or let them out.

She read it three more times before refolding it and putting it back in the box.

You'll know which one is the right one. And don't forget, you can follow more than one dream at a time.

She never even went through any of the other things inside the box.

The same toughness that keeps you from crying also keeps you from laughing.

CHAPTER NINETEEN

"YOU CAN'T JUST change your mind."

Decker was sitting in David's waiting room, Clancy, the newest puppy addition to the McBride ranch dutifully winding his leash around Decker's ankles as he sniffed the floor, his little stub of a tail moving ninety miles a minute.

"Morgan fell in love with him at the shelter over the weekend and I couldn't tell her no," Decker had said with a shrug, carrying Clancy into the office in one hand like a cell phone. *"She thinks he'll help Archer deal with the changes of moving in together now that we're married. She's insistent."*

David had given Clancy the once-over, and was now sitting on his reception desk, feet dangling, heels bouncing off the counter, the office closed for the day, Renee and Leo gone.

"I mean, can you?" Decker continued. "Change your mind?"

"I haven't signed anything yet," David said.

"You met with a contractor for the build-out."

"He hasn't even quoted me yet. We haven't gone over details."

"You got a loan."

"That I will use to open a place in Kansas City."

Decker lifted one foot, and then the other, to extract himself from the leash. Sarah, the office cat, hopped down from her perch next to David to check out Clancy. Clancy noticed her and came at her, tail wagging so hard his back feet slid on the floor. Sarah idly swatted him away; he squealed and ran back under Decker's feet.

"Vets are a dime a dozen in the city," Decker said. "You know that."

"I do," David said. "But Gracie is one of a kind." He slid off the desk and swooped up Clancy with one hand. He hugged the squirming puppy to his chest and scrubbed his ears with his fingers. "I have to do this, Decker."

Decker nodded, contemplated, then pushed the brim of his cowboy hat up with one finger so he could look his brother in the eyes.

"You've thought it through, haven't you?"

"A million times over the past three weeks."

"Then go do it," Decker said. "Go get her."

GRACIE SAT AT her desk with her head in her hands. It had been an extraordinarily long week. Long month, actually, but the week had been particularly brutal. Jem had been right about

Gracie taking so much time off, and Gracie had been right about Andrew being incompetent. She had so many fires to put out when she returned, she joked with Alicia, her administrative assistant, that she should have a red hat and carry a hose.

Plus, she just wasn't really into it anymore. The whole lot of it. The insane pace, the quick tempers, the arrogant attitudes. Had she ever been energized by this? She liked to think not, but then she would recall following David around the farm with a literal shotgun at his back and realize that, yes, she had not only been energized by it but had been a founding member of it. The OG Attitude Problem. She would laugh, if it didn't make her want to cry.

There were two sharp raps on her doorframe. She looked up; Jem stood in her doorway, one hand on her hip.

"Uh-oh," Gracie said. "I know that pose. What's wrong?"

Jem gave a fake smile, let go of the doorframe and swaggered into the office on her impossibly high stilettos. "What makes you think something is wrong? Can't I visit your office for good reasons?"

"Sure, you could," Gracie said. "But you don't. Not ever. And I know that hand-on-hip thing you do. Something is wrong. So, spill. What is it?"

Jem lowered herself into the chair across from Gracie's desk. "To be frank, Gracie, you are the problem," she said, primly smoothing her pencil skirt on her knee, almost as if she were already bored with the conversation. She picked at some invisible lint, then laced her fingers together. Satisfied, she made smug eye contact with Gracie.

"I'm the problem? How so?"

"How do I put this?" Jem said. "Oh, right, I know. Your heart is no longer in the game. You're soft and…nice now. Your edge is gone."

"My grandmother just died, Jem. Forgive me if I'm a little off for a couple of weeks."

"It's been more than a couple of weeks."

"I didn't know I was on a deadline."

"Andrew has been taking up your slack, and you know what? He's been doing a great job. Makes it harder to give you first shot at good projects, you know?"

Gracie rubbed her forehead. If Jem was trying to push her into a reaction, it was working, but she may not get the reaction she was hoping for. For the millionth time that day, she wondered what was happening in Buck County right now. If Ellory ever created a new flavored latte in honor of Norma's kitten. If Annie and Ben had learned to dance and become the talk of somewhere. How Sam and Betty were getting along on Decker's ranch.

What David was doing.

I can't do this anymore.

"What?" Jem asked.

Gracie thought she'd only thought the words, but she'd apparently said them aloud. And, she was surprised to learn, she wasn't sorry that she had.

She let go of her forehead, let her palms drop to her desk and let out an incredulous laugh. "I can't do this anymore," she repeated.

"What does that even mean?" Jem looked like the scared overgrown teenager Gracie had always suspected was hiding beneath.

"It means go ahead and give Andrew the good projects. It's fine with me."

"That's not a very winning attitude, Gracie."

"I don't care about winning, Jem. I don't even see this as winning anymore."

Jem tented her fingers together, staring over them like a cartoon supervillain. "You know what? I'm going to give you a pass today, because you're grieving. Grief can make people do weird things. And this…is weird."

Gracie's smile felt foreign in this office. Her cheeks were almost hesitant to hold it up. She wondered if it was possible that she'd never smiled here before. Not truly. "It is, isn't it? But in a good way. I feel good, Jem. You don't feel good?"

Jem stood and smoothed her skirt again. Gracie idly wondered how many skirts Jem literally rubbed into pieces and had to hold back a laugh. "No, Gracie, I don't feel good. I'll feel good when everyone is working to their full potential. I'll give you another week. After that…" She trailed off, dramatically shrugging as she walked away.

Her perceived mic drop moment.

Only Gracie wasn't interested in mic drops anymore.

"Have you ever eaten a blackberry directly off the bush, Jem?" Jem paused. "I don't know how or why, but they're sweeter. Have you ever watched a tractor pull?"

Jem looked over her shoulder. "Certainly not."

"To be fair, me neither. Not a real one. But I want to. The whole town turns out, so there must be something to it, right? I mean, I watched a pedal pull, and it was fun enough, but the tractor pulls… I would imagine they're loud and rumbly and there are clouds of dust and crowds cheering. Exciting stuff."

Jem frowned. "I'm really concerned about you."

Gracie giggled. "For the first time ever, I'm not. I'm concerned about you, though. I think you need to take a vacation. Just a little get-away."

"One week, Gracie," Jem said, then floated away, like a confused balloon.

Gracie couldn't help laughing. "Good thing I didn't tell you about the ranch sorting!" she shouted.

Alicia, Gracie's assistant, popped into her doorway, looking almost as perplexed and upset as Jem had. She was hugging a file folder to her chest.

"Everything okay?" she asked.

Gracie's laughter was dying away. "Yes, everything's fine. I'm sorry."

Alicia gave a tentative smile. "Don't be sorry. Sometimes I think this place could use a little lightening up. At least you're not kicking trash cans like Andrew."

"He kicks trash cans?"

Alicia checked over her shoulder and took a step inside Gracie's office. "We had to replace three of them while you were gone."

"You're kidding." Andrew had always been intense, but it sounded like his intensity grew to something else while Gracie was gone. Gracie was glad she had been gone and didn't have to witness it.

"I wish I was kidding." Alicia crossed the office and deposited the file folder onto Gracie's desk.

Gracie didn't make a move to open it. "Alicia, be honest with me. Am I like that? Like Andrew?"

The tentative smile returned. "You've never kicked a trash can."

"That's not what I asked."

"I've never had any problems with you."

Gracie sagged. "Also not what I asked."

"Listen, I get it," Alicia said. "You have to be a tough person to do the job that you do. You have to have a lot of passion. Sometimes passion spills over a little as other things and that's okay. That's what my therapist says, anyway." She chuckled.

Gracie sighed and opened the file folder. "Who is this?" She scanned the papers inside. "Real estate? I don't do real estate. How did this get assigned to me?"

"He asked for you."

"And you didn't tell him no?"

"He's actually here. Like, right now. He was insistent."

"Without an appointment." Gracie closed the folder and slid it to the edge of her desk. First a run-in with Jem and now a real estate client with no boundaries. She rubbed her forehead again. *I can't do this anymore…* "Get rid of him."

There was a pause. "I really think you should see him," Alicia stage-whispered.

"Why?"

"Just…"

"No. Alicia. I don't want to see him."

"This one you might."

"Ugh." Gracie let her forehead drop to her desk as her assistant left the room, giving her protests no heed whatsoever. "I don't do real estate."

"Hopefully you'll do it this one time, though," she heard. "I need help finding some commercial office space."

She knew that voice.

She slowly raised her head, wisps of her hair dangling over her face.

David McBride was standing in the doorway of her office.

Holding a bouquet of flowers.

He extended his arms as if to offer them to her. She still had said nothing, such was her shock to find him there in the first place.

"I'm moving to Kansas City. Hopefully to be with the love of my life."

CHAPTER TWENTY

None of what was happening made sense to Gracie. How had she gone from wishing she could see David just one more time to actually seeing him standing in her office with flowers?

"I'm sorry, what?" Every nerve ending was tingling. She had to remind herself to breathe so she didn't pass out. He was still holding the flowers toward her but was all the way on the other side of the room. She waved him in. "You don't have to stand there."

He brought her the flowers; they smelled amazing. Like fresh air and perfume and late September nights eating french fries after a tug-of-war. She felt woozy.

"I don't understand," she said. "You're moving your office? Here?" She gazed at the bouquet as if it held the answers.

"I'm moving myself here, too," he said.

"Why?"

"I tried, Gracie, I really did. I found a new place in Haw Springs. I was all set to sign the paperwork and get the build-out going. It was going to be a whole veterinarian hospital, so I could bring in some partners, hire more people. We were going to do a doggy day care." He laughed. "Can you imagine? A doggy day care in Haw Springs."

"Those are very popular…here," Gracie said, still in a daze. Doggy day care? What was even happening right now?

"The point is, I was all set to go. To fulfill my dream, my lifelong goals. Except…" He ducked his head. When he gazed at her again, she felt it all the way to her toes.

"Except…?"

He took the bouquet and gently laid it on her desk, then took both of her hands in his. "Except…it didn't feel like a dream without you. It felt empty and superficial and boring. I never had a dream of falling in love and getting married. I had a *plan*, and those things didn't fall into that plan. But then you came along."

"With my trusty shotgun," she said.

He grinned. "With your trusty shotgun. And you became my dreams and goals. My plan is incomplete without you. *You* are the plan."

"What are you saying?"

"I'm saying I can execute my plan—or some version of it—here, as long as I have you. None of that other stuff matters. I'm in love with you."

"How?"

"I don't know how exactly. I tried really hard not to fall in love with you. I failed."

"No, I mean how can you just change your life like this? Just decide to move to Kansas City and start over? Doesn't it scare you?"

"What scares me is the possibility of not being able to begin every morning looking into those beautiful gray eyes." He gazed at her so deeply she felt woozy. His gaze turned worried, and his hands loosened around hers. "Have I misread things? Do you not want this? Us, I mean?"

"No." She tightened her grip, turning their hands up and lacing her fingers through his. The giddy, giggly feeling was back. She could feel it begin to bubble up inside of her. "I want this. I want us. I love you, too, David. And I want it so much. I just don't want it here."

He frowned. "I don't understand."

She tilted her head back and let out a laugh. "I don't either, but I think it has something to do with a letter my grandma left me. I've been thinking *I can't do this anymore* for days… weeks… I don't know, months? But I didn't know what that meant, really, until right now in this moment. And now it's crystal clear. The clearest I've felt maybe ever. You're not moving to Kansas City."

"I'm not?"

"No. You're opening a veterinary hospital in Haw Springs, and I'm taking your old office on Main Street. I never put Grandma's farm up for sale. I couldn't do it. Because coming back to Haw Springs is the right thing. My right thing. I'm going home to stay."

He let go of her hands and, without a word, brushed her hair away from her forehead. He slid that hand up the back of her neck, burying his fingers in her hair, and slid the other hand around her waist. Slowly, he pulled her in for a kiss, then lingered with his forehead up against hers.

"Then let's go home."

* * * * *